C000212396

MELANCHOLY VISION

THE REVOLUTION SERIES AWAKENING

MELANCHOLY VISION

THE REVOLUTION SERIES AWAKENING

L. C. HAMILTON

atmosphere press

© 2021 L. C. Hamilton

Published by Atmosphere Press

No part of this book may be reproduced without permission from the author except in brief quotations and in reviews. This is a work of fiction, and any resemblance to real places, persons, or events is entirely coincidental.

atmospherepress.com

For my Mums, Dads, and my grandparents.

Author's Note

Have you ever tried to run away from responsibility, escaping and not caring what your family thinks? Or did you feel like an outcast, unable to fit in, so you'd rather speak to a doll and weird warlock? Welcome to *Melancholy Vision, the Revolution Series*, the world of Kilian and Jegor Lancaster, two magical investigators who have to deal with the exact same problems—just like us humans.

Melancholy Vision, the Revolution Series Awakening is the origin story of two cousins who live in Icon, the capital city of New Born Kingdom. A prophecy sends them on their next case; one with challenges, monsters, and relationship problems they never had to deal with before. Dive into the world of *Melancholy Vision* and explore the case and what is yet to come.

Melancholy Vision, the Revolution Series Awakening is an urban fantasy journey between monsters, love, hate, and the building of a society that is more or less fair.

I hope this book brings bravery, courage, imagination, and creation to you, wherever you are reading this. Now, it is time to discover a new world. A revolution is coming.

Are you ready to join?

"Like time, my texts are infinite."
– Warren Graham, *Life is Strange*

Prologue
Jegor

Why do you try, when you never know?

Icon, Doom District, 2005

Doom, as they called it, was a pitch-black area, the hood where dark magic happened. Rumours had it that this was the place to go, where demons and creatures woke at night. To Jegor, it was the best district to hang around, even as a young, fourteen-year-old magician. Jegor liked the dark, enjoyed the cold rain falling on him. The foggy streets gave him a comfortable feeling, where others would hide under their blankets behind closed curtains. If anything, darkness was like a friendly hand, ready to catch him when he needed it most. He remembered the day the ceremony had chosen him. The ritual every child had to go through at the age of four. The day his Magic League had chosen him.

Icon, the city where they lived, was the capital city of the world—New Born Kingdom. The magical population was only half as big as the human population. Not all countries existed in the magical world, as in the human world. Icon had similar architecture as old Victorian London as well as modern London. A few districts carried the same name. But the difference was shown by magic all around the city. Portals used to travel. Trading with objects and herbs instead of money. Silver was used as currency, but most magicians were interested in trading objects instead of using money. Silver was useful for essential things, like food and medicine. If it came to magical artefacts, trading was the popular option. Some magicians even traded with human objects like TVs and mobile phones. Unlike his cousin Kilian, Jegor had not really adapted to the modern ways. He had no interest in things such as MP3 players. The city was split in half when it came to the choice of modern culture and sticking to the "good old" magical ways.

"Good to see you again, my little friend." It was a rough yet charming voice that greeted him.

He looked at the person behind the counter of the shop he'd just entered. It was *the* magic shop around this area. *Fear's Potion Polka* was well known for all kinds of artefacts. Whether it was a healing potion, the cure to a broken heart, or "forbidden" herbs, Fear had it all, and he was well known for dealing with things that no one else would sell. He was a Korean-Russian warlock, one of the strongest in Icon. Every year, he got elected as member of the council, the political government in the city. Each city had one, ruled by magicians from all four Leagues.

"Didn't your mother tell you not to come here anymore?" Fear asked, an ominous glimmer in his eyes.

Jegor took off his hood and revealed a bald head. It fit his round face. He had lost all his hair the day the ceremony had chosen him—a price he had to pay for his magic. His eyes were dark grey, matching his simple black clothes. If there wasn't a special occasion, he would always wear black. It was one of the reasons children stayed away from him. He wasn't acting like society expected him to. And he wasn't as charming as Kilian.

"I don't care what Mother says. I am sick of taking royal lessons, while the important things get ignored. Everyone pretends that the dark magic never chose me." His voice wasn't angry, but it showed how tired he was of hearing the same things over and over again. He looked around. There were lots of shelves, decorated with weird artefacts. There were potions and herbs in different colours—green, blue, lilac, a very bright red. The labels told what each stood for—healing, poison, or essentials for certain recipes. Another shelf displayed books in different languages. The oddest book was the city guide for London. Fear didn't like the mortal world a lot, but he found it interesting to study the mortal ways of living, especially when it came to things all touristy. Next to the shelf of books was a collection of artefacts he had taken from other magical countries and cities such Madness, Aeropa, and Daarcemking. A skull with snakes coming out of its eyes. A black rose with vampire teeth. The claw of a werewolf, put into a green liquid to keep it steady. Every time Jegor came by, Fear had a new artefact placed on the shelf. The warlock was well-known for travelling all around the human and magical world.

"That is the deal you have to live with when it comes to your royal blood. Don't get annoyed. Your mother always hoped for you and Kilian to be in the decent section of magic. Yet the ceremony had another plan. Sooner or later, she will accept it. Don't focus your anger on something that isn't worth your time, young warlock." Fear looked Jegor in the eyes. Jegor had never seen eyes like Fear's. They were so dark that it reminded him of death itself. When Fear didn't choose to wear black jeans and comfortable jumpers cut so deep one could see his collarbone, he wore long coats with the most extraordinary embroidery. It was an expression of his Asian heritage, matching his light blond hair.

"I just wish she would treat me for once like she treats Kilian. He can do whatever he wants. Father is the only one who seems to understand me at home. But he's sick." Jegor looked at pile of folklore books. "Fear, my father is dying." He gulped. It was the first time he had said it out loud. Hearing the words made everything more real. The pain was manifesting right in his heart; a black needle that struck through his flesh to hit where it hurt the most.

From the early age of four, Jegor had learned to shut off his emotions, unlike Kilian. That was just one of the significant differences between them. Every child chosen by the ceremony of the old magicians had to go to the ritual of Merlin. It was the ritual in which every child with magical blood in their veins got chosen by one of the four Leagues of magic— Green, White, Red, or Black. Each of the Leagues stood for a different bloodline of magic. Jegor had been chosen by the Black League to be a Voodoo magician. Voodoo magic was one of the oldest, but it was a magic that went beyond blood rituals and stitching needles into dolls. It was the peak balance between sanity and darkness, juggling dark magic from an angle of perspective that most of them were not able to handle in the later years. Kilian had been chosen by the Red League to be a Trickster. Tricksters were the rarest magicians. They had the blood of the old warlocks in their veins. The Great Houdini had been one of them. The moment the cousins had been chosen, change had settled in the palace. The people started to talk. After all the generations, Jegor and Kilian were the first to bring change to the bloodline. None of their ancestors had been chosen by the Red or Black League when it came to the direct choice of heirs to the throne. It had been a fine line of Whites and Greens. They start to dazzle the palace and citizens into clouds of rumours. Jegor had been quick to adapt to the circumstances of always being watched and found his gaps in the system, just like Kilian. Though Kilian was the one who enjoyed the spotlight once in a blue moon.

Fear looked at Jegor, and for a moment, he couldn't tell what was going on the shopkeeper's mind. He had a blank expression before he moved over to a little box. He unlocked it and took something from within, closing the box with the help of grey mist coming out of his fingers. He walked over to Jegor.

"Open your hands, my dear friend," he stated.

Jegor opened his hands, and a moment later, he was holding a Voodoo doll. He looked shocked. "We're not allowed to have our own until we reach the age of sixteen," Jegor said seriously. No matter how annoyed he got with his parents, he was cautious when it came to following the rules. He never broke them like Kilian did—he only bent them.

Fear smiled briefly. "Of course you are not. And still, I decided to give it to you. The doll you are holding in your hands isn't any doll. It is *your* doll from now on—a friend, a helper, someone who you can talk to when I can't be here. His name is Carlin. An old friend gave it to me. He couldn't look out for him anymore. Most of the Voodoo dolls they're going to give you aren't even good to do real magic. This one is the right one for you. I was meant to give it to you later, but I've seen your magic, and you are far ahead of the other children in your year."

Jegor looked at the doll. It was white, the colour of a ghost. The stitches were black, spotted here and there with a little blood. One of its eyes was missing, while the other looked like a monstrous one. The lips were twisted in an insane smile. Jegor wasn't afraid when he looked at the doll. In a strange way, he felt connected. It was like it was looking at him. Before Jegor could say something, a strange noise interrupted the conversation, and he looked at Fear.

"Did you hear that?"

"Just the spiders I have to prepare for the coming lesson."

"Fear, spiders don't make noises."

Fear's expression changed, and he stepped closer to Jegor. He placed a hand on the shoulder of the young magician. "Sometimes, my dear friend, it is better not to ask so many questions. We all have secrets that we can only hide when one of us is dead."

Jegor didn't turn around again. Whatever he had just heard, he was sure that he would find the meaning behind the noise. For now, he stepped out into the dark night, a new friend by his side. Fear looked after him until he reached the next corner and vanished into the night.

"Your journey has just begun, my dearest Voodoo," Fear mumbled to himself, and walked towards the door that led to the cellar. He opened it and looked at the person sitting at the end of the stairs, a smile spreading across his face.

"Good Evening Maddison, let's begin with your lesson."

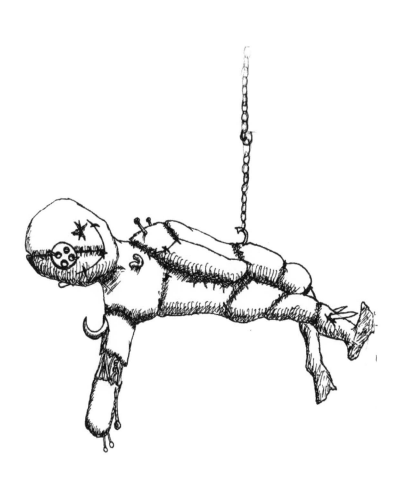

Chapter 1
Broken Seal

Magic comes with a price.
– F. F., "The Death and the Three Muses,"
The True Urban Legends

Icon, May 2018

Jegor was an early bird, even on a dark and hazy morning, not only because of his duty towards the palace but also so he had more time to practise. Like his cousin, Kilian, he had a private flat, where he spent most of the days in his life. He liked the palace, but there were certain rules at court and eyes that followed him wherever he went. In contrast with the black clothes he usually wore, his flat was decorated in white—white walls, white furniture, and even a white kitchen. Everything was well organized and furnished down to the finest details. He had a practise room just for his Voodoo magic, filled with artefacts and useful spellbooks. Vials containing different ingredients were neatly sorted on a shelf, right next to one lined with different herbs and animal skins. His bedroom had an extra detail next to the comfortable king-sized bed: a piano that he sometimes played before going to sleep. It was his form of meditation. Meditating was an essential key to keep the balance of magic within the magicians. If they didn't meditate, bad things could happen, starting from memory loss up to complete amnesia or insanity.

A dark voice well known to him appeared in his head. *Make your way to the palace. Something is going on.*

"And why is that, Carlin?" He glanced at the little Voodoo doll tied to his belt, where he also kept some vials and small weapons. The belt was the only extra accessory he wore. No rings, no necklaces. He was a simple man when it came to dress.

Kilian was the complete opposite and a sinner for fashion.

Jegor focused on the clock hanging above his bed. It was a magical clock, showing the nine time zones of the magical world. This morning, all of the zones had one thing in common—they had stopped at 11:44 A.M., Icon time. Jegor looked once more to Carlin. Whatever was waiting at the palace for him, he knew it wasn't a common case. Confirming his instincts, a message from his uncle Synclair via his smartphone arrived, telling him to come to the palace as quickly as he could. That could only mean his uncle Alegro, the king, was alarmed, and something was going on in Icon that had a big impact on the city.

Synclair was the only family member, apart from Kilian, who Jegor was really close to. His forty-five-year-old uncle was a Ghost, which meant he was able not only to see ghosts but also to communicate with them. As a Ghost, it was his duty to keep the balance between the living and dead. Whenever someone was going from this world, a Ghost's job was to make sure the person went in peace. Or, if they decided to stay, it was the Ghost's job to make sure the individual wouldn't cause trouble.

Synclair was one of the rare people Jegor truly trusted. Especially since he'd lost his parents, Synclair had always been there for him. Though his uncle wasn't interested in leading Icon. He knew the rules, he knew secrets and lies around the city, but acting as a sidekick was way more effective for him.

Jegor donned his long, black cloak before he left for the palace. As soon as he closed the door, his magical clock went on as if it had never stopped.

***

"Kilian, you need to wake up." A soft, female voice took the prince out of his dreamworld.

Kilian sighed and slowly opened his eyes. His green eyes seemed tired, but just for a moment, before he turned around and looked at the person next to him. She was beautiful and naked, but he had absolutely no idea who she was. *Last night must have been wild*, he thought, and put a fake smile on his face.

"How are you, my dear? Did you sleep well?" he asked the blond woman.

His memory slowly returned to him. She'd found him in one of his favourite pubs in the human world. He'd had to escape once more, to distract himself from his own problems, and there she'd found him.

"I'm wonderful. I could get used to this, you know," she answered.

"So could I. But as you know, a magician is always busy. I've gotta go." He gave her a kiss before he stood up.

To his surprise, he didn't even have clothes on, and Kilian was someone who usually didn't like to sleep naked. He observed himself in the long mirror and smirked a little. Kilian liked staring at himself. As he always used to say, "My parents did good work." His tanned skin, green eyes, and wavy brown hair with styled side cuts were a feast for the eyes of most kinds around him.

Within seconds, he had picked up his clothes—grey formal trousers, a white shirt, and a dark green vest. That was his classic look; there was always a hint of vintage about his style. The most iconic accessory was his blazer. Fitting the green vibe, the blazer was white with an ivy pattern. Some of the ivy had a golden border around it.

"I like you more without clothes," the girl said.

By now, Kilian was annoyed. She was a sweet girl but way too clingy for his taste.

One day, you will rule the magical world, and your nonsense has to stop. He could hear his father's words clearly in his head. He would never complain about growing up in a palace, but he also hadn't asked for all the duties that were yet to come if he were king one day. Being the prince who would lead one day was stressful enough. But there was no chance that Alegro would let him pass on leading the kingdom one day, even though Kilian had considered introducing this idea to the family at dinner once or twice in the last weeks. In his eyes, Kalimba would be much better on the throne. His younger sister was a natural leader. But also a woman—and a woman on the throne? That had never happened before in the internationally diverse bloodline of the Lancasters.

"So do I, but I need to go. Have a good day, my love." He stepped over to the bed, gave her a long enough kiss to make her believe he would come back, and then left the flat.

He walked along the streets of Greenwich, not far from the riverside. At least he had chosen a district that had a portal to his world. Luckily, he could use portals to go wherever he wanted, no matter if to the human or magical worlds. The portal traffic was watched by the council. Regardless, something was off this morning. Looking around, Kilian recognised the cars and buses were moving slower. His attention was caught by a girl standing in front of an electronic shop. She kept staring at the TV inside the shop as if she were hypnotized. Kilian stepped behind her to watch the TV as well.

"Terrible night for all the magicians out there," the little girl whispered. She didn't seem to be herself. The TV showed the corpse of a magician who had died last night—drowned while doing the legendary water tank trick.

Kilian froze. That wasn't a good sign.

"She isn't the only one. Nineteen others died as well." The girl turned around and stared at Kilian. She looked awfully pale, and something was wrong with her eyes.

"It has only begun, Prince Lancaster." Her voice was now dark and scratchy.

Before Kilian could do anything, the girl's body fell to the ground and vanished, like a drop of water hitting the ground. Kilian flicked his fingers, and in the next second, he was at the nearest portal. As a member of the royal family, he was growing quickly alarmed. He knew this was something that he and his cousin had to figure out, a new case on the doorstep.

***

The little girl appeared back in Icon in a dark alleyway, somewhere in the Doom District. Her eyes were still rolled back, showing only the white part.

"Did the trigger work?" a dark voice asked from the shadow of the alleyway.

"Of course. I will sent him a Vision that will manipulate his mind. He won't get good sleep for the next days," the girl answered, smirking.

"Well done. Envy is waiting for you at the Manor. Keep an eye on her, she has lately been intact with her powers," the voice ordered.

The little girl agreed, once again letting herself fall to the ground and vanish into nothingness.

***

"Where the hell is he again?" asked Alegro Lancaster, king of Icon and father to Kilian.

Alegro walked up and down while waiting with other family members in the main hall of the palace. It was a classic throne room, almost completely white except for the two big thrones for the king and queen. The thrones were silver with black cushions. Other than most rooms in the palace, the throne room was nearly plain, except for the giant painting of the family tree on the left side of the thrones that showed a diverse history and bloodline of royal members from all around the world. The throne room was used for any big event that happened in the palace, when the royal family changed the look of the throne room with the help of their magic. They made sure whoever came to pay a visit left with a mind-blowing memory.

"Is our brother ever on time?" asked Kennady, Kilian's younger sister. She was just sixteen, but she had a big mouth and a sharp mind. Next to her stood Kalimba, who was twenty years old and could be found in the garden of the palace most of the time, not only because she was a Nature magician, but also because she found it peaceful. Together with Kennady, she belonged to the Green League of magic. Kalimba was a Woods; her younger sister was an Element in the name of fire. She could control and use it, while Kalimba was in control of nature itself and gained power from everything that happened in nature. While Kalimba was known as the calm soul of the family, Kennady was known for the biggest conflicts. Unlike her siblings, she still had a lot to learn and was not in balance with her powers yet.

"Brother, relax. Kilian has probably seen what happened already. Let him be," said the soft voice of Synclair Lancaster. Unlike his older brother, Synclair knew how to control his temper, and when it came to Kilian, Synclair had learned to be patient and let the prince exert his free will since he was doing what he wanted either way.

Alegro rolled his eyes. Kilian's behaviour couldn't go on like this, especially when the rumours were true. His gaze wandered over to Tyana, his wife. She had been quiet the whole morning. Tyana usually had a calm nature, but there was a certain kind of quietness with her that meant something was wrong—he had learned that within weeks of finding each other, not long after Kilian's true mother had died. The moment Kilian's real mother, Amalia, had died, Alegro had changed. There had not been a day since that he wasn't making sure to keep Kilian in line and wish for the best outcome as future king. Years of harsh training and discipline had followed for the young prince. Rowen and Amadelia, Jegor's parents, had tried their best to help, along with Synclair and his wife, Leandra. But Kilian showed the same temper his mother had. She had been a Feeling under the Red League. The training with Kilian had only gotten better the moment Alegro met Tyana. As a magician from the White League, she brought the calmness the family needed. However, since then, Jegor's parents had passed and Leandra was not with them anymore. The king let out another sigh, feeling that his son had just entered the palace.

***

"I don't need to ask Carlin to tell you that everyone is waiting."

"It's always a pleasure to see you, Jegor, colourfully dressed as always," Kilian answered his older cousin, just entering the palace after the morning's encounter.

Jegor didn't react. Both cousins went on towards the throne room. Kilian knew that his father wouldn't be pleased.

"Did you hear anything yet?"

"It's everywhere on the news, Kil—even in their world. I went to the Market Square in the morning. Everyone is talking about it. The council has given a message to everyone to stay calm. They are waiting for our next move. Whatever happened last night isn't like the cases we had to deal with before."

If Jegor could look any more serious, it was at this moment.

"How is it possible that nineteen of us are dying at the same time? What kind of sick magic is that?" Kilian asked. He had seen higher numbers before. But this time it had hit his League. Kilian Lancaster was proud to be a Trickster. Nineteen of them dying at the same time didn't go unnoticed. Tricksters were visionaries, ones that pulled people into illusions, juggling the balance between dreams and reality. Kilian was alarmed.

"Are you serious or did you really forget the lecture of the seals?" Jegor asked.

"You are kidding me, right? If that happens, we're close to the end of the world, and I'm not ready yet to serve the crown like my father wants me to!" Kilian fired back. Unlike his cousin, Kilian had barely paid attention in mythology class. Urban Legends existed in his world, but his father had made sure that focusing on royal manners and status was a more relevant priority.

"Of course, that's the only problem you care about, you dramatic diva." Jegor sighed and opened the door to the throne room.

"Father!" Kilian said in a delighted tone, but Alegro didn't appear happy to see him in return.

"We'll discuss your behaviour later. For now, my duty is to give you the information about the case. Listen carefully. Time is now against us, and if we don't act quickly, we might lose more than we already have."

Jegor and Kilian exchanged a look. When it came to cases, there was no one else they trusted as much as one another. In this moment, both knew how serious this situation was, and yet still, both were sceptical.

"Go on then," Jegor said, and he could hear Carlin laughing inside his head.

"Last night, nineteen magicians died—at the same time, practising the same trick. It's none of our close friends. Some of them were very young magicians. It's a warning. Something is going on that I should have told you about years ago. I was arrogant in thinking nothing would happen—that the balance would stay."

Alegro focused on the two cousins. "I only gave you the lecture about the seven seals once, but now it's more than needed. Someone has stolen one of the seven seals that provide the balance between our world and the human world. Since the magicians got attacked, we think it must be either the Aquanda seal or Fenero. One of them provides the knowledge to magic. Synclair and I will investigate, but we are quite certain about this. The seal must have been at least removed, to make something like this happen."

"But I am a Trickster, and I still know the key to Houdini's oldest trick. Why didn't I get hurt?" Kilian asked, looking around. No one seemed to be shocked—not even his sisters. Kilian felt his tension rising inside and familiar anger crawling up his neck. Did his father really hide something that important from him? Kilian knew that mythology existed in New Born Kingdom. He knew that the stories humans told each other were all true. But the Urban Legends differed from the common mythology. No one could exactly tell when they had started; some rumoured them to be fiction, while others called them magic beyond New Born Kingdom.

"Exactly. Kilian shouldn't know big secrets anymore, unless there is something you want to tell us, Alegro?" Jegor's eyes went to the king. There was cynicism in his voice. Kilian knew he didn't trust his father. It had gotten worse since the day Jegor's parents died. He didn't blame Jegor. His side of the family had barely paid attention to him since Rowen and Amadelia were gone. Synclair, Kalimba, and Kilian were his only contact in the palace.

"Tell him, Alegro," Tyana Lancaster said calmly. "They are not children anymore, and if you don't tell, I will." She stood from her throne.

Synclair let out a little giggle. "I love the tense atmosphere in this family," he commented, and clapped in his hands.

"This is not funny, Synclair—"

"Exactly. It's not." Synclair cut off Alegro's words. "I've told you years ago you should educate them—that you should let them know every day, every night what can come for them. Jegor lost his parents. Denying that you won't lose one of them because of Kilian is selfish and foolish, Alegro!" Anger was written on Synclair's face. Kilian hadn't seen his uncle that angry since the last family feast five years ago. The situation was serious. Confusion riddled Kilian's face. Was his father seriously hiding something from him? Something connected to the Urban Legends? When Kilian had been working for the city and solving cases, had he been lied to, not knowing the bigger picture of the system he was living in? His thoughts were running wild. What was his father thinking? How could he treat them as the future of Icon and not explain what legend he was connected to? Something that was beyond anything he had been learning on his path of magic. Kilian's confusion turned into a bitter glare at his father.

"Your uncle is right. For the sake of both of you, I was hiding this too long from you. I made this a secret. We as a royal family together decided to treat it as secret, making sure to protect both of you from the reality in our society. But now is the time that you need to know. There is a legend—a legend that found its way to us when you were born, Kilian." Alegro took a deep breath and looked over to his wife.

Kilian saw Tyana nod and open her hands. She closed her eyes, mumbling a spell that materialised a parchment scroll in her hand. She took a deep breath before she started to read the words on the paper. "Every legend begins with a simple story," she started, and over the following minutes related the legend of Merlin:

Merlin's Legend

Every legend begins with a simple story,
but this one doesn't shine with gold and glory.

When the clock strikes twelve
and the case is broken,
the crown shall choose
when Loyalty has spoken.

Seven children are the key,
where one must set them free.
Time and Trust are the hardest task
when Love and Lies hide behind mask.

Don't wait too long
before the balance is gone.

Now take these words wisely.
Follow the path precisely.

Never cross a snake in the morning,
'cause if you do so,
Pandora's box releases the real show—

A show that no world can stand and see
when Apocalypse is free.

Kilian and Jegor both needed to process what they had just heard. The legend of Merlin had been nothing more than a fairy-tale to them back in the days when they were children. No one around the royal family had ever mentioned how important it was. It was folklore n the society, known in every League. Kilian and Jegor had always known it as something that would be read when they were younger. A magical goodnight story with no deeper meaning.

Kilian eventually found his voice. "How could you hide this from us? Making us believe these words were just another urban legend? And then you pretend that the only important thing in my life is to find a wife and have your crown on my head one day! Aren't you ashamed of yourself?" Kilian didn't scream, but his anger was written on his face, and his voice was under pressure. He was twenty-seven years old, and his father hadn't mentioned once that he was connected to any of this. Nor did his sisters, uncle—any of them.

He looked over to Jegor. Why was he so calm? "Did you know any of this?" he asked him, and for a moment Kilian felt like everyone in this room had hidden this.

"He didn't," Alegro said. "When we got the prophecy, it wasn't clear if it would ever happen. That is why I wanted you to focus on the crown. But disappointingly enough, you would rather sleep around, get drunk, and focus on magician shows in the human world!"

"Oh, Father, you make it sound like it's a bad thing," Kilian fired at his father. His emotions slowly took over. He was famous for investigating in this city. He was the face of the palace, the heir to the throne. He had met creatures connected to folklore before. Had seen dark shadows and fear in all forms. Kilian had learned how to separate folklore and mythology from fictional legends—or so he thought. Why had they been hiding this other than making it a secret for protection? Kilian didn't understand. What would the people say if they knew about this? Or did they know, and he was the only one that had been lied to? The future king was tangled in his thoughts, trapped between anger, confusion, and misunderstanding.

"Why are you so upset? I think it's pretty cool to be a hero," Kennedy said.

"Oh, shut up! Like you're one to talk. You would fucking throw up if a corpse with a ripped-out tongue would lie in front of you. You haven't seen shit as Jegor and I have, Buttercup. Or should I point out what fucking family tree of liars we have here? For what? What else have you been hiding for the sake of royalty?!" Kilian shouted, ready to throw a spell at his sister.

"Kilian, enough!" Tyana screamed, and everyone went silent. "I know you are upset, and you have every right to be. But your father and I both made this choice. If you want to be angry, you have to take your anger out on us. Nevertheless, you and Jegor are two of the chosen children and someone has removed the seal. Do you even realize what kind of responsibility is in your hands? For now, it's only one seal. But if another one is taken, it gets worse. The balance will overturn, and the human world isn't ready for us. They never were. It will lead to war and tragedy. People are confused and think it's been a tragedy itself that so many magicians died. But if another seal gets taken, the gap will get bigger. People will wonder and see behind what we see. You must protect that. You and Jegor need to find the children, whether you like it or not."

Kilian balled his hands into fists and swallowed hard. Why were they so keen on holding the balance together? Was it the hate against humans? What would be so wrong if both worlds mixed? Kilian couldn't stop thinking.

"How are we supposed to find the other children? And how do we know where the seals are to protect them?" Jegor asked.

Kilian gave him a death stare. How the hell could he be so calm? Did he really not know anything? Was he not at least a bit mad at all of them for hiding this?

"So far, from what we figured, the legend tells us that each child will have a Vision, Dream, or Omen about another child. We think the legend is now happening, so whatever happens next, you are connected. One of you is able to find the first child and the seals. We taught you everything over the last few years that you need to know as magicians. I'm praying to Artemis every night that she will protect you." Tyana seemed shattered. Kilian held back another fierce comment. There was not a single cell in his system that would bring empathy for any of them right now. Hiding something like this and making him look like a fool in front of everyone. If anything, they had only driven him further away by doing this. He wouldn't be surprised if his grandmother and father had something to do with this as well. The anger boiled under his skin.

"One more thing, Mother," Kilian said, ignoring his father. "Why is this sounding like a goodbye?" His voice was as calm as it could be right now. Even though she wasn't his true mother, Kilian liked Tyana. She had done her best to help him whenever she could in the past—especially when his father had nothing else in mind than pressuring him with duties towards his title. But that didn't change the fact that she had been lying to them as well. Treating this type of legend as a secret and not something as part of the Urban Legends hit hard.

Tyana didn't face Kilian. Something was wrong. Kilian had the urge to scream. Usually he tried to avoid family gatherings, but right now all he wanted was answers and the truth, regardless of how painful it was.

It was now Kalimba who stood up and looked at her brother. "The children of the seal all have one thing in common." A moment of silence stood between all of them before she continued. "They will lose someone close to them, most likely a family member."

Kilian froze. He couldn't believe this. Before any of them could say anything else, the prince had turned around and walked away as quickly as he could. Memories were running through his mind, pictures and moments he'd left far behind. But now he couldn't think of anything else. He saw his true mother in his mind, her corpse. It would happen again. He would go through loss, just because he was some chosen child who had to save the world for everyone's sake. How could they think it was okay to hide this mystery from him? He wasn't a teenager anymore, either. All these years of magic and practice he had taken for nothing but folklore. The palace and council were responsible for sorting the legends into the ones that were true and the ones that were fiction. Especially to separate them from the folklore that was also known in the human world. Kilian heard footsteps following behind him. He didn't have to turn around to know it was Jegor. There was no one else he would talk to after this new revelation of information.

***

Shoreditch was the district in Icon that never seemed quiet—not even in the early morning hours. It was loud, lively, and colourful. Like the area in the human world carrying the same name, Shoreditch was artistic. Street art decorated nearly every corner. Small markets for any kind of creative arts, pubs, and cafes were often the places for street magicians to perform their magic and entertain. *The Black Fairy* was one of these cafes, right in the middle of Shoreditch.

"Did you hear what he just said? He thinks Samhain is better than Yule! Did you put that into his head, Relayne?" Summer looked at her best friend in shock.

Ashton just rolled his eyes and continued to drink his chocolate milkshake.

"I haven't said anything, but I can't blame him for being right," Relayne answered.

Summer seemed like she wanted to slap at least one of them. "You two are stressing me out way too much."

"You will always be stressed," Ashton commented, and gave her a little smile.

"Oh, shut up," she said, but decided to give him a kiss on the cheek.

Relayne smiled. Seeing Summer so happy with Ashton made her happy, too. One year ago, Summer had introduced her to Ashton, and she'd never seen her best friend so happy. Summer was a twenty-three-year-old Feelings just like Relayne. The Feelings belonged to the Red League of magic. They were able to control, feel, and understand someone else's feelings. Summer's fawn brown skin and the black Afro contrasted Relayne's pale skin, freckles, and ginger hair. Ashton had similar skin to Summer's but more tattoos and curly, short black hair. His style was a mix between a skater boy and rock artist.

"So, Relayne, how's it going?" Summer asked.

Relayne looked tired; dark circles under her eyes, her hair roughly made into a messy bun. "I just keep on having this weird Dream all the time. I see these two guys coming into the cafe, and then everything gets blurry. I don't know." She sighed.

"Sounds like you need some fun time. You're putting more work into this cafe than you should. Even Relayne Parker needs a break once in a while," Summer said, and Ashton nodded in agreement.

"But the Black Fairy doesn't run on its own," Relayne argued.

"You need some better promotion. We can help you with that. Or we'll find you more workers so you can have your own life as well," Ashton suggested, and Summer nodded.

"Thank you, guys. You're the best. Mum would be proud to see that I at least have good people like you in my life," Relayne said, and her eyes went to a photo behind the counter. It showed her and Skylar when she was younger—two years before Skylar had died. Relayne had been eighteen when her mother had died. The circumstances were still unclear. After her death, Relayne had taken full responsibility over the Black Fairy. She lived in a small flat above the cafe. It was big enough for one person, and for her, it was more than okay.

"You can always count on us. And because of that, we have a surprise for you." Summer smirked.

The next moment, the door opened, and a person stepped into the cafe. She had long legs, a skinny figure, and curly, white-blond hair that reached her shoulders.

"Baelfire!" Relayne ran towards the beauty who'd just entered the place.

"Hello, baby girl. Summer promised me to not say anything, but I had to see you." A bright smile lit up Baelfire's face. She always had some extraordinary style and make-up. There was something weirdly crazy about her, the kind you wanted to get to know better. The person that was an inspiration to any pop artist out there.

"I have two tickets for the circus tonight, and you have absolutely no chance to say no."

"Really? But what if I do?" Relayne bit her lower lip, knowing Baelfire couldn't resist.

Before they could kiss each other, another voice interrupted.

"Excuse me a second."

Relayne looked over to the table where the voice had come from, then went to the table and looked at the person. Of course it was *him*. "Rose. I guess you wanna have your fave order besides *maybe* telling me how you always enter my cafe without me seeing?"

The man with the dark red hair and the left arm full of rose tattoos smiled. "Where would the fun be if you know?" he answered with a quiet but gentle voice.

"Same order? Or is there anything else you wanna tell me?"

Rose had been a visitor to the cafe since she had taken it over from her mother. Relayne didn't even know his real name. All she knew was that he was handsome, had tattoos, and always seemed to know more than anyone else.

"For starters, take care of yourself. In case you haven't realised who you are dealing or surrounding yourself with."

He didn't look up from the book he was reading. *Milton's Paradise.*

"Sure," Relayne's answered, then stepped away, wondering if there was any truth to his words.

***

Kilian looked outside the window. After the revealing news, he and Jegor had gone to Jegor's flat.

"As much as I'd like to give you your quiet time, we have a mission, a new case. The palace has found out that Aquanda was stolen—the seal deep down in the Thames. Whoever it was that took it must be powerful, since some monsters are down there. That also means now the monsters aren't controlled by the seal anymore, so we might have to deal with more deaths soon."

Kilian turned around and faced Jegor. "How in Merlin's name do you think I am capable of doing this? I have done nothing else other than losing myself the last year to escape the madness of the palace. Now everyone expects me to suddenly be a hero and do everyone a favour by saving them." Kilian shook his head. "And since it's not enough, because of this legend, I'm going to lose either my sister or mother. Unless they take my father; that would be a relief at last."

Jegor nodded, even though he knew Kilian did care about his father. But his cousin wasn't very sensitive when it came to his father and often released his pain with hate. "I understand that you're angry, but I also know that you love this world. No one loves magic more than you do. You're a Trickster, Kilian, and nineteen of your kind got killed last night. Don't pretend that it doesn't matter to you, because it even matters to me. These are our people, and someone is trying to destroy the balance. Each seal has its own purpose that keeps us separate from the human world. Imagine what happens when someone takes all of the seals. He or she could create a new world, enforce new rules, and, especially, break the shield between us and the humans. If we don't stop them, you're going to wish your father was your worst enemy soon."

A little laugh interrupted the discussion.

"In Houdini's goddamn name, how many times have I told you that Carlin needs to stop being a little creeper when we have serious discussions?!" Kilian shuddered.

Jegor smiled, and if that wasn't scary enough, the little Voodoo doll on Jegor's belt looked over to Kilian, as if it was the most normal thing in this room.

Jegor was right. though—Kilian loved this world. Magic was the reason he woke up every day. Just with no responsibility of being the future king. Sometimes he was wondering how it would be if his mother was still alive. If he would be responsible. She was probably looking down on him, sipping tea and laughing about the mess this society was. Especially the palace and council together. Kilian couldn't get the thought out of his head that there was more than just the secret of the legend. But for now it was enough to have him on the edge.

"Have you any idea where we should start? Unless you want spend another hour staring out the window while the world is burning down," Jegor interrupted his thoughts.

"No worries, princess. I certainly have an idea," Kilian replied. After all, it wasn't the first situation where he had been confronted with something in favour of his own discomfort. Most of the cases Kilian was disgusted about the creatures they had to deal with. White eyes, no eyes, rotten teeth, long tongues, no tongue, the creatures in and beyond Icon had a grotesque diversity. But back then it was the choice of council or palace work and, luckily, he was able to convince his father to start his training as investigator together with Jegor. One of the rare responsible things he did in his life so far. Kilian loved the thrill of an investigation, seeing the true faces of magicians and what they could hide. He knew that the system had gaps and problems, holes where people slid in and used it as opportunity to do something illegal. That's where he and Jegor did their work, finding these people and putting them into the prison underneath the council in Icon. But the young future king knew that this wasn't like any other case. This was a prophecy, something that had been written in stone, whether it was Merlin himself or someone else. If a prophecy was true, it meant magic of the old ages. The time where society had just formed itself in New Born Kingdom. Something that potentially had happened before or could happen in the form of another doomsday. Kilian felt his migraine rising the more he thought of the complexity behind this. But there was something that had happened lately that was a potential first clue to the situation.

"She was in my dreams last week. At first, I thought my creativity had taken over, but sadly, it wasn't any of my lustful dreams. She must be the Vision father mentioned. I am used to Dreams. But this was different. A Vision. I once met her when I was younger. Little did I know it was a magical meeting. But we shall see if she is now worthy enough to be one of us." Kilian started walking towards the entrance door. As a Trickster of the Red League, he was used to having the so-called Dream. All magicians in the Red and Green Leagues had them. But Visions were a privilege of the White League. Kilian had learned in his early teenage years how to separate a Vision from a Dream.

"What's her name?" Jegor asked.

Kilian turned around with a smirk on his face.

"Relayne. Relayne Parker."

Chapter 2
Relayne

And to hold the balance, he created the Feelings.
To give them the chance to make things better and right.
– F. F., "The Dollmaker," *The True Urban Legends*

After Baelfire's arrival, she, Summer, and Ashton left Relayne to work. For once, it seemed to be a calm day at the cafe. Relayne had heard what had happened in the news, and being at work meant being distracted from the dark reality. It wasn't the first case where magicians were killed, but not so many at once and not so many Tricksters. Rose still sat in his corner, not showing much interest in conversation. Sometimes she wondered if he had a bigger purpose for being here. But then, he was probably just another lost soul trying to escape the problems this society brought to anyone living in the magical world.

Not everything was good, and there were still too many differences between the four Leagues. It wasn't just the difference related to poor and rich; it was also about being treated right, no matter what bloodline or magical power ran through their veins. Or the fact that most of the council members were from the White League. The only equal circle was the head of the council, put together as eight members from the society, two of each League. Everyone else underneath was a White or Green. It had taken nearly six months, after the death of Relayne's mother, to get the licence for the cafe. Relayne didn't like the council, but what could one magician do in a complicated political system like Icon's?

Next to Rose's table sat two siblings, Alicia and Flynn, who came here once in a while to have a good start in the morning before they went off to do their magical duties in Icon.

Relayne wanted to bring a coffee to another customer when she realised that time had stopped in her cafe, and only she could still move. She looked around and saw two strangers sitting at her counter.

They weren't strangers, exactly. She knew who they were. Everyone in the city knew them.

"How come two princes are visiting me here?" she asked, biting her bottom lip.

"To correct you, first, I'm not a prince. Kilian is," Jegor stated, and gave her a gesture that told her to sit down with them, so they could talk.

Relayne went over to the counter and sat down on the other side. Why were they here? Did they want to ask questions about her mother? Had she forgotten to pay a bill last month? Where they on a hunt for their newest case?

"We make her nervous. I don't have to be a Trickster or Feelings to know that," Kilian commented in amusement, which prompted an annoyed glance from Relayne.

"Guess it's true what they say about your big mouth," Relayne said. She crossed her arms.

"Fierce. I like that. Do you even remember me in the slightest?"

"Should I, Kilian? Besides the fact that you belong to the royal shit court, I don't see any reason I should remember your face. Or do you wanna tell me you're the same boy who wanted to help me years ago?" Relayne asked. As a Feeling, she could remember any person or creature that she had ever been connected to, though it was her decision to choose if she wanted to remember the connection. Kilian being the prince and soon-to-be king was something she had clearly not forgotten. Even if she wanted to, he was too often presented in media and their daily life.

Relayne saw Jegor glance at his cousin. The Feeling raised an eyebrow.

"Don't hurt my feelings, red witch," Kilian said with slight cynicism.

"Luckily, our bond is nearly black, so there isn't much to hurt," Relayne answered. She looked over to Jegor. Being able to remember connections was one thing, but seeing the connections between people, shown in the form of strings, was another. Depending on how close someone was or felt towards each other, the colour of the string changed. Colours could vary in all shades of the colour theory. Grey or black usually meant there was nothing at all or the connection was broken.

"Can you tell me now why you're here? I'm running this business, and at the moment, freezing my customers doesn't help at all." Relayne wasn't sure if she even wanted to hear what they had to say. It was true that Kilian's emotion string was nearly black, but there was an underlying magenta that left Relayne with concern. The one between her and Jegor was green, which stood for nothing more than simply knowing him without having any stronger feelings.

"You're one of the chosen children of the seal. Kilian saw you in his Visions. And if you noticed, last night, magicians died, because one of the seals was removed. The prophecy about us, the children of the seal, is now happening. And we need your help to fix the balance before more people die."

Relayne remained silent. This couldn't be true. She was supposed to be one of the children? It was only an Urban Legend that her mother had told her, nothing that she could ever imagine being true at all. She knew that there were legends that existed and others that didn't. But Relayne belonged to one of the lower classes, where there was no access to certain details within the magic system.

"But how do you know that I am the one? Now and then, magicians have Visions. That doesn't mean I'm the one who's in charge of your misery." Relayne was too sceptical to easily believe this. Maybe she had done something wrong towards the palace, and now the royal family was trying to test her. Or the council. She wouldn't be surprised.

"She has a point, Jegor," Kilian said, looking at his cousin. "Besides, someone from the street? Really?"

Relayne was tempted to throw something at Kilian.

"You lost your mother, right?" Jegor asked Relayne, staring at her intensely.

Silence was Relayne's first reaction, before she spoke up. "I did. But does that have anything to do with the legend?"

"The prophecy told us that every child had a loss inside their family. Someone who was close to them died—or is going to die. How did your mother die, Relayne?"

Relayne swallowed hard and looked down at her feet. She remembered that Summer had once been visited by a council member named Joseph. She had been through the same thing as Relayne, losing her mother, too. Relayne knew there was no way she could avoid the talk. People above her would always get the answers, one way or another. Relayne felt cold sweat running down her back and clenched her fists she looked up to the royal family members.

"She was sick—very sick—from one day to another. Nothing of that made sense. She kept on telling me that there was a reason she had to go," Relayne told them, breathing faster and voice shaking slightly. "So if that's the reason, I don't want any of this. Magicians like me have to fight for everything in this society, while you drink tea and get the best support for everything."

Kilian couldn't help but giggle. "Instead of blaming the royal family, you should work on yourself. It's easy to judge others when you only know one side of the story."

Relayne balled one of her hands into a fist and hit the counter, her eyes starting to glow red, showing a sign of her abilities. "One more word, and I'll make you shut up," she said.

"Try me. But in Houdini's name, you wouldn't dare to fight me," Kilian said quietly, in a tone that was still provocative.

"Enough of this," Jegor interrupted. "I can understand your anger and your mistrust in us. But this isn't about the classes of our society. This is about much more than you are seeing at the moment. The first seal got removed and made magicians worldwide lose their memory and ability to do certain tricks. If this goes on, more terrible things will happen. We don't know who has done this, and it's on us to find out and protect the world we live in before more damage is done. You come from a dark side, Relayne. I can see it, and I get why you're hurt. But you're not the only one who has been suffering, and I live under this crystal-clear palace, which you think is so on top of everything."

Jegor stood up and walked away without another word. Relayne and Kilian looked at each other one more time before Kilian went after his cousin.

Time resumed in the cafe, and Relayne took a deep breath. She looked over to the picture of her and her mother before her gaze met Rose's—as if he had seen what just happened.

***

"You need to do something about this," a dark, rough voice said to Baelfire, who stood near the Black Fairy, which Jegor and Kilian had just left.

"Why should I make her join them, when she can join us?" Baelfire answered, looking over to the shadows of the street from which the voice came.

35

"This is not how it's going to work. She needs the struggle to see who is best for her. You can do that, right? She loves you; make her join them."

Baelfire sighed. "She loves this overdramatic image of me. I'm literally the most extraordinary person she knows, and that she admires. I wouldn't call that love at all. But fine, *wolf*. If you say so, I shall have a talk with her."

The shadow left with a creepy laugh. Baelfire took a cigarette out of her jacket and re-entered the cafe.

***

"Hey, babe." Baelfire faced Relayne with a smile.

"Didn't you say you were busy until tonight?" Relayne asked, preparing new orders.

"Plans have changed, and I wanted to look after you. Did I just see right that you had a visit from the royal highnesses themselves? Kilian is indeed attractive, and I wonder if I should be worried about anything?" Baelfire raised an eyebrow and glanced at Relayne with a cheeky smile.

"He is a spoiled brat. That's all. Looks don't make anything better. But yes, you have seen it right. They basically wanted to hire me for a new case. They told me I'm involved in something much bigger than everyone else seems to know about. Can you believe that? Me being the next superhero? I don't think so, not at all." Relayne sighed.

"Okay, first, stop being so harsh on yourself. Just because society makes you believe you're not worth any of this doesn't mean you're not. Your mother always told you, you were meant for something bigger, for something better in Icon. Maybe she knew what was going to happen."

"Jegor said the reason she died is that I'm involved in this. How do you feel about something like that? I killed my mother, Baelfire." Relayne took a deep breath. Saying it out loud felt even worse. Even if it wasn't true, it was a hard pill to swallow.

Baelfire grabbed Relayne's hand. "You didn't kill your mother, darling. Sometimes fate decides what's going to happen for us. Your mother taught you the best as long as she could. And look who you are—a young, strong Feeling who is just at the beginning of this journey. If you're a puzzle piece to this whole thing that's going on at the moment, don't run away from it. Magic comes with a price, and sometimes we have to pay for it. Don't tell me you don't love the world we live in. I can see it every day that you love your ability. Maybe now is the time to make something great out of it and show them what you're worth. If you're the one who can change things, why don't you try?" Baelfire started smiling.

Relayne leaned over the counter and gave her a long, thankful kiss. "Sometimes I wonder how you made it into my life. But then, we have these moments, and I know exactly why you're in my life." Relayne let go of Baelfire's hands. "If I start this journey, I'm not sure if I can still see you as much as I want to. What if I can't cope with the fact that I might be losing you too?"

Baelfire giggled a little. "Darling. You will never lose me. I will always find my way back to you. But now you need to go and find them before it's too late. I know you can do it. And while you're away, I'll take care of the cafe."

"Thank you, Baelfire. I owe you something."

Relayne was still unsure when she left the cafe behind. Though she had to try and see. That was the thing about magic. It came with uncertainty and opened ways to the unknown.

Baelfire looked after her girlfriend and sighed. She knew how to take care of the café, but she wasn't sure if she was ready to see Relayne less, and walking next to Kilian Lancaster.

***

"So what are we supposed to do now? And why the hell did you take me to Doom?" Kilian asked, looking around. Doom was the darkest district in Icon and well known for most of the magic of the Black League. The sun didn't shine as high as it did in the other districts, the water was darker, and the night was longer.

"My Vision was my room. But not in the flat I live in. It was a different building. I didn't see a person. Could be that this room was a connection to a place that we have to find."

Kilian rolled his eyes and sighed. "Oh, brilliant. Now we're one with a magical house. But why in Houdini's name in the most disgusting district of them all? How are we supposed to find motivation here when everything is so dark?"

"I think it's suitable," Jegor said, and showed the slightest hint of a smile.

"All right, Frankenstein. I'm sure you can tell me where the house is?"

"Maybe. Carlin might wanna help me out here?"

The Voodoo doll looked up to Jegor. *If so, does that mean I can walk you to the house?*

"No, he certainly can't. And also, get out of my head! I've told you many times!" Kilian seemed frustrated.

"Let him be. The only person he ever really speaks to is me," Jegor said defensively.

Thank you, Jegor. But I do annoy Kilian on purpose.

Jegor couldn't help but smile once more.

"What did he say?" Kilian asked, but Jegor just shrugged his shoulders.

Only a true child can find it; that's for sure.

"I think we need to work together on this. Give me your hand," Jegor said, facing Kilian.

"It's been a while since we worked together." Kilian reached out his hand.

Jegor took one of the little knives from his belt and made a cut in his hand and another in Kilian's. He put their hands together before he closed his eyes and started to mutter words in Latin—a common language for the Black League and their spells. When he opened his eyes, they were completely black. Nocturna, the spell he was using, was a basis for the Black League to either see through walls or in the dark. All four Leagues of magic were able to use the same basic tricks to have it easier in life until they got sorted into their League at the age of four. The first years could show tendencies of the Leagues, but it wasn't until the ceremony when magicians became a part of the social system and started to learn the magic within the League that had chosen them.

Jegor tried to focus. He let his gaze wander, exploring the nearby area. Other than the inside of the houses nearby there was no direct hint, creature, or building that seemed odd enough to follow.

"Kilian, I could use help. Carlin, that counts for you as well."

"Fine then," Kilian answered. While still holding the blood bond that made it possible for Jegor to see through walls, he took a billiard ball from his jacket. It was a dark violet one with an eye on it. He threw it in the air, where he made it stop, casting a spell that turned it into dust. Once materialized, the dust spread out, turning into different numbers—coordinates, to be exact. Tricksters were able to use all kinds of gambling artefacts to turn them into useful things. Billiard balls were often used for organisation and direction. Pulvisara was a spell used to find coordinates.

"It's hidden," Jegor began to say. "Otherwise, I would be able to see it right now."

Strong magic comes with it. We probably need a key.

"And how the hell do we find that key?" Kilian asked Carlin.

"I can help," a female voice said behind them.

Both turned around and looked at Relayne.

She held a red key in one of her hands, the handle shaped like a heart.

"How delightful. Guess you finally came to the conclusion that we're the better company?" Kilian couldn't hide his satisfaction.

"No, not really, Kilian. And if there is one of you who I trust, it's your cousin. But if this stupid piece of paper decides to choose me, I'm willing to take the fate and make this world a better place."

Jegor and Kilian exchanged a look. While Jegor seemed impressed by her showing up, Kilian had to hold back a laugh.

"She has a point," Jegor said before Kilian could do anything, and the three of them moved on towards the direction of the coordinates.

"Your ego is really a burden, little red rose," Kilian said with a sigh.

"She is, for once, someone who doesn't immediately believe anything you say, Kil," Jegor answered.

Relayne smiled. "Your cousin is right. Just because you came a long way with your charming, sexual attitude, you don't have to think I'd fall for someone like that."

Kilian gave them an indignant look. "I'm not only good-looking. I'm also very clever and charming in my mind."

Oh yeah, certainly you are.

"Shut up, Carlin!"

"Who is Carlin?" Relayne asked.

"His little doll. He can speak and do so much more that you don't wanna see," Kilian explained, before all of them stepped into the street where the house was supposed to be.

"There's nothing here—not even hiding behind a spell." Kilian looked around.

"What about the true believer rule?" Relayne said.

"Might be a thing," Jegor said. "Whenever there seems no way, keep the spirit," he continued, repeating one of the main rules in New Born Kingdom.

"So you're saying our imagination will lead the way?" Kilian asked, raising an eyebrow. He didn't seem convinced. It wasn't that he didn't believe in the rule, but it seemed too easy. He also wasn't sure if the key Relayne was holding was the one opening it.

"Whenever this rule happens, we get tested. Remember the time we had to find Kennady when your parents went away? We couldn't find her anywhere, and you were on the verge of freaking out," Jegor reminded his cousin.

"I don't think I want to repeat that stressful situation," Kilian commented shortly.

All of them started to focus on their abilities. Jegor took a deep breath and closed his eyes. He was more focused when he closed his eyes due to his inner balance towards the Black League. Kilian took a deep breath, simply staring into nothingness, while Relayne made her hands into fists and stared at the sky. A long moment of silence passed between the three of them. Jegor thought of pure darkness, the one thing that had always surrounded him. Kilian thought of the endless possibilities that he had as Trickster between playing cards and illusions. Relayne thought of Baelfire and how their meeting had been one of the most magical things in her life.

After a while, something slowly began showing itself—a very long staircase made out of dark wood, leading up in the air, to something that none of them could see yet.

Jegor opened his eyes. "I guess we are all seeing this?" he asked, glancing at the other two magicians.

Relayne nodded, and without waiting any longer, went up the staircase, followed by the two cousins.

Up in the air, none of them could see the ground. That's why the house was placed in the Doom District; it was the darkest district and the house was only possible to access by the ones who proved to be worthy. A few houses like that existed in this area, covered by strong spells and curses.

Relayne looked at the door. "There is no lock," she stated.

Jegor looked over her shoulder. "Guess your key has another meaning, then," the older cousin stated.

"Great. How do we get inside? Abracadabra? Knock-knock, here is Johnny?" Kilian asked.

"I guess we have to do something," Jegor stated. He contemplated the burgundy door. "We need to show the house that we have a right to be here. That's usually blood sacrifice or giving a gift." Jegor grabbed his knife. He made another cut in his hand, then pressed it against the door. A creaking noise followed—the door opening itself. Jegor stepped through and the door closed behind him.

Kilian did the same, leaving Relayne the knife to follow after him. But the moment she did the same and put her hand on to the door, her hand started burning. Relayne groaned and shook her hand.

"What the hell?" she mumbled, and looked at her hand, seeing a symbol. She had seen a symbol like this before on a poster and sticker somewhere near the Underground of the Doom. Relayne blinked a few times. The symbol on her hand was gone.

"One more try," she said, pressing her hand onto the door again. This time it worked and Relayne entered.

The moment they all entered, magic began to reveal itself. It was big and bright inside. A long floor ahead granted access to different rooms. Jegor closed the door behind them and made his way forward. There wasn't much decoration, just a hall stand with three hooks that had little nameplates over them. Their names were written in there, leaving four other spaces. At the end of the hall, there was another staircase leading up, but the access was closed by a green, magical barrier.

"We have a living room and two bathrooms down here, along with a kitchen. My room is on the right at the end, and Kilian, yours is next to Relayne's at the beginning," Jegor explained after he'd explored. Each of the doors had a name tag as well. So far only three were named, like the ones above the hooks.

"How can the house know we're here? That it's us?" Kilian asked, unsure what to think about all this. Of course, he was excited about a whole new layer of magic. But on the other hand, it was hitting him that the prophecy was true, and there was a lot of weight lying on his and his cousin's shoulders.

Because Merlin himself made this house. He knew you would come. This magic goes back beyond to the days when most of the magicians had to hide.

"Great, now a doll gives me life advice." Kilian sighed, and it looked like Carlin was giving him a happy smile.

"However, the house knows us and that we are meant to be here. We have a new home now." Jegor stepped away and went into his room, closing the door.

"And you tell me that I have no charm," Kilian smirked at Relayne before he went into his room.

Relayne sighed before she stepped to the door marked with her name. She could feel a connection before she even touched the door handle. Her heart was beating faster, and finally she opened it. The view awaiting her took her breath away. It was a room full of red, white, and black decorations.

As if the house could read my whole desires and true wishes.

She closed the door behind her and started to look around. Everything was vintage. There was a giant photo wall with pictures of Ashton, Summer, and Baelfire over her white, king-sized bed. A cherry-red wardrobe had more space inside than appeared possible from the outside. There was even a desk and place for her tattoo drawings and other creative things she had in mind. When she looked over to the bookshelf, she could see that there were books that were supposed to be on the floor in her flat over the cafe.

"All my belongings are here as if they always had to be," she whispered to herself, stepping over to the window. She was sure she wouldn't be able to see anything because of the dark fog that was always hanging over the Doom District—but she was wrong. The window gave her a view over the district in a marvellous way. Dusk had just fallen, and she could see how the street lights were starting to glow. In the distance, she saw a tentacle coming out of the Icon River. The Doom was well known for some scary creatures who inhabited the area. The window gave her a perfect perspective over the city she had grown up in; a clash of cultures, from east to west and north to south. There was no similar part in Icon. Each district had its own architecture and atmosphere.

Relayne stepped over to the bed and sat down before she let herself fall to the back. She started smiling and closed her eyes. In this moment, she felt free and was sure she had made the right decision, ignoring the weird incident right before she had entered the house.

***

Baelfire checked the clock in her hand once more. It was half-past nine in the evening, and the show had already started. Relayne still wasn't here.

"She won't come. I could have told you, but that would have ruined your day already."

Baelfire turned around and faced the person who was standing in front of her—a tall, charismatic man with remarkable cheekbones and dark brown hair that was short and styled to the back. He was wearing a long black coat, which was closed and didn't reveal anything else besides his on-point black leather boots.

"Spare me, Polikarpowitsch," Baelfire hissed, looking into his eyes. "Just because she is with them doesn't mean she will forget about me. Or is there anything you didn't tell me before you made me convince her?" Baelfire trusted him, but Pieotr was well known for not telling the whole story.

"Since when do you call me by my surname?" He sounded amused.

"Only if you play me. You know how bad this can end for both of us. Don't you have anything better to do? Looking after Maddison, *Pieotr*?"

"She is with her monster." Pieotr seemed disgusted.

"So it's boredom that's leading you to me?" Baelfire raised an eyebrow.

"Not really. I just walked by and saw you suffering. Ever thought of coming out to her?"

"Are you kidding me? She loves me like this." Baelfire laughed.

"She does. But she's now with a prince. Have you seen Kilian Lancaster?" Pieotr took a pack of cigarettes out of his coat.

"She wouldn't fall for someone like that. That's not the Relayne I know," Baelfire answered quickly, crossing her arms.

"He has something that you have as well. Think about it." Pieotr walked away.

Baelfire looked after him, mixed feelings stirring inside her. She knew that Pieotr wouldn't expose her in any way, but he was right. And that left her with a bitter feeling. Baelfire focused on the tickets to the circus before she burned them and left the place.

***

While Baelfire didn't attend the show, Alicia and Flynn were in the middle of it. The two Vestergaard siblings were regular visitors of the circus. Alicia was less interested in the circus than Flynn, but for the love of her younger brother, she went with him anyway. Flynn had ash-blond hair and light blue eyes. Alicia's hair was nearly white, while her eyes were grey.

"Oh, it's starting," Flynn said with a grin. He had a silver ring piercing on his left lower lip, which complemented his friendly smile even more.

"I hope we're going to see blood," Alicia said with a smirk.

The circus was well known for the best illusions in town. Every year, the group of magicians who led the circus changed, but each member had first-class skills and was very creative. No storytelling was the same. This year's topic was the urban legends, the ones that were told around Icon and other big cities.

The light in the tent went off. An instrumental soundtrack started playing: an oboe setting the scenery, flowing together with the friendly strums of a harp and the crystal-clear chirps of birds. A fairy-tale dream. Shortly after that, green, lilac, and orange lights appeared around the audience. The room was glowing, revealing the setting of the storytelling—the Woods, one of the five districts in Icon, known for magicians belonging to the Green League. Flynn couldn't hold back his excitement. Beautiful magicians bending their genders, dressed as fairies, dwarfs, and other species appeared. One of them began to tell the legend of this evening. Flowers, trees, and other typical plants of the Woods grew in the show arena. A spectacle of glooming and breath-taking colours. Alicia smiled the moment a pack of wolves came running into the arena. Her focus went to a magician dressed as a dark creature.

Must be the villain of tonight's show, Alicia thought to herself. The next moment, he was nowhere to be seen. Confused, she blinked a few times, but the magician was gone.

"Did you see that guy in the right corner? He was very tall," Alicia asked her brother.

"Hmm? No. Sorry. My eyes are all on the beautiful fairies," Flynn answered.

Alicia tried once more to spot the magician she'd seen. But he didn't show up during the rest of the show, leaving Alicia with a weird feeling.

Chapter 3
Forbes

He can be under your bed. He can be next door.
Wherever he is, he will find you and get you.
– F. F., "The Crimson Eater," *The True Urban Legends*

Relayne woke up feeling sweaty, her blanket strewn beside her bed. It was morning, and she had just woken up from a very intense dream. She looked around before she realised she was in her new home. Relayne let herself fall back onto the bed and tried to calm her breathing. *You've been here before, it's just been a while.*

Something felt different—as if she hadn't really woken up. In her dream, she had been running along dark corridors, running away from something or someone that was hunting her. She hadn't been alone. Relayne was sure she'd heard Kilian's voice as well, and that didn't make anything better. Was it a Dream or a Vision? She ran her hands nervously through her hair. Anxiety crept up her chest, on the edge of taking her breath away. Still in shock, she got out of bed. It was time to talk with Kilian and Jegor. She needed their help.

***

"Morning, sunshine," Kilian said with absolutely no enthusiasm, not even looking up from the newspaper he was currently reading. Not that he was actually interested in what the local newspaper had to say in nine out of ten situations. However, since a new case was running, Kilian was relying on any resources he could find.

"What time is it?" Relayne asked.

"It's three in the afternoon. We tried to wake you up earlier, but we couldn't even open your door. Did something happen? You look as pale as a ghost," Jegor stated.

Relayne nodded. "I had a Dream, maybe a Vision. I was down in a dark chamber, and I was running away from something. You were there with me, Kilian. The smell was absolutely disgusting, as if something had died. I have no idea what this means, and I couldn't see clearly but I knew I didn't wanna turn around. Fear was in the room, as if I could touch it, I was so scared."

"Have you ever seen a chamber like it?" Jegor asked.

"No. But I know it was under a familiar building. At least it felt like it."

Kilian put away his newspaper and faced Relayne. "Have you ever done a spell that helps with finding places?"

"No. Usually my feelings and the connection towards something or someone work for me. That's how Feelings work, you know," Relayne said.

Kilian raised an eyebrow. "I like your sassiness. Let's get ready and find what you were looking for."

***

"So, how are we supposed to find the next child?" Relayne asked as they walked through the Doom District, trying to find a hint that would lead them towards the chamber Relayne had seen in her Dream.

"One of us has a Vision. I saw you in my Vision, so it's either you or Jegor. Unless we have something else, like a magical hint that points out who's next, I guess." Kilian sighed. Committing himself to this whole journey was still stressful for him. He could lose one of his family members any day, and whoever it would be, he knew it would be another slap in his face. He loved his sisters, even though they didn't spend as much time together as they used to. They'd all grown older, and with their different abilities, they'd gone separate ways. Though Kilian was lesser connected to Kennady. The Element of fire had her own head and, compared to him and Kalimba, Kennady was playing along with the royal rules.

For someone from a rich family, it was easier to learn new abilities. More wealth meant better mentors and schools where they could practise. Lesser wealth meant that it was a long, tough road of self-study and three schools that provided the bare minimum for each League. Some magicians who had to go that way even died. Having a look at the situation from this point of view showed Kilian that there was, indeed, a gap in the system, and not everything was as perfect as his father had always wanted him to believe. He wasn't blaming his father, for once. This was more a question of the system itself. What were they hiding? How could someone pass a seal like this? What kind of magic was used to do such thing? Kilian had not let go of the fact that his father had made the legend a secret.

When Kilian was younger, he had to study hard day and night. It was horrible for him from the day the ceremony had chosen him to be a Trickster. Tricksters were rare in this world. And since this case had started, that was even more true. The mortal world still believed that people like Houdini were just magicians who knew the secret behind the stage, but it was real magic. Houdini used to be one of Kilian's idols when he was younger. He was so fierce and brave, though somewhat insane. By now, it was a name that seemed like a curse, since everyone tried to compare him to someone else. Of course, Kilian had a big ego, but he would never compare himself to someone like Houdini.

"There it is. That's where the feeling is coming from. Do you see the red sparks? They're dancing around the doorstep." Relayne pointed at the door of the shop.

Kilian froze and Jegor let out a big sigh. Relayne looked at them, confused.

"What is it?" she asked.

"Let's just say it's not the first time this old friend is involved in something," Jegor answered, and the three made their way into the store.

***

"Fear's Polka Potion," Relayne whispered to herself when she entered the shop. A wave of different smells wafted towards her nose, and the next second, she sneezed.

"If that isn't a lovely—" Fear stopped when he looked at the trio. His focus was now on Relayne. He was staring at her—no, he was *observing* her, as if she were someone so special, so magnificent, that he couldn't believe she'd just entered the room. He walked over to her instantly, took her hand, and gave her a gentle kiss on her hand.

"You, my *dear rose*, are exactly the person I've been waiting for," he whispered, and Relayne couldn't help but shiver.

"Okay, Romeo, hands off," Kilian said.

Fear giggled in amusement and looked at the prince. He was a bit taller than Kilian. "Scared that, for once, I'm in the spotlight?"

"Enough of this nonsense," Jegor interrupted. "Fear, we're here because we're looking for a chamber where something or someone is hiding. We don't know yet. Can you help us out here?"

"If she's included, I'll do anything," Fear said, and winked at Relayne, which made her blush. She was used to comments like that from her customers, but there was something about him—his charisma and the way he looked at her, as if they had known each other for a long time.

Kilian seemed to be more annoyed. He'd never trusted Fear in the first place, and now he was acting like he knew something they didn't. Fear liked doing that, and even though he had helped them multiple times in the past, Kilian never considered Fear to be a friend.

"What can you tell us?" Jegor asked.

"Nothing to be exact. But I've seen the news as well, and since I'm a member of the council, we're literally not talking about anything else. No one knows who is behind all this and what is happening at the moment. I can tell you that it's nothing good when the seals are involved. I had to do a patrol and even get myself up to Madness. Can you believe it? Naughty magicians up there; I can tell you that for sure. Anyway, everything seems to be in order. Whoever stole the first seal wasn't on their own. We found out that the guards had been killed by the monster that was protecting the seal. So this person must be a very strong magician, probably capable of more than one League."

Fear went to a shelf to look for something.

"More than one League? But then this person must be registered. Everyone has an orb at the magic council, especially those who are able to do more than one League of magic. These things save everything from the moment the ceremony has happened," Kilian stated.

Relayne felt another shiver running down her back.

Fear looked at her once more. "You're a bit naïve, Relayne, if you think people aren't capable of doing something illegal in this city. This whole glory system has more gaps than Kilian is able to swallow billiard balls!"

"Pervert," Kilian answered sarcastically.

"What happened with the monster?" Jegor asked, ignoring their banter.

"We don't know yet," Fear said. He held a key in his hands, taken from a box. "Whoever did this has this monster under control now. That's one of the big problems we're working on at the moment. The monster left a message that was quite brutal—blood all over the floor and on the walls, rolling heads, if you know what I mean." Fear sighed as if he had been stressed out by choosing today's dinner menu. "But there was a clue that we found. There was something written in blood—it said *Superbia.*"

Now Jegor was holding his breath for a moment. He was hardly concerned about most things in life. While Kilian had contacts around the upper circle of society, Jegor knew his way around the underground. Each district had one. It was the lowest area, the circle where anyone was living that was bending rules and crossing boundaries against the law of Icon. You could only access the underground if you knew someone living there.

"Seems like you know something about this?" Kilian questioned his cousin.

"There are rumours about a group in the underground. I never paid attention to anything like that because there are so many of them. There was one name that came up more than one time—*the Seven Deadly Sins.*"

Relayne felt more uncomfortable every second. She had heard of underground groups as well, but luckily, she'd never been in contact with any of them so far.

"I've heard of them, too. But so far, we know nothing more." Fear pointed at the key. "That's the key to my chamber downstairs. You can check it out, but all I have are two dark corridors with boxes and potion stuff."

Kilian took the key and looked over at the others. "I guess it's enough if only two of us go. In case something happens," he said.

Fear snickered, and Jegor nodded.

Relayne went over and, together with Kilian, went down into the chamber. For a moment, it was completely dark. Relayne flicked her fingers and red matter in the form of little bubbles lightened the corridor.

"Of course he doesn't have a light switch like every normal person," Kilian murmured. He started looking around.

Fear was right. There were lots of boxes. Some were filled with herbs, others with liquids. Relayne started to look around as well.

"Let's just have a quick walk around, and then we can go back," she suggested.

"Yeah, but, darling, you took us here. Something must be here, and I'm not sure if I wanna find out what it is," Kilian said, concerned.

"Why are you so worried?" Relayne asked. "Someone like you doesn't really seem to be scared of anything."

"Have you never heard the urban legend about the Crimson Eater?"

"You mean the monster that lives in the shadow to snatch children and eat them?"

"Yes. Where do you think something like that would live if it had to choose a place?"

"Well, fair enough. But, Kilian, we are not kids anymore, and that legend is still a legend."

"Guess Fear was right, with calling you naïve." But if Kilian hadn't been lied to, it wouldn't surprise him as much if Relayne couldn't see the difference between the true and false legends. His attention went from his thoughts to her when Relayne suddenly stopped, and he bumped into her.

"Why are you stopping?"

"I stepped into something," she said.

When the red lights focused on the ground, Relayne saw a trail of blood that led towards the end of the corridor. Her heart started beating faster, and she swallowed hard. She turned around to talk to Kilian, but when she did, he wasn't standing there. In the next second, she could feel heavy breathing behind her.

"Oh shit," she said.

The creature was a head taller than her. The skin was rotten, and the smell was even worse. It had a broad mouth, sharp teeth, and eyes that scared Relayne even more. She wasn't sure what it was, but when she tried to see what the monster was feeling towards her, she couldn't even see a string. That was unusual. Without waiting any longer, she turned her back towards the monster and started running. She ran until she bumped into Kilian, who seemed to be as scared as she was.

"Where have you been?" he asked.

"Where the hell have *you* been?" she asked, glancing behind her, sure the monster was still there. But there was nothing. Her face was paler than before. "There was this thing behind me, just like in my Dream. It looked horrible."

Kilian grabbed her by the hand and went with her upstairs. He locked the door and cast a spell to make sure the door would not open. His breath was rapid, and whatever he had seen, it had scared him as well.

Jegor glanced at them. "What happened in there?" he asked.

"We saw the Crimson Eater," Kilian said, even though he wasn't sure. But the feeling was the same he'd always experienced when it came to this creature. "Why did you not warn us, Fear? Did you wanna see us dead? Is that why you sent me down there?" Kilian was furious.

"Calm it, prince," Fear hissed. "If I wanted you dead, I could do it on my own. I told you the truth when I said there was nothing down there. So what exactly have you seen? I have a back door that leads to the outside. But it's impossible to open under normal circumstances."

"Well, spoiler alert, whatever that was, it got inside!" Kilian answered.

"Let me check." Fear undid Kilian's spell and went into the chamber.

A few minutes passed before he came back and closed the door again. "You're right. Someone has gotten into it. But whoever did that is now gone, and so is the monster. Can you describe it to me? How it looked? I don't think this is coincidence." Fear walked up and down, from one shelf to another, trying to figure what could have happened.

"It looked like a wendigo—but worse. As if it had something human inside," Relayne said. She could still feel the breath on her neck and see the big, white eyes.

Fear went over to Relayne and put one hand on her shoulder. "Let me look through your eyes. If I can see it in your memory, I might be able to tell you what you just saw," he said in a calm voice.

Relayne's breath was still coming fast, her body quivering and cold sweat running down her back.

Fear took her hands and looked her in the eyes. "Breathe in and out. You're with us, with me. No one's gonna harm you anymore." His voice sounded even softer, treating her as if she were the most valuable person in this room.

Relayne's breathing calmed and she stopped shaking. Kilian and Jegor exchanged a suspicious look. One of Fear's hands wandered towards her cheek, and then he closed his eyes, still holding her other hand. Relayne stiffened again, but just for a moment as Fear looked into her memory. He stepped away and spoke something in a foreign language.

"What? What is it that we saw down there?" Kilian asked, even if he wasn't sure he wanted to hear the answer.

"You saw the monster—the monster that was supposed to protect the seal that is gone now. But something was different. It had changed. The monster of Aquanda was a wendigo that we were hiding in a cache down the Icon river palace where the seal was hidden. But in that case, the wendigo would have directly attacked you. Wendigos feast on human and magician flesh. This one was observing you, as if it had its own will. Someone must have done a magical experiment on it, and whatever it is now, it is more dangerous than before."

There is something else. Ask him.

Jegor looked down at Carlin and then at Fear. "What about the monster in general? You seem a bit tense, Feardorcha."

Fear faced Jegor and the two others. "I wouldn't tell this to anyone else, and I wouldn't tell you if I didn't know you were connected. Four of the seals are protected by strong monsters that the magical world hasn't seen before. One of them is now free and surely in the wrong hands. It must have been turned by the magic of the seal. Otherwise, I can't explain this transformation. However, there are three other big monsters. And I can only give you this piece advice; you'd better find them first, before they find you. Don't give them a reason to see you as target. They won't harm you unless you give them one."

Kilian rolled his eyes. "Fantastic! Are we done now? After all this crap, I'd rather have a glass of wine."

Fear smiled at Kilian.

"The Crimson Eater is one of them."

Kilian went paler than before, and Relayne froze.

When the three of them left the shop, Relayne didn't look back. She knew the things that had happened in there were just the beginning. Her eyes were focused on the streets, though the posters of missing people didn't go unnoticed, plastering walls and lanterns. A shiver ran down her back—she had seen them before, though not as much in the other districts. Were the monsters the behind the disappearances? Relayne didn't dare to imagine. She followed the cousins back to the house in silence, while Fear's words about her naivety echoed inside her head.

***

"How was my first impression?"

"Delightful. You've been excellent with following my orders," the young woman answered, speaking to the monster that Kilian and Relayne had just seen. She was nearly as pale as the monster itself, with long, wavy brown hair and a body shaped like a glass doll.

"Thank you, master." The monster sneered, showing his long teeth.

"It's time to give you the full potion to make you even bigger and better. Come on now, Misfitress. It is time to have a bath."

The woman walked away, while the wendigo went into the shadow and followed her silently.

Chapter 4
Underground

She knew she couldn't exist just like that,
she needed a reason to breathe.
– F.F., "The Story of Balance," *The True Urban Legends*

Alegro was sitting on Tyana's bedside. Right after they had announced that Kilian and Jegor were involved in the prophecy, she had felt weaker. For a while now, her circulation didn't seem to work as well as it used to.

"You keep on looking at me as if I were already dead," she whispered quietly to her husband, smiling softly.

Alegro sighed. He held one of her hands. "I feel like we could have avoided this by telling them earlier. I was trying to protect them, but maybe I was wrong. Synclair wanted me to open up the moment his wife got killed. Now look where we are. I think I lost Kilian." Certain guilt riddled his face, and on second glance, Tyana noticed dark circles under his eyes. Sleep was rare these days, and there wasn't a moment where he didn't think about the future and what would happen.

"You did what you thought was right. Yes, you are a harsh and tough leader, but that was the way you always chose to raise your children. And look at them—all of them are beautiful and strong magicians. Even Kennady is growing into a wonderful woman. If you keep on living in the past, you won't be able to face what is coming. I am dying, Alegro. But I knew what I was getting myself into the moment I married you." Tyana faced him with a brighter smile than before.

Alegro remained silent for a moment and then nodded and gently kissed her hand. "I will stay with you. Synclair can do the rest of the work today." Alegro's voice was soft, yet he didn't smile. There were certain things Tyana didn't know and he wouldn't be able to tell her, even in her last hours.

***

Synclair had taken on the rest of the duties for the day. There was always something to do in the palace. Most work was connected to the council.

"If you need a break, I am more than happy to take something off your shoulders," Kalimba said, interrupting the Ghost's thoughts.

Synclair looked up from his paperwork and let out a sigh. "I am pretty sure you are having a better time in your botanic garden than sitting at this desk," Synclair answered.

Kalimba sat down on a chair near him. "I do. That makes me the calmest of the family." She grinned.

"And the smartest woman of the family," Synclair added with a chuckle.

"Tyana will be gone in a few hours, I can feel it," Kalimba said. Her voice was gentle. Being balanced with nature meant that she was able to feel movements within nature. Most of her days, Kalimba worked in her botanic garden. Whenever she went out, she dealt with business around the Woods.

"Yeah. Alegro and I have prepared her ceremony as best as we could. I would like you to give her the last speech. I'm not sure Kilian and Jegor will be there and even then I am sure you are the better choice for words," Synclair said. The dark colour under his eyes revealed how tired he was. There was always a problem in the palace. Kilian and Alegro's fights came on top of everything else.

"I know that this is just the beginning," Kalimba stated. Her gaze wandered to the big window that revealed a look inside their garden. "I sometimes wonder how mum would have handled the situation. The system, the law," she quietly confessed.

Synclair couldn't help but chuckle. "She would have thrown Kilian and Alegro in a room together, locking it by spells so neither of them would get out before they wouldn't have sorted their shit out," he said. "Kilian has her temper, you have her kindness." A melancholic smile spread across his face. He was dwelling in old memories—back in the days when the whole family was still together.

"Would you say it was a better time? Back when mum was alive?" Kalimba asked.

Synclair looked at her, taking a deep breath. "No. We just thought less about tomorrow and lived more."

***

Baelfire stretched, revealing some skin and tattoos around her hip under the pink shirt that said "Go hard or home" in neon green font. Her ice-blonde hair was straightened, falling over her shoulders. Big pink hoops and neon pink fishnets matched her black leather shorts and Dr. Martens. The look was rounded out by her outstanding make-up and fake fur lavender coat.

"Fuck, I feel underdressed," a voice interrupted Baelfire's thoughts.

"You always will when you are standing next to me, baby-girl," Baelfire said with a bright grin, and pulled her friend Alva into a hug. Alva was a bit shorter than her. She had a brown-to-blonde ombre look, freckles decorating her skin, and a silver nose ring. Dressed casually, she wore a black hoodie, black ripped jeans, and green sneakers.

"I'm glad you had time, though, I am bored as fuck," Baelfire said, giving Alva a kiss on the cheek. Baelfire loved affection—giving or receiving.

"Trust me, working in the council is also something you don't want to do all day," Alva said.

"Hope you didn't start this threesome without me?" a husky voice interrupted the two magicians.

Baelfire rolled her eyes. "Can we not do something on our own for once?" she asked, annoyed.

Pieotr laughed. The half-Finnish, half-Russian Blood shook his head. He was dressed in a leather jacket, short blond hair styled to the back of his head. His finest detail were his cheekbones.

"You didn't even make the effort to dress well," Baelfire complained.

"Everyone looks good in black, especially me," Pieotr fired back.

"Well let me know when you guys managed to swing your dicks, I'm on my way," Alva said. She vanished into the wall in front of them.

"My lady," Pieotr said, bowing in front of Baelfire and holding out a hand. Baelfire slapped his hand away and walked through the wall. Pieotr followed with a laugh.

On the other side of the wall, all three landed at a crossroad that had posters flying and flapping around in the air. All of them showed different fonts and directions. They had officially entered the Underground of the Doom District. The area looked urban, full of stalls and shops that screamed *obscure*. The Underground in the Doom District was famous for never having sunlight. Instead, the area was lightened by lanterns filled with coloured matter that made the area glow; a neon-shivering aesthetic that asked you to come closer and take a look at the forbidden fruit behind the mirror, far from the glorious surface society that Icon mostly presented.

Since the news that one of the seals had been stolen had gotten out, more and more people made their way to the Undergrounds to get off the radar of the council. The Undergrounds were just one gap in the system that made it capable for crime to happen. Though, lately, that had also happened above the Undergrounds, around the city.

"Follow me," Baelfire said, leading the way, confidently swinging her hips. It didn't take long for her to catch attention. Baelfire ignored the looks—she knew she would never fit in. She had stopped trying a long time ago.

Alva's eyes were focused on the shops, taking in the area and trying to remember where they would go. Pieotr had lit a cigarette, enjoying the smoke inside his lungs.

"That's the place I saw the sins group symbol a while ago," Baelfire said, and pointed at a small cafe. It looked decent from the outside, with a few wooden chairs with matching black tables. Nothing to be seen from far through the windows.

"Could have been just kids, spraying the symbols on the wall," Alva said.

"Or it could be someone that knows something. I wanna check it out," Baelfire said. She walked over to the door, where she met a guard, dressed in a suit. That alone was unusual—guards being a clear sign of gang activities in the Underground.

"Sorry sir, may I pass?" Baelfire asked in a friendly voice.

The guy looked her up and down. "If you show me some skin, you may," he answered, curling back his lips to reveal a dirty grin.

Alva, standing behind Baelfire, lunged forward, ready to fight, but Pieotr grabbed her arm and shook his head.

"And what if I don't?" Baelfire asked, voice still friendly.

"Then my friends and I will take care of that," the man answered. A few more men had appeared behind him.

"I see. Sorry for any inconvenience, sir. I just thought you might have some connections to the sins. But as it seems, you are just sad men who like to beat up girls at night." Baelfire turned around.

The man's eyes started glowing and he quickly grabbed after Baelfire. Pieotr stopped him, moving in front of the girls, no emotion on his face.

"I think you heard what my sister said. But I still think you owe her an apology as well as any other women you have touched before," Pieotr said, his voice cold and threatening.

"I don't owe you any shit—" the man began to say, but his voice raised into a scream.

"Oh, what is it?" Pieotr asked, looking down on him. Alva was walking past them, into the cafe, closing the door. Screams and sounds of fighting followed shortly afterward, the other men begging Alva to stop.

Pieotr looked over to Baelfire, waiting for a signal to get involved. Baelfire looked to the men then back to Pieotr, winking. A second later, the man held by Pieotr began to crumble, the blood fading out of the man's system before the cracking of bones followed. Pieotr didn't stop until the man was just a mess of bones and skin. Baelfire laid a hand on his back. Pieotr got up and the door to the café opened, Alva standing in the door frame, a pile of corpses behind her.

"Thank you, guys. Let's fuck off, I'll clean up," Baelfire said. Pieotr and Alva started to move. Baelfire looked at the cafe. The friendly look from before was gone. And the darker her eyes got, the higher the flames started to dance around the café. Baelfire vanished into the fire, catching up to her friends.

Chapter 5
The Legend

And his heart was heavy. Maybe too heavy to keep another burden.
— F. F., "The Dollmaker," *The True Urban Legends*

After the incident in Fear's shop, later in the evening, Kilian and Relayne sat in the living room. Jegor was nowhere to be seen. Kilian didn't bother looking for him, knowing that his cousin needed his space from time to time.

"Why were you so protective when Fear looked at me?" Relayne asked, eating her pasta.

"Darling, you may wanna hook up with whomever on the street from your circle, but Feardorcha Forbes is the worst catch you could ever make. This guy has something going on that I haven't figured out yet. But since we're teammates and need to stick together, I just made sure you didn't do anything that you would regret afterwards."

Relayne rolled her eyes. "Thanks, Mother. Didn't know I needed your permission to do anything with anyone," she said, making it clear she didn't like overprotective behaviour.

"That warlock is dangerous. He's a friend of Jegor's, but I never trusted him. For some reason, he also knows about my worst fear. And if that isn't worrying enough, I don't know what is." Kilian sighed and put the last card on top of the house of cards he was building, listening to some music on his old

MP3 player. Kilian's interest in electronic things had started the moment magicians had adapted to them. Some magicians refused the human electricity and internet wave that had influenced New Born Kingdom. But the nineties generation especially enjoyed them.

"Is that Killer Queen? Didn't know you have good music taste."

"You don't know a lot about me, Red," Kilian said, facing her now. "Instead of being so sassy, why don't you see this as an opportunity to ask me for advice?" he suggested, giving her a serious look.

"As in being my teacher? No thanks. All you do is make arrogant comments about me as a street magician anyway."

Kilian flipped one of the cards and brought the house to fall before he stood up and walked over to Relayne, sitting next to her. "You can judge me like everyone else out there. Or you can actually start working with me. We fall under the same League. The Red League is our home. We may come from different families, but the magical bond is the same. I might be a Trickster, but we and the Feelings aren't so different. Or do you wanna tell me the string is still black?"

"For sure, if you continue," Relayne hissed. "I have no reason to trust you, even if this legend has decided for us to do this together. I want to change the balance and do what's right. That doesn't mean I have to be close to you or whatever."

Kilian rolled his eyes and sighed. "And you're telling me my ego is big. Have you heard yourself? Why don't you believe in yourself?" he asked, confused but also seriously interested.

"Because people like your father and the whole upper class always made me believe differently. Look outside, Kilian. People like you and I will never be the same, even if the League brings us together. While you were learning in the best classes of the city, us street magicians only have two to three choices of schools, if even. My mother taught me more on her own. Tell me how that's fair?"

"It's not. I get where your anger is coming from. A lot of things are going the wrong way."

Relayne glanced at him, impressed that he agreed with her. Kilian started to realise it more and more since he had been told that he was part of a prophecy. The palace wouldn't have made it such a big secret if there wasn't more to it. This was something about the system and beyond any investigation they had conducted.

"Maybe that's the reason people are trying to change things. They want a revolution because your family and the council aren't listening," Relayne answered.

"A revolution never ends well for anyone. I don't know as much about politics, as Jegor does. But there could be changes beforehand. A revolution brings more misery than gain," Kilian said, and made a face, as if he was remembering a situation connected to this topic.

"How many times have you seen *Les Miserables*?" Relayne asked, and for the first time she saw Kilian smile. He had a beautiful smile.

"Feardorcha was the warlock who was at my ceremony," Relayne said, changing the topic. "I remember him talking to my mother. But I didn't understand what was going on, of course. It was only until years later when my mother mentioned Feardorcha in connection with my father."

"Let me guess. Your mother never told you who it was," Kilian said.

"Ten points for Slytherin," Relayne answered sarcastically. "She always said he was a mistake; that's all. My mother was a White under the name of the gods' magic. Loki was her leading god. That was why it was possible for her to teach me so many things. She had a strong belief, and Loki gave her everything she asked for, being there for her and making her the strong witch she was."

Kilian nodded. The god magicians were the rarest under the White League. If the ceremony chose that path for a magician, a certain god would choose the child and lead them from there. It was the hardest path to follow the rules of a god, to do rituals and always perform well for the gods. Kilian was happy that he'd never had to go that way. He had seen enough of what his stepmother went through. As far as he knew, the gods were the same as the ones in the human world, but not including the monotheistic beliefs. Rumour had it that there were new gods in the magical world. Kilian had never paid attention, not feeling any kind of connection to religious magic or beliefs.

"It explains why Fear was so fond of you. Does that mean you trust me now?" Kilian mocked.

"My family's past is nothing I would hide from anyone," Relayne answered.

"Fine. Let's talk about your understanding of Urban Legends, then. Have you ever heard of the monsters of the seal?"

"Not until it was mentioned in the shop earlier," Relayne replied.

Kilian smirked. "I see. Let me enlighten you about the real enemies we have to face soon."

He walked into his room and came back minutes later with a giant book.

"Is that the black magic timetable?" Relayne asked, focusing on the book.

"Don't be stupid. That's only for witches who are either a Green or a Black. This, my dear child, is *the Beastarium of Icon* I got for my eighteenth birthday. It includes every monster that I and Jegor have ever met or believed existed. As soon as we believe, the pages get filled with new information, which has helped us in the past when we worked on cases. Most of the knowledge comes from Jegor, since he spent way more time in the Doom District than I did. That's where sixty percent of the monsters live. The rest are somewhere else in the city. Dwarves and elves are included as well. They belong to the category of species that lives among us and don't try to harm us. The last pages are the monsters that belong to the most dangerous category. The facts come only clear as strong black ink, when we found proof of monsters. That way we can separate what's real and what's just in our heads or fiction in the sector of Urban Legends."

"See, this is clearly one thing that should be accessible to all Leagues," Relayne commented on the Beastarium.

"If it would be, people could use that to their advantage. Jegor and I need it for our investigation, to figure things out quicker," Kilian said.

He opened the book and took a deep breath. He wasn't sure if he wanted to see what he was supposed to see. But sooner or later, he would encounter this creature of his childhood nightmares, and he needed to be prepared for that fight.

"Misfitress. That's the creature I saw down Fear's hall," Relayne said when she saw one of the last pages.

There were two drawings. One showed Misfitress in the form that Relayne had seen, and the other was much bigger and scarier, with wide, white eyes and a big mouth with sharp teeth and a long tongue that could strangle a person. The description said that he was nearly three metres tall if he was standing straight. Long black hair fell down over his raw-boned body. His claws were nearly as sharp as his teeth. Relayne swallowed.

Misfitress is a creature that was captured to protect one of the magical seals. Under a magical curse, formed by dark magic, Misfitress got his own free will. From that day on, he wouldn't harm anyone around the seal unless he had a reason for a target. Just like any other wendigo, he feasts on flesh, both human and animal.

"The book says that Tress was already different. How can it be that I have seen him so human, then?" Relayne asked.

"I've only seen Tress once, and that was enough to make a giant step around him. Whoever has control over him must have used a forbidden curse to make him human," Kilian explained.

"That's possible? Literally everyone can be Frankenstein and create their own monster," Relayne said. A shiver ran down her back.

"No. The balance provides that forbidden curses get reported as soon as someone is doing them. But if one of the seals was stolen, there must have been a gap where no one would notice it," Kilian explained.

Relayne nodded before she turned the page and gasped.

Kilian took a sharp breath. "I absolutely hate this thing," he hissed, and Relayne looked up at him.

"Why are you so scared? I mean, it does look...creepy." she said, her voice calm, since Kilian seemed tense.

Kilian looked at her, debating for a few seconds if he should let her know. They were partners now. If he wanted her trust, he had to speak up. At least a little. "I was haunted by this thing in my dreams when I was a child and teenager. Jegor even tried a Voodoo curse on me, but nothing worked. It's like my one and only archenemy that I could never get out of my head." He stopped. "That's all you need to know for now," he said bluntly. Kilian was generally more open about things in life, but when it came to his worst fears, he tried to avoid the topic as often as he could.

"I understand. I don't have a reason to trust you other than this connection, and the same is true for you," Relayne answered him.

"Thank you," Kilian said, and Relayne walked away.

Kilian looked after her for a moment. Relayne might have felt the struggle inside him or that something was going on. He had told her just the tip of the iceberg, but there was much more to it. Kilian took a deep breath. For some reason, he had been close to telling her everything—as if there was no barrier between them. Kilian thought back to the moment they had met. Even though he had been jealous that day, something had happened after he'd left her and her mother. The nightmares about the Crimson Eater had stopped.

***

"Flynn, we need to get ready for the party," Alicia called to her younger brother. Usually he was the one excited for parties.

"Flynn?" Alicia asked again, knocking on the bathroom door of the flat they shared.

Flynn swung the door open and looked at his sister. He was paler than usual, and his eyes were red, as if he had been crying.

"Is everything okay?" Alicia asked.

Flynn nodded quickly. "Yes. I'm just a bit overwhelmed with emotions. Since the breakup, it happens once in a while that I still think back to the good memories with me and her, you know." Flynn tried to smile, but Alicia could see that he was struggling.

"We don't have to go out tonight, if you don't want to," she suggested.

But Flynn shook his head in denial. "You know how the people in the Woods are. They are always up for a party. I can sit here and drown in my misery, or I can go out there and enjoy my life as best I can, with the coolest sister in town." He grinned, and whenever he did that, it was hard for Alicia to not smile.

"Fine then. Let's go. I'll make sure you have a good night," Alicia said.

Flynn pulled her into a hug. He was the kind of brother who gave good hugs whenever they were needed. But right now, Alicia felt he was the one who needed it. Since Flynn was taller than her, she just leaned a bit more into it, without losing too much air.

"I love you, no matter what," Flynn whispered, and kissed her on the forehead.

She couldn't see the tears welling in his eyes again, but she could feel that this wasn't just any kind of hug. It felt like a goodbye.

***

Relayne had gone to her room after her conversation with Kilian and the Beastarium. She wanted to distract herself and escape. Maybe it was too much of a burden for her to handle. Maybe she couldn't stand all this pressure. When she looked at her drawing, she dropped her pencil and let out a gasp. She hadn't realized what her lines were connecting, and now she was staring at another drawing of the Crimson Eater. Just looking at it made her shiver. It had no eyes but it felt like the drawing was watching her. The skin was a dark red, and she was sure that, when it opened its mouth, there were plenty of teeth, ready to bite and break bones. The other drawing in the Beastarium had shown that it had a long black tongue. The body reminded Relayne somehow of a giant lizard crossed with a snake. She swallowed and closed her sketchbook. This wasn't her idea of an escape.

Relayne grabbed her phone and tried to call her girlfriend—Baelfire could help her get things off her mind. But the call went to voicemail.

***

Baelfire looked at her phone but ignored it. She didn't want to talk to Relayne.

"Pieotr told me you had some trouble in town?" a blond woman interrupted her thoughts. Baelfire looked at her. She was stunning, with sharp cheekbones, straight hair falling to her hips, dressed in an emerald dress.

Emerald—the nuance before poison.

"It was nothing. Just another gang that tried to make noise for nothing. Or more like the wrong motives," Baelfire said with a shrug.

"I know how this can get to your head, silly," the woman said, walking closer. Gently she placed her hands on Baelfire's shoulders. Baelfire raised an eyebrow before she grasped the woman's hands in a soft gesture.

"I was serious when I said you and me are over, Amber," Baelfire said.

Amber chuckled. "I know. Does that mean I can't be here anymore to support you?" she asked, releasing Baelfire's hands. She turned around smoothly, hips swinging, walking with confidence. "Enjoy your evening baby. I can tell you that she isn't thinking of you the way I did." Amber walked out of the room, leaving a bitter feeling inside of Baelfire. The Element of Fire ignored the rest of the calls from Relayne for the night.

***

"Jegor," a rough voice whispered.

He turned around, still trying to figure out where he was. It was a forest, dark and foggy—a place he'd never been before. He could barely see, and when he looked down, Carlin wasn't at his belt. What was happening?

"You need to follow the right path to make the right choice. If you don't do this, none of you will find the person you're looking for. You must go on your own, or everything is lost, just like your mind."

***

Jegor woke up, cold sweat running down his back. He hadn't even slept. He'd done one of his meditations to find a balance between the black magic and his normal mind.

What did you see? Carlin looked at him from his bed.

"A Vision. I think it was a sign for the next child. But it's gonna be a task as well. I have to do this challenge on my own—even without you." Even though Jegor knew it had been a Vision, his heart was beating fast. It was common for him to see Omens. Visions left a different feeling inside of him; something uncertain, something that he couldn't hold because it didn't belong to his League.

Carlin fell off the bed and rolled over to Jegor before he stood up again and faced him. If Carlin was able to seem concerned, he was in this moment. But then his face changed again, and he smiled.

Does that mean you're gonna leave me alone with Kilian?

"If I have to. Let's get ready, the world is counting on us."

***

The Woods were stunning. During the day, everything was beautiful. The nature was blooming and inviting, depending on the season. Most of the Green League magicians lived here. The Woods, having the same name as their district, were well known for nature magic, while the Beasts could handle everything, including animals. They could speak to the animals, understand them, and some of them could even turn into a beast themselves. Since it was the beginning of spring, little butterflies were flying around and glowing in the dark, in all the colours that the Woods had to show. The most extraordinary species lived here and showed their cultural expression within the woods. No matter the colour or heritage, the Woods were a warm and welcoming place for everyone.

"I really don't know if it's a good idea to have a party here. Literally every one of them is probably high, and a virgin as well." Alicia moaned and rolled her eyes. She had decided to dress as casually as she could, to avoid most of the Woods, who were looking for someone to hook up with.

"You wouldn't mind having a virgin, would you?" Flynn asked, sass in his voice.

"I owe you something, so we're here now. Let's have fun, I guess?"

Flynn gave his sister a kiss on the cheek and went into the centre of the party.

Alicia looked around. Lots of magicians were wearing flowers in their hair or leaves from the trees. She was a White under the name of Tyr, the northern god of war and fire. With a sigh, she stepped over to the bar to get a drink. There was lots of punch and colourful cocktails, and it was hard to say if there was anything without alcohol. It wasn't that she wasn't in for something like that, but in a group where she didn't feel that comfortable, she would rather stay sober. Alicia never liked the Woods. There was something about this district that made her shiver. Maybe she had read too many fairy tales when she was younger that made her believe there was a big bad wolf hiding somewhere.

"Looks like you could use good company," a guy with brown hair said to her with a smile.

Alicia tried to smile back, but it didn't look convincing. "I was actually just getting a drink before I find my brother again."

"Oh come on. Have a little fun," he said, grabbing her arm.

Alicia froze and faced him. She realized that his lips were purple, which didn't seem normal. "I wouldn't hold on if I were you," she said. His hand had started to get red, as if someone had thrown hot water over it.

The guy swore and let go of her. "Bitch," he hissed, and went away.

Alicia sighed, grabbed a drink, and went on.

***

After two hours, the situation was still the same for Alicia. Her brother was having fun. She could see that, and didn't blame him at all. His girlfriend had broken up with him a week ago. He wanted distraction. Since both siblings had lost their parents a year ago, Alicia looked after her brother more than usual. She knew she was too protective, but she couldn't lose him, too. Even though she had a pretty tough nature, the death of their parents still lingered in her mind. The council had told them it was an accident and a tragedy, but Alicia didn't believe them. Something had happened that everyone was trying to cover up for some reason she hadn't figured out yet.

Bored after her third drink, she started wandering around the Woods—not too far from the party, but far enough to have a bit more freedom. The fairy lights in the trees were beautiful, and the laughter and music in the background ensured a nice atmosphere.

"Seems like I'm not the only one who's bored by all this nonsense."

Alicia looked around for the voice that had interrupted her thoughts. There was no one—or at least not for her to see, until a person emerged from a tree. Alicia blinked a few times just to make sure she hadn't had too much to drink.

"Yes, I am that guy who walks out of a tree, like a chameleon," the stranger said with a smirk, before she could ask. He was quite tall, with ginger hair and freckles dancing over his cheeks. His skin was pale, and the outfit he was wearing—a dark green shirt and grey jogging trousers—told Alicia he was a Wood. He wore a green bandana in his hair, which gave him a bit of a wild look.

"In what kind of sense would you make yourself look like a tree instead of dancing?" Alicia questioned him, still trying to understand what she'd just seen.

"I like to scare people when I'm bored," he said, and shrugged his shoulders. "I'm Petyr, by the way, and you must be Alicia Vestergaard. Your brother is quite a visitor in this area. I guess he has a thing for ladies who are drawn towards nature." Petyr sounded amused.

"I guess the trees have told you my name?" Alicia asked. She sighed. *Great, another nature magician.*

"Whites under the name of the gods are rare. It doesn't happen every day that I meet someone connected to Tyr. The books say he's one of the hardest to impress. Is that true?" Petyr asked, avoiding her question.

"Why should I tell you?" Alicia asked, raising an eyebrow.

"I'm just curious. Wanna have a little fun now?" Petyr tilted his head, giving her an intense gaze.

Alicia looked around. There wasn't anything else that would entertain her tonight, and for some reason, this stranger didn't feel like a stranger at all. "Let's go then. Show me what Woods call a real party."

***

It was the middle of the night when Alicia realized how late it was. Petyr had shown her that there was a lot to explore the deeper they got into the Woods—a lake with a waterfall, tree houses up in the crowns of the trees, and fields with fruits and vegetables. It wasn't too bad after all when someone knew the way around. And eventually, Alicia had made her point clear that she wouldn't mind sex, shortly after ending up on top of Petyr and marking him with a few hickeys; a hot ride followed by choking the ginger magician underneath her. Both of them were now lying in the grass and looking at the stars in the sky.

"I should go and find my brother. By now, he doesn't know how to get back to our house," Alicia said after a while, fixing her clothes.

"Isn't he old enough to find his way home? Or with someone?" Petyr sat up and faced Alicia.

"I would say yes, but under the circumstances, with things quite criminal at the moment, I don't wanna let him walk alone. If the balance isn't safe, it can also mean more monsters are around us," Alicia explained. She stood up. "Thanks for showing me the area. The forest isn't too bad, I guess." She leaned forward and gave him a kiss on the cheek, which made Petyr smile.

"Anytime. I like fierce company and sex. My house is nearby. Is it okay for you to go back on your own?" Petyr asked.

"I should be fine. I remember the way you showed me," Alicia said with confidence.

"Good girl. I'll see you when I see you." And with these words, Petyr disappeared as if he had never been there.

Alicia chuckled before she went back to the party. She could still hear the music, but not as loudly as before. The path had little lights along the way, yet it was dark enough to make Alicia feel uncomfortable. She couldn't really say why. A second ago, she hadn't felt afraid at all.

Nothing better than anxiety, she thought to herself, and started to walk faster. For some reason, she couldn't stop thinking that something was watching her. She suddenly realized she wasn't on the path anymore. How could that happen? Alicia was sure she had been on the right path. Panic rising, she looked around. The lights were gone, and it was now completely dark. Her breathing got faster, and she clenched her hands into fists.

"Alicia." It was a whisper that reached her ears. "Alicia. Didn't your mother tell you it's rude to come to a place without an invitation?"

Alicia didn't move. It wasn't the first encounter with a monster, but the whole atmosphere gave her a different feeling—something she had never felt before.

"You're such a beautiful creature. I wouldn't mind you, but every territory has its rules, and you didn't follow mine at all. What a bad girl." The whisper turned into a clear, soft voice.

Alicia had the feeling that someone or something was standing behind her. She didn't dare look.

"Take it as a warning, my dear child."

She felt breath on her ear. It made the panic worse. She could also smell something, a mixture of pine needles, cinnamon, and something rotten. Cold sweat ran down her back, and all she could do was hope that whatever was behind her didn't do anything else.

Alicia was lucky. Suddenly, everything returned to normal, and she found herself on the path, the music and little lights swelling around her. Alicia could move and breathe normally again, and so she started running until she was in the light of the party and surrounded by people again. Luckily, it didn't take her long to find Flynn, who was, indeed, a bit drunk.

"Hey where have you been?" he asked, tipsy and in a good mood.

"We need to go home, now," she said, and Flynn could see that something was wrong.

"What happened? Where were you?" He drew his sister away from the crowd.

"I can tell you everything on the way home. Can we just go, please?"

"Yeah, sure. But tell me at least what happened to your neck?"

"What do you mean what happened to my neck?" Alicia asked in confusion. She had only left marks on Petyr, not the other way around.

Flynn took out his phone and opened the front camera.

Alicia gasped and let out a little scream when he showed her the photo. It gave her proof that something had happened in the forest. Imprinted in her neck was something that looked half like a human hand and half like a claw. Alicia focused on her younger brother and took him by his hand. She didn't look back until they had left the Woods.

Chapter 6
Haunted

And when he comes for you,
he will take it and leave your loved ones with misery and pain.
– F. F., "The Bogeyman," *The True Urban Legends*

"I never liked the Woods. Most of them are crazy people and I have a bad memory about an elf who wanted to sleep with me once." Kilian was anything but excited for this trip. Jegor had told Relayne and his cousin what he had seen in his Vision. After a short discussion, it was clear to them that they needed to start searching in the Woods.

"Is there anything you *do* like in this district?" Relayne asked Kilian.

"Places with style, my dear, not the most famous place for drugs," Kilian said with a sigh.

"Not every nature magician takes drugs. You're judging everyone again. As much as you hate your father, lately you sound too much like him," Jegor added to the conversation.

Carlin gave a little giggle.

Kilian just went silent and stepped away from them.

"He's stressed. We don't need any more arguments," Relayne said to Jegor.

"I'll quote you on that the next time he's taking your temper to the next level," Jegor answered. He went on towards the Woods ahead of them. Nothing looked dangerous at all in the day. It was the opposite. The area was friendly, and everyone seemed to be happy around here. Relayne used to come here when she was younger. Elves, dwarfs, goblins, nymphs, sirens. They all had their place within the Woods. The League was most common to have the biggest diversity in looks, skin, and height of their species.

"Is it true that elves have a certain charm that makes you believe anything?" Relayne asked now, still looking around, observing the area.

"Some of them, yes. Depends on how good they are with their magic," Jegor replied.

Kilian had his eyes on a group of young Beast ladies who were just learning new spells.

"Jegor," a friendly voice shouted.

"Petyr, good to see you," Jegor answered, quite formally.

Petyr stepped closer to them before he focused on Relayne and Kilian. He made his hand into a fist in front of Relayne, and when he opened it again, a red rose bloomed out of it.

"The trees told me they're your favourites." Petyr smiled.

Relayne smiled back, taking the rose.

Kilian rolled his eyes and stepped in front of Relayne before Petyr could do anything else. "We're not here for your little charming tricks. Anything curious happened lately in this place?" he asked, embracing his investigator side.

"It's very good to see you as well, Kilian," Petyr answered sarcastically. "And besides the fact that I had a nice evening with a White yesterday, nothing happened at all. Unless you wanna tell me there is something wrong with the Woods that I don't know about yet?" He looked at the cousins questioningly.

"I had a Vision of a forest and a path that I had to go on alone to find someone, the next child of the seal," Jegor explained.

"So the legend is true," Petyr said. "I found three corpses near the lake yesterday, quite unusual for our area."

"Excuse me? Three corpses and you tell us everything is normal?" Kilian raised his voice, glaring at him angrily.

"It's normal to us. If something in the Woods happens, it's a balance of nature. But the amount of corpses is not. If a person dies in the Doom District, no one seems shocked. So why is it different here? We have a balance as well, and nature takes what it takes whenever the time has come," Petyr said in a calm voice.

"Can you tell us who the corpses were?" Jegor asked.

"No. They had no faces," Petyr answered.

"No faces? That sounds like the tale of the Bogeyman," Relayne said.

"Enlighten us. I'm sure only Jegor knows," Kilian commented, while Jegor nodded.

"Actually, you aren't the only one, Jegor," Petyr corrected with a cheeky smile.

"In the tale, a girl gets haunted by a ghost in the forest. Not a ghost, exactly," Relayne explained. "It's the king of the Woods, also known as Bogeyman. He has the ability to control the Woods, and bodies if he wants to. He is well known for taking faces away."

Petyr smiled at her. "Someone has done her research," he said, pride in his tone. "But if my little rose here is right, we have a much darker problem than any of us could see coming." His face grew as serious as the other three.

"Acer is supposed to be one of the protectors of the seals and the right-hand man of the king of the Woods," Jegor said, looking at Kilian.

"I guess it's your task to find him, then, and make sure the seal is safe," Kilian answered his cousin.

Jegor looked back at Petyr, who seemed to be thinking about something. "Can you show me the darkest path?" he asked. "I have a feeling I'm closer than I should be." There was a constant feeling around him, like something was in the air or something was watching him.

"Of course I can. Meet me when dawn hits the treetops," Petyr said, and then disappeared.

"How can you trust him? He could be a part of this. Do you even realize that?" Kilian couldn't hide his mistrust.

"Don't be stupid, Kilian. You don't like him, and that makes you blind, because he is a better magician than you are. I came here for a reason, and I have a task to fulfil. In the meantime, you and Relayne need to continue to find the others or see about the other seals. Can you do that for me?" Jegor asked roughly, making it clear that he had no time to discuss any further relationship problems.

"Give me a reason why I should leave you alone with him," Kilian argued.

"Because I think he might be one of us. But as we both know, Petyr isn't someone who lets himself into things like that, until someone makes him believe."

With these last words, Jegor stepped away, leaving Kilian and Relayne alone together.

***

"I still don't like the fact that he's doing this alone," Kilian said after Jegor had left them.

"Stay calm. I guess you are more worried that we have to look after *him*." Relayne pointed at Carlin, who now hanging around her belt.

I like you, Relayne. You understand me.

"Congratulations. You are now friends with Chucky," Kilian said sarcastically.

"Jegor is one of the strongest Voodoo magicians. Let him be. Everything happens for a reason," Relayne answered with a sigh. Kilian could be really stubborn and protective—at least from what Relayne had seen so far. Maybe that was a good thing, though; at least he showed he cared about his cousin.

Together with Kilian, she was now walking along Icon River, which led directly towards the Doom District.

"The water looks blacker than usual. Is that also because of the stolen seal?" Relayne asked, inspecting the water.

"Perhaps. The Icon River has a lot of monsters you probably haven't seen at all," Kilian said.

Relayne could only imagine what was deep down in the river. Most of her lifetime in Icon she had spent her days around Shoreditch. The more she started to discover about this legend and city, the more she realised how she had never paid close attention. She had been comfortable living in her own safe bubble of society. Her thoughts got interrupted when Feardorcha bumped into them on the next corner.

"I knew I would find you. You need to come with me, I have guests for you," Fear said, and his voice revealed he was under pressure and in a hurry.

"Guests?" Relayne asked him. "We just came out of the Woods."

"I know. Two siblings are waiting in my shop, and one of them might be connected to all of this. She had an encounter with the monster of the seal, and that's usually impossible, unless there's a bigger reason to it. She should be dead by now, but for some reason, she is fighting against what happened to her," Fear said seriously.

"Wait. Are you telling us another giant monster has been released?" Kilian snapped.

"Follow me, and you'll see what I mean," Fear said. He turned around and didn't wait for them to follow him.

***

Kilian and Relayne entered the potion shop. Alicia was lying on a mattress on the ground, pale and feverish. The imprint on her neck was now a deep black and spreading down her arm, which made it look like she was poisoned. Flynn knelt next to her.

"Flynn, Alicia, these two are Kilian and Relayne. Tell them what happened, and I shall brew the potion you need to make her better. If you really had an encounter with the King of the Woods, you're lucky you're not dead already." Fear started to wander around, gathering a few things before opening a spellbook.

Relayne looked at the siblings, taking a few seconds to recognize them—they used to be customers in the Black Fairy.

"We were just in the Woods to have a fun evening. I wasn't focusing, so she went on her own. I have no idea what happened then, but she told me that there was a creature that spoke to her after she left the guy she was with that night," Flynn explained. "This is all my fault. She always protects me, but I never really take care of her. I had a Vision a while ago that showed me your faces. What is happening?" Flynn's voice was shaking, as was his whole body.

Relayne and Kilian exchanged a serious look.

"Let me explain, Kilian. You look after Alicia," Relayne said. She took Flynn aside.

Kilian sat down. When he put a hand on Alicia's cheek, he could feel how cold she was, even if she looked like she had a high fever. It was costing her a lot of energy to open her eyes, but she faced Kilian.

"His name was Petyr, and whatever haunted me followed after I left him," she said very quietly.

Kilian's face showed his concern. Petyr seemed to be involved in all of this. But could one of them be the next child, too? Flynn had mentioned a Vision before. The last Vision had been Jegor's, and he had seen the forest. Not that Kilian would complain, but he needed to make sure this wasn't a trick. The prince could feel the pressure on his shoulders. *Stay focused and trust your abilities*, he thought to himself.

"Did you have any Visions or Dreams in the last days?" he asked Alicia.

Alicia shook her head slightly. "Only my old nightmares of losing my parents and that something happens to Flynn."

Kilian nodded and focused on the mark the creature had left. "We will make sure that you stay alive," he said, trying to be strong.

***

"You can't blame yourself for going to the party," Relayne told Flynn. "Magic has its own way, and with everything that's going on at the moment, you can't take that on your head. If you and your sister are involved in this, there's a reason all this is happening. But I have to say, I've never seen a mark like this. Have you ever heard of the urban legend of the Bogeyman? If anything like that is happening, she might lose her face." She couldn't hide this detail from him. He was Alicia's brother, and he needed to know the details.

Flynn swallowed hard. "She literally spent her whole life protecting me, especially since we lost our parents. We are both wild children of magic, but she was always responsible for everything. She once even got into a street fight against some idiots of my magical class back in the days. Whatever happens, I can't lose her, Relayne. She means everything to me. So if there is anything I can do, I will."

Relayne nodded and glanced at Alicia and Kilian before she stepped over and sat down at Alicia's side as well. She could see the pain she was suffering.

"Kilian, can you hold one of my arms?" Relayne asked, pulling up her sleeves.

"What are you doing?" Kilian questioned.

"I'm trying to take away some pain until Fear has the potion ready."

Kilian nodded and took her arm. Relayne closed her eyes, and when she opened them again, they were glowing dark red. She took one of Alicia's hands and started to concentrate. The moment they touched, Relayne let out a hard breath as she was hit by the pain Alicia was enduring. Kilian had to lean against her to make sure Relayne didn't fall back. Alicia's breath quickened at first, but then she calmed as Relayne took the pain from her.

"Let go, Relayne," Kilian said when he saw that her eyes were turning black—she was taking too much pain inside her.

"I can't," she said with a sharp breath. "Something is holding onto me."

"Out of the way!" Fear had walked over, and with a jolt, he set Relayne free from Alicia and gave Alicia the potion directly, until she had swallowed the whole thing.

Alicia passed out, and so did Relayne.

"It works," Flynn said when he looked at the imprint, which was now getting smaller, shrinking until it completely disappeared, as if it had never been there. Flynn released a deep breath. But it wasn't one of relief. Slowly he stepped away from the scenery and made his way out of the store.

***

An hour later, Relayne woke up. It took her a moment to realize where she was. Fear had taken her to the sofa in his flat. She looked around and saw lots of magical artefacts. Just like his shop, it all looked a bit chaotic and unorganized. Herbs, potions, and books were lying around. Papers, letters, and other documents were on the ground. Some of them had Fear's handwriting on them. Others seemed to be lists for potions or documents from the council. When she looked up, she could see more herbs and artefacts hanging from the ceiling. The room offered a mixture of different smells, and she felt like she'd just woken up in the middle of the market square, where all the local magicians sold their wares.

"I see you're awake." Fear stepped over to her and gave her a cup of something. "It's good for the immune system. Drink all of it and then go to your house. Flynn and Kilian are on their way. Our young prince thinks Flynn is another one of you."

Fear's voice was so soft that Relayne couldn't imagine him being mean or evil in any kind of way. Seeing his flat and him like this made her understand why Jegor was friends with him. Not only because of the Black League, but because the atmosphere that came with it made her realize that both magicians had the same common interest in everything unusual.

Relayne nodded and drank the whole cup. It tasted a bit too pepperminty for her taste, but it made her feel better within seconds. She stood up and looked around once more. In a strange way, she felt comfortable in his flat.

"Thank you Feardorcha," Relayne said and put the cup down.

"That's all right, my darling."

***

As soon as Relayne left the flat, Carlin caught her attention.

We need to find Kilian and Flynn. Something's wrong. Have you not felt it?

"What do you mean?" Relayne asked the little doll.

Fear was trying to tell you something without saying it. Hurry. We need to find them. Flynn isn't the child.

Relayne looked at Carlin, shocked. "But how do you know?" she asked, feeling pressure rising inside her.

Think about it. Alicia was always the protector, and she just survived an attack of a seal monster.

Without answering, Relayne started to run. She had to catch Flynn before he could enter the house. She didn't care which dark path she took and kept on running. She had to catch them before anything bad happened. Relayne ran as if her life was depending on it. Rushed by adrenaline and panic, she was red matter in the wind, only stopping when she entered the street where the hidden house was. She could see that Kilian and Flynn were both way too high up the stairs.

"*Kilian!*" she screamed, but knew neither of them could hear her.

Under pressure, she reached the first step. But it was too late. She heard a cracking noise, and a second later, a body was tumbling down the staircase and landing next to her. She let out a scream.

Flynn had been rejected by the house.

***

The moment Flynn fell down the stairs, Alicia woke up in the shop and let out a scream. Fear came down from his flat, but before he could reach Alicia, she had left the shop and started running, following her instincts towards the street where it had happened. The amount of pressure and emotions were overwhelming her. This couldn't happen. Not after everything she already had been through. Not in this town she'd once loved so much. It had been one thing to lose her parents, but losing Flynn—that was something she couldn't take. *How am I supposed to keep going when you're the last one that keeps me sane?* Alicia thought to herself and kept running. All she had done was attend a party, have some fun, and try to enjoy the social life that her brother loved so much. Was Petyr the reason she was going through this? The mark on her neck, the poison inside her body. Tears burned at the edge of her eyes. Alicia had been careless. Now her brother was in danger. With a last sprint, she reached the corner of the street where her instincts had led her.

Quickly she ran up to Flynn. Kilian and Relayne were sitting next to him. He had a weak pulse, but was still alive.

"What happened?" Alicia screamed. "What did you do to him?" Overwhelmed by emotions, Alicia couldn't calm her voice.

Kilian, still in shock, couldn't find words. Relayne glanced at her.

"Alicia, you need to be calm. He's still here with us, but we need to bring him to Fear before it's too late," Relayne said, as calmly as she could.

"Calm? Your royal highness literally just killed my brother!" Alicia fired back. She had seen it. An Omen. Something that could have been prevented.

Relayne had to focus, taking a deep breath so as not to be trampled by Alicia's emotions.

"It wasn't me. It was the house!" Kilian tried to defend himself. "I didn't know that there was a rejection spell! And he told me that he was the one."

"Whatever," Alicia hissed. She pulled Flynn up with all the magical power she had inside her. "Tyr, I beg you. Give me strength and don't let me lose him. I can't lose someone else. I just can't," she whispered.

Together with Kilian, she started walking her brother back towards Fear's shop. Relayne went with them, and as quickly as they could, they were back at the potion shop.

"Fear, we need your help!" Alicia said in panic.

Fear stepped over to Flynn, now lying on the ground. "I can sense that he is close to dying. What in Merlin's name did you do?" he asked. In his many years as a magician and with all of his knowledge of magic, he had seen a lot of things. But even Feardorcha Forbes did not know everything.

"Kilian tried to bring him into the house. But he wasn't meant to go there. It was me. I was the one who was supposed to enter the house." Alicia tried to hold her tears back. She couldn't even look at Kilian.

Relayne took Kilian by his hand and went with him to the back of the room before things could escalate more.

"His inner magic is keeping him alive, but I need to know what happened," Fear stated.

"I saw it. An Omen. He got rejected by the house because I was supposed to be the one. I don't understand why this is happening. But it was me that had to go there," she explained, wiping her tears away, the guilt in her voice clear. "Please tell me you can save him. I'll pay whatever I have to pay, do whatever I have to do. Just don't let him die," Alicia begged the warlock.

"There is something I can do. But a rejection spell like this can't be fixed like any other spell. The injuries would be fine, but it's his mind. Not even I can fix that." Feardorcha focused on Kilian and Relayne for a moment before he looked back to Alicia. "If I save him, he won't remember anything. If I don't, he will die."

Alicia looked at her brother. *Why is this happening?*

"So it's amnesia or death? Either way, I'll lose him," Alicia whispered to herself. She stood up and ran over to Kilian, swinging her fist. "You did this!" she screamed, but couldn't reach him. Fear had stopped her and was drawing her back.

"I was tricked," Kilian said. "Someone manipulated my thoughts, and I wasn't careful to realize that. But if you wanna blame someone for this, then find the person who did this—not me." He left the shop, followed by Relayne, and faced her outside. Mixed emotions battling on his face, he tried to find words. Someone had tricked him. But Flynn had made sure that Kilian believed him. Did he know something they didn't know?

"Flynn said to me that he was the one. He was sure. And so was I, because someone set something into my mind. I don't understand any of this yet, but what if—"

"Flynn was trying to protect Alicia? Sacrificing himself to keep her from being the child?" Relayne finished his thought.

Kilian nodded but couldn't say it out loud. Alicia was on the edge of killing him either way, and even if Flynn knew what was going to happen, Kilian hadn't even had the chance to help or protect him, blinded by the pictures he had seen.

Inside the shop, Fear calmed Alicia down.

"You need to make a decision. Now!" he said, knowing it wasn't easy. Time was against them.

"Let him live," she answered quietly. "And when he wakes up, make sure he goes to a safe place. At least I can be sure that no one will harm him anymore." Alicia looked once more at Flynn before she left the shop.

Chapter 7
Acer

But even a king is looking for love.
– F.F., "The Bogeyman," *The True Urban Legends*

As soon as the sun began to set, Jegor met Petyr in the Woods, where Petyr leaned against a tree, not bothered at all.

"I am surprised that you didn't even bring Carlin," Petyr stated.

"They will kill me straight away if I don't obey their rules. If there is something I respect, it is nature and everything that comes with it," Jegor answered.

Petyr could see that the Voodoo magician was still tense and that meant something.

Jegor was rarely anything but calm. But this task was bigger than anything he'd ever had to deal with in his life as an investigator.

"You just have to walk in. The Woods will lead the way, and I am sure Acer will find you before you can find him. Whatever you have to face inside, make sure to keep your sanity. Woods don't like it when Black magicians take over their territory—they are somewhat allergic to your kind," Petyr explained. He couldn't hide his smirk. Even though he loved the Woods folk and had been living with them for years, some of them had their own heads and rules to live by.

"Don't worry," Jegor said with confidence.

And before either of them could say anything else, Jegor plunged into the Woods. Petyr looked after him, then turned in the opposite direction, not knowing what would happen next.

***

The moment Jegor entered the Woods, the trees closed behind him, blocking the way back and forcing him to move forward. Jegor could hear whispers and quiet voices, none of them clear. For a while, he just kept walking, and nothing around him seemed to change—other than the Woods getting darker, until he could hardly see his own feet anymore. That's when he stopped, taking a deep breath. He needed to trust his instincts and not rush anything, or the Woods would decide for him.

"Acer, holy ghost of the Woods and right hand to the King of the Woods, show yourself if you're awaiting me," Jegor spoke loud and clear.

It wasn't the first time he'd had to find Acer. Sometimes he came to the Woods to speak with him, get advice, or train. But Acer only showed himself if he had reason to. Some magicians had never seen him at all and still thought he was just another urban legend.

A couple of minutes passed, leaving Jegor with nothing but the voices, until a creature stepped out of the shadows as if it had been there the whole time.

Acer could walk in the shadows, which meant he could become shadow himself and watch people and creatures whenever he wanted to, following them as shadow. His form was a combination of rotten tree and human body, reeking of moss and death. Jegor looked up at the two-metre tall creature, which was now facing him. He couldn't ascertain if Acer was watching him or not because he had no eyes, only a wide, stitched-up mouth. He only opened it when he was ready to eat—once a year, at least three human bodies.

You came at the right time, following what I have sent you, Acer said, the voice only in Jegor's head just like Carlin's.

"I had a feeling it was you. I haven't had the pleasure of meeting the king himself so far. And as we both know the Woods—other than Petyr—don't really like me as a guest," Jegor answered politely, his hands behind his back in a sign of respect.

Acer let out an amused laugh with a slightly hysterical undertone. *Indeed. Some of the elves have been asking me if they can have a piece of your skin,* Acer told the Voodoo magician, facing Jegor with a grin.

"Since time is running, what task is it that I have to fulfil?" Jegor asked.

Acer focused on Jegor, walking towards him. *You need to answer to the truth trial of the King of Woods—three questions where you have to be completely honest. Just you and the Woods. There is no way of lying, so think wisely before you answer. If the king senses your honesty, you will be free to go and will be able to leave the Woods without any harm. If not, I am not gonna spoil the surprise of what happens to you,* he said, amusement in his voice. He brushed one of his fingers over Jegor's face.

Jegor didn't flinch or make a noise until Acer had stepped back.

"Are we ready, then?" he asked. He could feel the pressure inside. Kilian was the one for emotions; therefore, the King of Woods must have picked a task that was pointing out one of his weakest spots.

As you wish. The first question is, if you had the chance to kill one of your current family members, who would it be? Acer slowly paced in front of Jegor.

Jegor knew that the Woods wanted to know his darkest secrets. Everything that would happen in the Woods was something that would always be here. The whispers and voices he had heard before were secrets and lies, hiding within the trees and leaves.

"Cassiopeia," Jegor answered, his face stoic.

Acer clicked his fingers, and nothing happened—a sign that Jegor had spoken the truth.

Well, well. The big problem. Who would have thought? Next question: who do you think is the true king that should sit on the throne?

Jegor could feel the pressure inside him rise. It wasn't a secret that Jegor and Alegro didn't get along well, but speaking about the king in a manner of disrespect was unacceptable, especially to the council. Even though the palace always had the last word on decisions, the council had a big word towards it as well. The truth could cost Jegor his job. He gulped, taking a deep breath before he answered.

"No male Lancaster in the current regime," Jegor answered.

Acer clicked his fingers, taking the answer to the trees. And again it was true.

A little giggle escaped Acer as he faced Jegor one more time. *I can feel your imbalance. Black magicians do suffer the most when it comes to being sane or not. One last question, are you ready?*

Even though Acer had asked, Jegor had no choice but to answer the final question. Cold sweat ran down his back, his hands balled into fists and his breath heavy.

"One more question," Jegor answered.

Acer nodded and fully turned towards Jegor, very close to him now. *Have you ever been sexually attracted to someone?* Acer took his time pronouncing every word, cautious into detail, to provoke Jegor more and making it feel like stitch of a needle right into the Voodoo's heart. The needle stitch that was too familiar for Jegor.

Jegor could feel the pressure pushing to the edge inside him. While he was hearing voices around the Woods, it was all in his head now—insults, laughs, screams. Everything was a wild mixture, all of it pushing his mental health to the brink of shattering, allowing insanity to break through and take control. He closed his eyes and tried to calm himself, but in the next moment, the pressure pulled him to the ground, and his breathing became even heavier.

You just have to say no. That's all. Don't be like that again. It's okay. There is nothing wrong with it, Jegor tried to tell himself. But thoughts ran amok through his head. And that wasn't all. Pictures and memories ran through his head as well.

Acer looked down on him. *The time is ticking, Mr. Voodoo,* he said.

Jegor looked up to the creature, and the pressure written on his face. He knew that the King of the Woods was using this weakness, since Jegor had gotten in trouble because of it. Especially as part of the Royal family, Jegor's love life had brought up in more than one discussion. Ignoring the voices in his head, Jegor found his way back and stood in front of Acer. "No," he finally said, trying to pull his inner pressure under control.

Acer clicked his fingers for the third time. But this time, the trees answered.

They say you are not telling the full truth, Acer stated.

"But that was my honest answer. I have never been sexually attracted to someone. I don't care about sex."

Before Jegor could continue, Acer had pressed one of his hands in front of his mouth. *Silence. The king will decide what is going to happen now,* he said.

Jegor could still breathe, barely, and the pressure inside him had now crossed lines. He could feel his body shaking, and the only thing holding him to the ground was Acer himself.

After a couple of seconds, the trees grew quiet again. Acer focused on Jegor and let go of his mouth.

You are allowed to go. The king wanted to deliver this message to you.

Jegor stepped back and took a deep breath. He didn't understand—why was the king suddenly trying to help him? Too many questions circled through his head.

"Thank you," Jegor said firmly, then turned his back on Acer.

But Acer stopped him before he could leave the Woods. *The king's most important pieces of information are the relationships between people and the emotions that come with it. Whoever this is you are trying to cover, you might succeed in front of anyone else, but you can't run away from yourself. Think about it. If you need me in the future, find me. I am your friend, after all.*

Acer receded into the shadow from which he had emerged, and the trees opened up again. Without waiting any longer, Jegor left the Woods, finally able to breathe again. With every step, the voices in his head got quieter until there was only silence.

***

Jegor returned to the house after his task. It had been tough, but other than being left with mixed feelings, there had been no further damage. This task had only been about him. And whatever that meant, Jegor was sure to find out more soon. Nothing ever happened without a reason in this city.

"I'm back," Jegor said, loudly enough for everyone to hear. He stepped into the living room and saw Relayne watching TV, Carlin on her shoulder.

"Where's Kilian?" he asked.

"In his room. And so is Alicia. She is the next child. There was an incident earlier. Kilian got tricked by someone and thought Flynn was the child that was meant to be with us. But it was Alicia, and so the house rejected Flynn and nearly killed him. Fear is helping him, but he will wake up with amnesia and won't know who Alicia is anymore."

Carlin rolled himself down from Relayne's shoulder and looked up at Jegor. *Good to see you. Can I hang around with you again? Relayne is lovely. She let me watch* Gossip Girl.

Jegor seemed confused for a moment, then took Carlin and let him hang on his belt. "Thanks for letting me know. I'll speak to Kilian," Jegor said, and left Relayne alone.

***

"Before you say anything, I took the blame. I was too focused. For once, I thought I had the next clue, the next hint for this. But I didn't. I was wrong, I got tricked, and I nearly killed someone. This all got underlined by the fact that Flynn made me believe it was him. Maybe he knew something, but that doesn't change the fact that I let him run right into it," Kilian said, looking out his window, refusing to face Jegor.

"I am not here to blame you. I wanna know how you got tricked," Jegor answered. He walked closer to his cousin.

"Someone gave me a wrong Vision in my mind. I have no idea how it's possible. But the Vision made me believe I could take the win out of this—that I could say I made this, like a feeling of glory," Kilian explained, certain guilt in his voice.

"So you wanted to find the next child to look better than me? Kilian, this isn't a game," Jegor admonished harshly.

"I know, Jegor. But you didn't see what I saw. I was a hero in my mind. So whoever did this took my jealousy as an advantage and made me believe things that were not true at all." Kilian tried to explain his choice, but his voice betrayed him.

"This sounds like a Mind who got into your head. But this would be a very strong one if she or he made you believe that you knew the next clue. Whoever we are dealing with is an equal enemy to all of us," Jegor said, calmer now, and Kilian turned around to face his cousin.

"We need to find out who we're dealing with. Otherwise, we can't go on. We need to find his or her weak spots, and when I figure out who did this, I'll make sure they get the right punishment," Kilian vowed. He turned back to the window and Jegor left the room.

***

Compared to Relayne's, Alicia's room was less colourful but more practical. The moment she stepped inside, it had reminded her of the Scandinavian hut in Denmark she and her family used to visit in the human world when she was younger, and nostalgia had hit her hard.

Next to her bed was a little desk and, standing on top of it, a small white lamp and a picture of her and Flynn. Just thinking of him was like taking a knife to the heart. Kilian had been tricked, just like all of them. Alicia couldn't help but replay the situation over and over again in her mind. How could she have prevented this situation? And how could she be part of a legend? Just because she was here didn't mean she was directly going with it. But going back to her home wasn't an option anymore, either. She had nothing left other than material belongings that connected her to her old place. One of her hands went to the necklace she was wearing. It was a symbol of Tyr, the god she was loyal to—the god who had it in his hand to give her strength and power whenever she needed it.

"Tyr, make me find a way to make this right. Help me overcome the pain. That is all I'm asking for. If I have to live, I need to be able to overcome this pain," she whispered and closed her eyes.

The other hand touched the window, while her breath was calm. When she opened her eyes, she could see the silhouette of her brother in the window. He was back at their flat, looking a bit tired, but all his wounds seemed to be gone. Alicia's eyes teared up. Flynn was safe, and that was all that mattered for now. She turned around and walked over to her bed. Sleep was now the key to facing whatever would happen next on this journey.

Chapter 8
Petyr

And the King of the Woods wasn't alone. He had a right-hand man,
who would always follow him in the shadows.
– F. F., "The King of the Woods," *The True Urban Legends*

It was a new day when Petyr woke up in his treehouse. After the events of last night, he wasn't as calm as he was usually. Jegor had mastered the challenge of the Woods, which had made Petyr think. Nothing in the Woods happened without a reason. Maybe Jegor was right, and Petyr had a certain connection to all of this. He had seen a few rotten flowers and had found the corpses near the lake, but he never would have thought he was connected to all of this. Petyr was a perfectionist of the nature magicians. People came to him if they needed his help. He understood this world better than most of them did. Perhaps it was the fact that he was over three hundred years old. Nature magicians were the only magicians who could live long if they learned their magic fully on their own and became one with nature. Petyr had paid that price a long time ago, when he had been just twenty years old. His wish was to keep his younger spirit, which was excited by everything that smelled like an adventure, with good humour, good moments, and many beautiful ladies by his side.

But over the years, Petyr had also seen anger in different ways—people who joined armies and fought against each other. It was brutal. Perhaps that's why he had been so blind over the last few weeks. He was hoping this war wasn't happening. But now it was right on his doorstep, and he couldn't escape any longer. The Undergrounds in each district had shown signs of revolt before. Petyr moved more around the Undergrounds than the common areas. The Seaside and Woods were known for bigger trade in their Undergrounds. Petyr liked to wander around these Undergrounds, where there was no hierarchy, each with its own rules. Some had been made by magicians, and others by non-humans. The pile of no-name corpses had been growing on the Seaside. Rumour had it that they weren't even residents of Icon. But Petyr had not looked further into it. He should have known better.

Even worse, he was a part of all this. He was one of the children. Last night he had been haunted by a Vision—something that wasn't common for his League. And Alicia had been part of it. Petyr had heard stories before, about the spirits haunting the Woods, and there was one Urban Legend he couldn't get out of his head. The Bogeyman. The evil spirit and King of the Woods. No one had ever seen him before, but everyone told different stories about him. Some said he was responsible for all the deaths in the Woods and the missing children. Petyr even used the story to scare his lovebirds once in a while, but never had he thought there might be something true about it connected to the legends of the seal. One thing was the Urban Legend, the other was a prophecy.

Dressed in black boxer shorts, he stepped over to his window to look out into the forest. He loved his treehouse. It was his cosy escape room whenever he needed peace. Decorated in green, orange, and brown, it matched his wardrobe and connection to nature. Loads of pillows scattered the area, piled up so he could relax in nearly every corner. With the help of his magic, no one was able to get inside unless Petyr allowed it. It was already hard to find in the Woods.

Petyr surveyed outside. The sun barely shone through the tops of the trees, a calm awakening of the nature around him. Too calm for his taste. Something was going on, and even though he didn't like the idea of being part of a prophecy, there was no way to avoid such a thing. He had seen refusal of prophecies before. None of them had a good ending.

***

"Come in," Alicia said. She didn't turn around—she had a feeling it was Kilian. The White focused on the big blackboard in her room where she had put up lots of notes, anything that might be useful. After getting some sleep since the latest events, Alicia had started putting the pieces together. She wouldn't rest until she'd found the person responsible for her brother's tragedy.

"We need to talk. If you wanna work together in the future, you can't ignore me," Kilian said. His voice was calm; he hadn't come here to fight.

"I know," Alicia said, and turned around. "As much as I would like to kick the shit out of you, it's not your fault. I see that now, and it was my temper that took over. Flynn is everything I have left, and now he's gone now. Whoever did this to you and me has no idea what is waiting for them. But that doesn't change the fact that I need to know why I am part of this."

Alicia looked determined. It was the spirit of Tyr leading inside her.

"I honestly agree with you," Kilian said in relief. "I know none of us can turn back time. But just to let you know, you're not alone. The tragedy of this whole legend is that we all need to go through loss. This can either bring us closer or divide us, but we need to find a solution for all of this."

Alicia nodded. A piece was missing to her. Everything had happened so fast. "Have you lost someone yet?" she asked, now with certain curiosity.

"I lost my real mother when I was young," Kilian began to say. Alicia focused on the Trickster. From what she had seen so far, he was an open person. It seemed that he was able to talk about anything easily—almost the opposite of Alicia, who always made sure that the person in front of her wasn't holding a knife behind their back.

"But I don't think that ever really got to me, since my father was a strong leader," Kilian continued. "He didn't give me the time to be sad, and it took him only a year to find a new wife. Don't get me wrong. I love my stepmother. She has been nothing but kind to me since they found each other, but together with him, they have been lying to me and Jegor. My cousin lost his parents around the same time I lost my mother, and all they said to us was that—"

"It was a tragedy and no one can tell you the real answer," Alicia finished his sentence. "That's how I must have lost my parents. The curse must have happened to all of us at the same time. Whoever we lost, we can't explain why or what exactly happened." She sighed and looked at her board. "I tried to put a few things together that came into my mind—where we found each other, where we used to live, and the places of the seals according to Jegor. I'm trying to get an overview to figure out who did what to us. Relayne told me what happened down in the chamber in Fear's shop. I don't think we have only one enemy here," Alicia explained to the prince.

Kilian studied the notes on the board. "You're smart for a White of war," Kilian said, quite impressed. "But why do you think it's more than one person? What if it is only one?"

"The thing Relayne saw downstairs in the chamber was a real monster. Controlling a monster like that is dark magic, so it was probably someone from the Black League. The person who used you for manipulation was a Mind from the Red

League—which makes at least two enemies we have to fight. But what if there are as many enemies as children? It's all about the balance, like the legend says."

Kilian slowly nodded, processing the new information. Alicia really had focus. "You might be right. I will pass this information on to my cousin, so he can mention it to my uncle. In that case, we need to hurry and find the others. Our enemies won't sleep and are probably on the hunt for the next seal already." He started for the door

"Kilian," Alicia said, causing the Trickster to stop and turn around again. "When we find the person who did this to us, I'm gonna kill them."

Kilian hesitated but then slowly nodded. "I understand. If that's what you have to do to sleep better, I won't hold you back."

***

"Thanks for helping me with the boxes, man," Flynn said with a grin.

"No problem, mate. I know how exhausting moving can be," the other guy said. He was more trained compared to Flynn, capable of carrying heavy boxes without a problem.

"Yeah, I don't even remember how my ex and I broke up. Everything happened so fast and suddenly I got a letter from the council that I needed to move houses, and here we are." Flynn shrugged.

"I see how it is. Anyway, I gotta keep going. Welcome to the Seaside, Flynn," the guy said.

"Hang on, I didn't catch your name," Flynn said.

The guy turned around once more and smiled. "It's Taylor."

Flynn smiled. "Thank you, Taylor, I owe you."

***

Relayne took a deep breath. A shiver ran over her back. Her eyes saddened, she focused on the Black Fairy Cafe. She hadn't been here for a few days, and even when Baelfire said it was okay, she felt a certain guilt tying a knot in her stomach. But the cafe was running, so what was there to worry about? Maybe it was her anxiety trying to get to her.

"Missed me?"

She turned around to see Baelfire smoking a cigarette, wearing the uniform of the cafe, which didn't make her less beautiful. The sleeves were rolled up, revealing a few tattoos.

"I always miss you. Is everything okay?" Relayne asked with a smile. Usually she would have hugged or kissed her, but there was a certain feeling she could sense emanating from Baelfire. Something was different.

"Sure, everything is fine. The cafe is in good hands—just like you with your new mates, I guess." Baelfire couldn't hide the jealousy in her voice.

"Did I miss something, or are you jealous?" Relayne asked.

"I was just wondering if a prince is better company for you," Baelfire answered, her voice deeper and a bit rougher than usual.

Relayne eyed her girlfriend. Someone had gotten into her head. She could see that the colour bond between them had changed, and by the way Baelfire was looking at her, it was clear that something had happened.

"Let me fix your feelings before you say something you don't mean," Relayne said in a calm voice, stepping towards Baelfire.

"No, Relayne. That's not how this works. You can't fix everything and pretend it's okay. Just because you have the ability to do it doesn't mean I want it. I want to feel angry and frustrated right now. I am trying my best to make things work for you. And in the past, it was always the time that stood between us. Now you suddenly have to save the world, and however we're gonna turn it, we'll never have the time we need for us to make things work in the way we want them to work," Baelfire fired at her.

Relayne felt her heart drop, tension rising along her back, shoulders hunching up. "Do you wanna break up with me?" she asked, her voice on the verge of breaking.

"I don't *wanna* break up with you. I *have* to break up with you to make things work and make it easier for both of us. If you have the weight of the world on you, you shouldn't waste your time with someone like me anyway. I will be just another romance in your history of wrong guys," Baelfire stated.

Relayne looked at her with a mix of confusion and shock. "Who did this to you? You've never said anything like this to me before, never." Her voice had risen in volume.

"That's because I put your happiness first, just like right now. It's easier for you to leave me when you hate me. So go now. I'll take care of this place with Summer and Ashton, like I promised you. But don't come here ever again if you just want to see me. We're done." Baelfire ended the conversation and turned around. She left Relayne alone and went inside the cafe.

Relayne looked after her before she stepped away. She had seen how the connection between them had turned from a light red into a dark one and then slowly into a black line, as if they had never spoken to each other. Angry and pained, Relayne left the place that had once been her home. The farther she stepped away, the more sadness ran over her, followed by a cold feeling—the breaking of her heart.

***

"What do you think about all this nonsense?" Misfitress said in a low, dark voice. Just because he was capable of being human now didn't mean he could understand any of this—and especially not why humans did certain things.

"It's human love, Tress, something you don't understand yet," Maddison said to her monster. She threw her cigarette on the ground before she stepped on it.

"When can I finally do something that is less boring?" Tress asked, a little glow in his white eyes. He was ready to do something bad; the only thing holding him back was Maddison herself.

"Soon, my dear friend. But for now, you have to be patient. The boss wants us to hide at the moment, and if we don't do that, you know it's gonna be more dramatic than necessary." Maddison reached her hand out and stroked Misfitress's head. He was way taller than Maddison was. That alone gave him the advantage to make people—magician or not—feel uncomfortable. She gave him a little smile. "You need to get into your human form soon. There's a social event we have to attend. The magical council will decide what they want to do about the current situation," she explained.

"And you're going to make them believe?" Tress asked.

"That's how politics work. The real enemy has all the strings in their hand, and in this moment, that is me. Now come on. We still need to find you an evening snack." Maddison left, followed by Misfitress, who growled before he slowly stood up and went after her.

***

"Did someone just knock on the door?" Kilian asked, looking at Jegor and Alicia. They were all sitting in the living room together, talking over the information Kilian and Alicia had just found discussed.

"I think so," Alicia said. She stood and went to open the door. The house would protect her if someone tried to break in like this. After Flynn had been rejected, Jegor and Kilian had made sure to find out any information about what the house would give them. The house had its own rules. Mostly the rules were to the children's advantage.

"I knew it would be you," Petyr said with a little smile at Alicia. "Can I come in?"

"Dare to come in, if you don't mind amnesia or potential death, if you aren't the next child of the seal," Alicia said.

Petyr stared her in the eyes before he stepped towards her—inside the house. "I know when the time has come and people need me," he said with a wink.

Alicia rolled her eyes and closed the door. Both of them went back into the living room.

"Of course it had to be a nature magician." Kilian sighed, not happy in the slightest that it was Petyr. Whatever Merlin or whoever had written this legend must have had a soft spot for mocking someone like Kilian. The prince was missing his excessive nights, just to have something else on his mind.

"Sorry to disappoint you, Kilian. I promise, I won't touch any girlfriend or boyfriend near you this time. Besides, Alicia has an eye on me anyway," Petyr said with a laugh. He sat down on one of the sofas.

"I've heard that. And just because we had a magical night under the stars doesn't mean I fancy you," Alicia said, sitting next to him on the sofa.

Petyr still seemed amused, while Kilian couldn't care less about their interaction.

"As I can see, we are missing someone?" Petyr asked, looking around.

"Relayne went out to see her girlfriend. But she should be back by now," Jegor replied.

"Don't worry, boys. She's probably having a good time right now," Alicia guessed.

"However, since I'm here now, enlighten me about everything I need to know," Petyr said, ready to take on whatever would come.

Chapter 9
Acquaintances

"He comes at night and if you fail to obey, he takes everything."
– F.F., "The Eyekeeper," *The True Urban Legends*

Relayne didn't stop until she found herself in a very dark side street of Shoreditch. Her thoughts and anger had taken over, and all she did was run until she was out of breath. She had thought she could handle this whole situation—that everything would be fine. But little did she know how wrong she had been. What would Summer and Ashton say? Would they see it the same and sooner or later ditch her and avoid her? She had considered calling Summer, but what would she say? That saving the world was too tough? That she wanted to give up on the world for Baelfire?

Tears streamed down her face when she sat down on the cold ground. Was magic really worth the price? Was this whole journey worth the pain? How could she save anyone when she could barely handle her own life? One of her fists hit the wall in front of her, again and again. Her hand was bleeding, but due to her magic she didn't feel the physical pain unless she wanted to. Relayne looked at her hand. She wanted the pain, wanted to feel something other than the confusion and overwhelming anxiety of the last days. She was shaking, breathing fast, and again her fist hit the wall. This time she whined, letting the pain flood inside. Baelfire wasn't here to fix her this time. Summer and Ashton probably had better things to do. A loud sob escaped her lips. Her hand was drenched in blood now, but Relayne didn't care. She wanted this to end. Wanted the pain to be stronger than this responsibility resting on her shoulders. She was ready to smash her hand against the wall, but before she could do more damage, someone stopped her.

"Don't hurt yourself just because you are hurting right now," the person said, pulling her up.

Relayne didn't want to look—she knew exactly who it was, since she had known him as a customer of her cafe before. "Why the fuck do you care, Rose?" she asked, sobbing and annoyed.

"Calligan from now on. I'll take you home before you do anything stupid," he answered.

"I don't have a home anymore," Relayne tried to protest.

"Not yours, idiot. Mine of course," Calligan said.

"I always thought you were one of those magicians who spend their time in my cafe until it closes and your real dark magic work begins."

Calligan sighed and focused on her. Right now was not the time to have a discussion with her, even though her nature as a Feeling made it quite difficult.

"If you really think that, think again. I was there for you," he explained.

Relayne couldn't follow. Her mind and body felt weak, and all she really wanted was this pain to stop. Without saying anything more, she let Calligan do his thing, hoping in silence that the pain would stop.

***

"Are you fucking insane?"

"Stop yelling at me, Quinn!" Calligan hissed, settling Relayne on the sofa in his flat.

"Sorry, may I remind you that Cami is gonna fucking chop off our balls? We are on a mission and you suddenly decided to save the love of your life?" Quinn continued. Quentin Foxgrove n was one of Calligan's best friends and a known hunter in Madness, one of the rare cities with hunter activity. The ash-blond, slim hunter wasn't nearly as tall as Calligan but, as he used to say: *I can still kick your ass, no matter my height or weight.*

"Can't you see that she is hurt?" Calligan asked, annoyed, and grabbed a healing kit from one of the drawers, along with as a serum that would help Relayne calm her mind.

"It's really stressful when you think with your dick. I said what I said," Quinn scoffed and walked out of the room.

"Where are you going?" Calligan demanded.

"Doing our mission, you twat. One has to get the job done!" Quinn yelled back.

Calligan quickly ran after him, grabbing Quinn's arm and stopping him from going further. Quinn looked like he was ready to punch Calligan.

"You need to be careful out there, okay?"

Quinn rolled his eyes. "Thank you, *boyfriend,* but I have been in this business longer than you," he snapped.

Calligan chuckled and ruffled Quinn's hair. "I'll make sure that nothing gets in between on the next missions. That is a promise," he said, and held out his little finger.

Quinn looked at the hand and back at his friend's face. "I am not going to pinky promise over your love-driven ass!"

"Come on Quinn, we always do it!"

Quinn hesitated before he intervened his little finger with Calligan's. The taller hunter grinned.

"Fuck off, Rose!"

"I love you too!" Calligan yelled after his best friend.

***

"Are you really telling me she just slept here and you didn't touch her at all?"

"Yes, Brixton. Now get your curious ass away from her and help me to clean up this mess. How about you make the empty wine bottles disappear?" Calligan answered his white Persian cat, which was wearing pink heart sunglasses as if it was the most normal thing. Brixton had once been his best friend, but after certain events, he had turned into a cat.

"If you weren't so ungrateful sometimes, it wouldn't look like a mess here," Brixton moaned.

"I have better things to do. Magician business instead of watching Netflix the whole day," Calligan answered drily. Brixton was a classic diva, no matter if cat or magician.

"Hey! Do you know how hard it is when you have to wait another year until the next season of *Stranger Things*? This is some real frustration," Brixton said, offended.

"Just make it look more...liveable," Calligan demanded once more before he sat down next to Relayne.

Calligan had helped her last night, making sure she got some rest. Under normal circumstances, he would have never taken her here. It was way too soon, and in general, Calligan didn't like visitors in his own home. There were many reasons for that, but Brixton was one of the main ones. Quinn and Jester, his hunter friends and partners were the only ones he usually allowed in his place.

"Relayne, you need to wake up," Calligan said, slowly running his fingers through her hair. The way she was sleeping seemed so innocent, but Calligan knew better. Being a visitor of her cafe on a daily basis had shown him multiple sides of the Feeling.

"What happened?" she asked in a sleepy voice. She didn't seem to realize where she was or how she'd gotten here.

"You went mental. I helped you. That's it. But now you need to get up. The world counts on you, and the others are probably looking for you." Calligan helped her up from the sofa.

Relayne still had yet to realize where she was, but slowly her memory from the previous night returned—including the fact that Calligan Rose had helped her.

"Why the fuck did you help me?" she asked in confusion, suddenly more awake.

"Because I was just walking by. A thank-you would be nice, but I didn't expect that," Calligan answered.

"I just don't understand it. We rarely ever spoke. And it was a dark corner; I remember that. So nice try for telling me you just walked by," Relayne shot back.

"You're still a bit weak. Find the others now and stop asking questions that make me feel uncomfortable," Calligan said. He put an arm around her to lead her towards the door. He knew that this would happen; it was exactly why he shouldn't have taken her to his house yet. He could hear Quinn in his head: *I told you so, brother.*

"You can't just kick me out and think I won't remember this," Relayne stated.

"Well yeah, but I can still kick you out. Leave now, Relayne," Calligan answered in a more serious voice. He opened the door, shoved her through it, and slammed it behind her before she could even think of coming back in.

"You are so dramatic sometimes," Brixton said from the other room.

"Shut up, Brixton!" Calligan called back and sighed.

Relayne, on the other side of the door, was still confused. Suddenly she was standing in the street where the house of the children was hidden. She turned around, but there was nothing anymore. Calligan had used a portal to keep the location of his house a secret. Confused and annoyed, she started walking towards the house of the children.

Chapter 10
Stranger

And if you find someone you love, the balance can break you easily.
– F. F., "The Dollmaker," *The True Urban Legends*

"Jegor, it's good to see you," Synclair said with a smile.

"I'm here to discuss the current situation. How is everyone doing?" Jegor asked.

"The usual. Alegro is constantly with the council having discussions about the current situation. Tyana is getting worse as it seems, and Kennady and Kalimba are fulfilling their usual tasks. No one really knows which step they want to take next. Do you have any clues as to who we're up against?"

"Not really. Kilian had a bad encounter and got tricked in a nasty way. Whoever this is must have used the day when the balance struggled. Otherwise, I can't explain to myself how it's possible for the council to not realize what kind of magic is used here," Jegor explained.

Synclair agreed. "As soon as we find out who we're up against, new rules will be introduced for sure. Alegro is on his anger path once more, so I can see that everyone who's involved in this will get a wanted poster with a nice amount of money on his or her head. This is so old school, but most of the council members seem to agree with this nonsense at the moment." He said and let out another sigh. Bringing back old laws from Icon and other magical cities wasn't a good thing in his eyes. It would only bring more cruelty and gaps for people who needed a chance to get rid of problematic people.

"But death threats haven't been made since the last century. If we're up against a group, there will be people who will follow them, and there will be much more loss." Jegor couldn't help but show his anger.

Synclair agreed again. "I see it the same way. If you ask me, I think it's already too much that we're allowed to torture people inside the palace and council, if necessary. If too many people get killed at the same time, the other side won't balance, and we as Ghosts will have the problem of keeping them under control. It's like a new opening to a haunting season." Synclair was one of the magicians who could see, speak, and control ghosts, the latter only possible if the magician had a strong, healthy internal balance. The Ghosts belonged to the minority of the Black League. Being a Ghost brought a lot of responsibility, not only for magicians, but for the other side they had to control. Though the balance of magic was a forbidden topic in society, magicians were trained to lean towards the good side of magic. The thought of dark magic alone was something that could get people in trouble—another reason why Jegor was treated differently inside the royal family. He was capable of dealing with both the good and bad sides, something that was against the rules. And something the public didn't know. If the royal family was good at anything, it was keeping secrets.

"Whatever you can do, make sure they don't choose the path of death. It would be a massacre, and at the end of the day, we might even kill the wrong people. This can't happen, not in the name of the palace and for the future that Kilian has to carry on his shoulders," Jegor said. Despite his calmer tone, it was clear that he was still angry. After everything they had fought for over the last years, this was something that could ruin their structure and society for sure.

"I'll do my best. Go back to the house now, Jegor. The palace was never your comfortable place anyway," Synclair said, smiling again before Jegor left the room.

***

"—and that was the time when I had my worst encounter with an elf," Petyr finished his story, and Alicia laughed.

Kilian was hanging around in the living room, but his thoughts were somewhere else. There was hardly a moment when he could think clearly. He knew he soon had to face the loss of another family member. The world was counting on him. And the last encounter had shown him how serious this was. Whoever they were up against, Kilian knew now that this wasn't child's play.

"I'm back." Relayne's voice interrupted the scene. She stood in the doorway of the living room, facing the other children.

"Where have you been?" Kilian snapped.

"I had a bad encounter last night. My girlfriend broke up with me," Relayne began.

"And you think that's a reason to leave us alone and not tell us where you've been?" Kilian argued.

"Kilian!" Petyr warned.

"I didn't know that I signed a contract to tell you where I am at all times," Relayne fired back.

"You have a responsibility towards me, towards all of us," Kilian said. "If you can't take that seriously, why do you think we should care if something happens to you?"

"Oh yeah. It's my fault once more? Do you even listen to yourself? You're a selfish bastard who's always had what others wanted—a perfect life, a perfect family. How could you know in the slightest how it is to lose someone so close to you?" Relayne shouted, completely missing the balance between her own feelings and Kilian's in the room.

Before he could say anything, she left and went to her room.

Kilian stared at the spot where she had been standing and then turned around and took a deep breath. Two magicians of the Red League could be a toxic combination.

"That was a dick move. Go after her later and apologize," Alicia said.

But Kilian refused. "Her stubborn head and temper will get us in trouble one day, I tell you." He, too, went to his room and slammed the door. He knew he had mostly overreacted because his head was full of thoughts, but that didn't make her retorts hurt less. There were enough people out there who saw him as the spoiled prince.

"Don't worry. They can't see yet how deeply connected they are," Petyr said to Alicia before continuing his stories about all the magical things that happened in the Woods.

***

It was dusk when Jegor returned to the house. Just when he'd wanted to leave the palace, it had happened—Tyana had lost her life. As a Voodoo magician, he was able to feel and sense certain dark magic, but he couldn't see ghosts unless they wanted him to see them. Synclair's face had changed, and his uncle was hardly someone who got surprised or changed his facial expression in shock. Even though Kalimba had predicted Tyana's last moments hours ago, the White had tried to hold on to her life as best as she could.

Now it was on him to tell Kilian. But how could he tell him that after yesterday? Kilian was going through a lot at the moment. Jegor also wasn't the best choice when it came to emotional messages. He had never really been emotional since the day his parents passed. He'd always found a way to deal with things in his own way and to not shed a tear for anything. He had improved this strength with his magic. It was a cold wall that he had built up over the years, something he could use to his advantage. Some cruel magicians were still using torture when it came to investigations, but someone like Jegor would never say a word, no matter what pain he was enduring.

"Jegor, something happened," Alicia said when she walked out of her room and into Jegor, who had just entered the house.

Petyr had retreated to his room upstairs and hadn't been seen since his storytelling.

"I know. But you go first," Jegor answered.

"I had a Vision. I saw a girl, and it was on the Seaside. I think it might be a clue." Alicia still seemed upset about what she had seen.

"We will figure things out as soon as I tell Kilian what happened," Jegor answered.

"Excuse me?" Kilian interrupted, just coming out of his room.

Jegor faced his cousin.

"Anything you wanna tell me since you've been to the palace?" Kilian asked.

"I think you should sit down for this," Jegor suggested.

"Just say it," Kilian answered, rushed. He felt like he knew what his cousin was about to say.

Jegor sighed. It wasn't the first tragedy within the family or between the two cousins, but he hated to be the person to bring the news. There was no right moment for this, and waiting any longer wouldn't change anything, yet he felt guilty for giving Kilian more bad news after the latest events.

"It's Tyana, Kil," Jegor began to say, focusing on his cousin. "She died."

***

Kilian didn't say anything for a long moment. What was there to say, anyway? He knew that this would happen sooner or later. There was this feeling inside him, like a feather that was touching a sense he hadn't felt before. It was making him numb. Kilian nodded and turned his back on Jegor. "Thanks for telling me before Father had the chance to do it," Kilian said firmly.

"It's okay. Let us know when you need something or if we can do anything for you," Jegor answered, and Alicia agreed.

Alicia hesitated, arms moving up quickly before she shoved her hands into her pockets. Kilian looked at her and shook his head. A hug wouldn't fix the death of his stepmother.

Without a word, he went back into his room. He needed some time on his own.

Jegor turned to Alicia. "You said you saw a girl on the Seaside? You need to tell me more details now."

"She wasn't alone. She had a shark with her. But he was also human, so probably a Beast, I guess," Alicia explained.

"That's a Crossing. Some Woods and Element magicians have the magical ability to turn themselves into animals as well. Or this person might be cursed by the sea. Do you think we need to prepare ourselves for a fight? Or can we simply find her?" Jegor asked.

"We don't need to prepare for a fight, but we need to hurry. I saw the second seal, and I think she knows where it is. She is the key to the Woods."

Jegor was already at the house entrance.

***

Shadra looked at the ocean. She loved the noise of the waves and the horizon, with different colours every day. It was her home, her safe place. She didn't want to be anywhere else in this city, even though her heart beat through and through for Icon. She had grown up in this city. Shadra had no idea who her mother was, but her father, a pirate and a magician, had always told her she was the most beautiful woman and the reason Shadra had long, curly turquoise hair. Her skin was pale, nearly white, the price she had paid as an Element of water. She could communicate with the animals under the sea, and most of the time she was with her best friend, Ferguson Julio Gomez. He was also an Element of water. Beyond that, Ferguson was a Crossing—someone that could change into an animal or run around half-human, half-animal.

Shadra had been staring at the sea when Ferguson jumped out of the water. His favourite form of sharks was a white shark. Once on land, he returned to his human form.

"And did you find a good snack?" Shadra asked with a smile.

Ferguson grinned, showing rows of sharp teeth. Some of them were still stained with bits of blood, which gave Shadra the answer she wanted to hear.

"Next time you should come with me," Ferguson said, his Spanish accent reverberating.

"I know. I just had to do some negotiating for my dad. He's coming into town soon, you know. And as I know him, he has a big deal between the pirate crews."

Pirate crews still existed in the magical world. They were the reason why the magic council had to define a new law this year. It forbade them to sail around in the human world. Pirates in the twenty-first century? That would be too much of a culture shock, and if the humans realized that the pirates could also use magic, it would lead to too much trouble.

"Usually he leaves me a letter by this time. I'm not sure if something has happened to him," Shadra said. Letters were traditional within the family.

"It'll be fine. He's a strong man who raised an even stronger daughter. Don't worry too much," Ferguson said calmly.

Shadra tried to smile as they walked along the beach, but deep inside something was telling her that it was different this time.

***

"Wow, it's been ages since I've been to the beach," Petyr said. He was happy and excited to be here. Usually, he had too much business to handle in the Woods to even go to the Seaside District.

"We're not here for fun," Jegor said, and Petyr rolled his eyes.

"I know that. Doesn't change how beautiful this area is," Petyr answered.

The sea was indeed gigantic, and its colour changed depending on the season. At the moment, it was the light green of spring. The sand was a mild rose colour, littered with shells in different shades. The end of the beach was lined by beach houses and towers, opposite which sat a giant bay area, within which you could see shipwrecks serving as play-places for the younger people to have thrilling bonfire nights.

"Will you recognize the girl from your Vision if you see her?" Jegor asked.

"I think so. She had very bright turquoise hair," Alicia said.

"I could use some nature magic, but I think it's on Alicia to find her," Petyr added.

Alicia nodded and looked around. There were lots of uniquely-dressed people in this area. It was more open, some magicians drawn to the sea, wearing fishing nets, shells, or other sea accessories.

"Let's split up. The faster we are, the better for us," Jegor said, and the search began.

***

Meanwhile, Kilian emerged from his room. He still didn't know how to handle the news about his stepmother, so the best idea, at least in his eyes, was to ignore it all—or to distract himself. He went to the kitchen and mixed himself a magical, strong cocktail. It had been a while since he'd had alcohol. It wasn't that he wasn't used to it, but every time he got drunk, his father told him things he didn't want to hear. He was over twenty years old and not some rebel teenager who didn't know what he was doing. Kilian knew *exactly* what he was doing, and that was the point. He would rather live a creative, chaotic life being himself than be on the throne and forced into a wedding he didn't want in the first place. Kilian adored women and men in both ways, but his father would never understand that.

"You'll be breaking the glass if you hold on any tighter."

It was Relayne, again, who interrupted his thoughts.

Kilian let go of the glass just to pick it up a second later and drink the whole mixture. He sighed in relief and faced Relayne. "Why are you not with the others?" he asked.

"I didn't realize they were leaving. I was, rather, punching my pillow after your lovely words," Relayne answered in a too-friendly way, showing him that she hadn't forgotten what he'd said to her earlier.

Kilian rolled his eyes. "Don't be salty. It can't hurt that much," he said, hoping the alcohol would show its effect quickly.

"You don't even think of an apology, do you?" Relayne asked bitterly.

Kilian didn't answer for a moment, then he turned around and faced her again. "I guess when your stepmother dies, there are a few things that you don't really care about," he said in a very sharp tone.

"Your mother died?" Relayne asked, shocked.

"Yes, she did. So long, farewell. But how could you know? You don't care about me enough to ask in a sensitive way. So I don't care enough or at all about your life," Kilian answered, as if he was pointing out facts.

"You care enough to be worried when Fear tried to charm me," Relayne hissed, rooting through the fridge.

Kilian needed a second cocktail if the conversation was going to continue like this.

"It's okay," Relayne said. "I get it. Some of my kind hate your kind. But we're not all like that. So stop looking at me as if I'm the one who hurt you. We're in this together. All of us have lost something or someone. It's on us to protect our city and our kind now. Don't you see that?" After Baelfire had broken up with her, she didn't want another argument, especially one that would last long.

Kilian took a sip from his second cocktail. "Oh, believe me, I do see that. I see it probably better than everyone else. Since I was four years old, I've been told how to rule a kingdom, how to choose wisely, and how to be on the throne one day. Father had nothing else in mind. No social circle besides the children who had high blood, so they could look and choose who I should marry one day. Don't get me wrong. Who wouldn't love to have power and the crown? But the way they raised me, the way they made me look at things, that's something I can hardly let go," Kilian explained. He wasn't afraid to show emotion, even though it came with a bitter taste that he once more had to explain himself—not to mention the nights where he tried to escape and simply forget the weight on his shoulders. He drank as much as he could before he had to breathe. Finally, he could feel the effect of the alcohol going through his veins. Magic could be handy, especially in this case. The numb feeling from earlier was still with him, though; he couldn't explain it.

"But why did they never consider Jegor? He seems to be calm about everything." Relayne was trying to get the bigger picture.

"Calm? His parents are dead, he has no normal friends, and he talks to a Voodoo doll!" Kilian exclaimed, raising an eyebrow. Maybe she was weird too, but her facial expression didn't change. Relayne seemed serious. Kilian sighed. "It's in the royal law that only the first son of the first next family string can wear the crown. If Synclair would have chosen children his child would have been the next heir to the throne. Jegor has no right in that sense. Also, if you're a woman, you are fucked." Kilian drank some more.

Relayne nodded. "That makes sense, even though I think your royal system needs to be reconsidered," she said.

"Why are you trying so hard to understand me? Us?" Kilian asked, looking her in the eyes.

"Because it's not your story alone. I lost my mother, and I don't know who my father is. But for some reason, Merlin—or whoever wrote the legend—included me in all this. So we need to find a solution. No one of us wanted this or are here because we signed up for this. But we can't just look away and pretend this society we live in is okay. You're angry about your family? Fine. Take advantage and use your position wisely. You and Jegor have access to one of the most important positions in this hierarchy. The only position that stands against it, is the political council. It's in your hands, Kilian," Relayne told him, her eyes going slightly red. Inner rage combined with passion came through her words.

Kilian didn't break eye contact as Relayne spoke. He reached for one of her hands. Relayne wanted to pull back, but hesitated when she was hit by a warm wave of his emotions. Kilian led her hand closer to his face before he blew a gentle kiss on her hand. His gaze met hers, and there was something different in his eyes. Relayne could feel her heart beating faster. Kilian let go of her hand and stepped away.

"Thank you, Relayne," Kilian said, and returned to his room. The numb feeling inside him had changed. It felt like a flame that had just started to glow.

***

Jegor was walking on his own towards the shipwrecks on the Seaside. Alicia and Petyr had gone in the other direction, which led them towards the living area. Petyr was right. The area was beautiful. Alicia tried to remember the girl and what she had seen, but her Vision had only shown her that this area was right.

Last time she had been here, it was with her brother. A certain pain jolted through her body. Just because she was now with people who were with her in this didn't mean losing Flynn hurt less. In the end, it was better—at least that was what she tried to tell herself to sleep better. If he didn't know her, no one could hurt him because he was connected to her.

A cracking noise took her out of her thoughts. She looked down and saw that she had stepped on a green shell. She was about to continue on when she noticed a little note in the shell. As she bent down and plucked up the note, a smile crossed her face. It was written in Danish.

"What is it?" Petyr asked, curious.

"It's the clue we needed. Sometimes gods can show the perfect path," Alicia answered.

She concentrated, and the little note began to sway above her hand. She whispered something in Danish before the note started to burn, little sparks flying around in a circle before forming an arrow that pointed towards the shipwrecks.

"Guess Jegor's intuition wasn't too bad either." Petyr grinned, grabbed Alicia's hand, and changed direction, heading towards the shipwrecks.

Chapter 11
Shadra

And if you were lost at sea, he would come and find you.
– F. F., "The Captain," *The True Urban Legends*

You always said you're not a beach person. Why did you not send your cousin? Carlin asked Jegor, hanging on his belt as usual.

"Kilian is obviously not in the best place. If I sent him here, he'd end up sleeping with a mermaid or who knows what. I can't risk our case by him being a mental wreck."

Carlin laughed a little. *I'm not so sure if it was clever to leave him alone with Relayne.*

"I don't care if they end up together, as long as they don't ruin anything for the future," Jegor said, and looked around. For some reason, he liked the shipwrecks. It was quite dark around here, and the smell of the sea was stronger. A few people ran around, but in looking closer, Jegor was able to see they were the outcasts of the seaside community. Some of them were homeless, and others came here because they didn't fit in with the posh sea people who lived in their lodges and beach houses. Jegor remembered that he'd once made a deal with a pirate in this area. Most of them were at least good with giving information.

"Any clue where to start, Carlin?" Jegor asked his little doll now.

Let's go in the darkest bits. We like it there, don't we?

Jegor showed a glimpse of a smile and went on to one of the bigger wrecks. He could hear some teenagers playing around with magic and trying new tricks.

Look up. There's a girl with turquoise hair.

Jegor followed Carlin's advice and saw her. She looked quite young. She wasn't necessarily a teenager, but if she was older than that, she was only at the beginning of her twenties. Jegor approached the wreck, but something felt wrong. This was too easy. He looked to his left, and in the next moment, something was jumping out of the water—a giant white shark, coming in his direction. Thanks to his fast reactions, Jegor avoided the giant shark, who now turned into a Crossing—half-shark, half-human. Jegor put up his hands, trying to signal that he hadn't come here to make trouble.

"I'm not here to fight," Jegor said.

"Is that so? What does one royal highness want from a girl like my friend?" the shark asked, showing his teeth.

"Something important. Don't give me a reason to fight. I'm here for a talk, nothing else."

Ferguson looked at him. It wasn't clear what he would do next. Then he turned into a complete human and held out his hand. Jegor took it and nodded.

"My apologies, my royal prince. We had some incidents lately, and with everything that is going on, I want to make sure that no one harms her or does anything else. My name is Ferguson Gomez. Pleased to meet you, Prince Lancaster."

"It's all right. And no need for the political correctness. Call me Jegor."

A Scottish name and no accent? Carlin interrupted in their heads.

"Family trees and their national origins. Similar to the Lancasters, I guess?" Ferguson asked, looking at the Voodoo doll. Jegor nodded. Their family tree was indeed a mess of nations and names. Some had blood-related connections to their names. Others had been named after their great ancestors or historically important magicians.

After he introduced himself, Shadra came down from where she had been perched and eyed Jegor. "Is he a friend of yours?" she asked Ferguson.

"Shadra, this is Jegor Lancaster. He belongs to the royal family, and he is here to speak with you," Ferguson explained.

Shadra's cheeks went red when she realized she hadn't paid attention to the person standing in front of her. She wanted to curtsy, but Jegor just waved it off.

"I'm not here to speak about royal business. I'm here to speak about a prophecy. One of my...let's say *friends*, saw you in a Vision, and we think you might be the next potential child of the seal," Jegor explained to Shadra.

Shadra and Ferguson exchanged a look. While Ferguson seemed to have calmed down, Shadra felt like someone had just hit her with a frying pan.

"A prophecy? Me? I'm just a normal Element magician. I've spent all my life basically on the seaside and rarely in the city. How can I be the person you're looking for?" Shadra asked. She couldn't hide her emotions, which were overrunning her. Mostly curiosity was running through her body. Her fingertips tingled, an exciting feeling going through her body.

"Magic doesn't always make sense. It does what it does," Jegor said.

"He's right. I saw you, Shadra." A female voice interrupted the scene as Alicia and Petyr walked up. "I saw you diving and your friend by your side. I think it must be you since I saw something else. You were the one who knew where the next seal was. Have you ever heard of that? Merlin's legend?" Alicia asked.

"The seven seals that hold this city and everything else together? My father once told me the story, but I never thought it was more than an Urban Legend. Are you gonna tell me that I'm a chosen one?" Shadra asked with a giggle.

But none of them were amused.

"Excuse me. It might be my inner child who doesn't believe in anything like this. I always admired Urban Legends because they seemed to be the only thing that were somehow not real in this world," Shadra explained.

Petyr stepped forward, closer to her. Before he could reach her, Ferguson stepped between them. Petyr looked at the shark and smiled. "Don't be overprotective. We're here to help her," he said.

"It's okay, Ferguson. His charm doesn't work with me," Shadra said.

"Thank you," Petyr said, smiling as Alicia giggled at the comment. "I know this seems crazy, and as someone who is very mature and grounded, I couldn't believe it myself. But the world we're living in is changing at the moment, and if you're one of the people who can change that and do something important in life, wouldn't you want that? Being a part of something bigger than waiting for your father to come home?" Petyr asked in a calm voice.

"I didn't mention my father," Shadra said, looking at him in surprise.

"You didn't have to. The sea is telling me things. I'm a nature magician and, therefore, the person who probably understands you the best," Petyr said. He reached out his hand. "Come with us, Shadra."

Shadra looked at his hand and then at Ferguson. "I need a moment," she said, and stepped away with her friend.

"I'm not sure why someone should be interested in me or what I'm doing," she murmured to Ferguson. It wasn't that Shadra didn't love the smell of a new adventure. Since her father was a pirate, there had always been some kind of adventure in her life. But this was much bigger than all the stories and adventures she had discovered before.

"It's not about your place and where you're coming from. It's about the things you're gonna do for the future," Ferguson said with a sigh. "I tried to protect you as long as I could, but you're nineteen now. Before your father left, he told me that a secret about you—that you were gonna do something greater than you thought one day. I never figured out what this could possibly mean but this seems too coincidental to not follow along."

Shadra swallowed. Perhaps Ferguson was right. "I'm not good with social interaction. You know that. You're the only person I really have, and wherever I go, there is usually trouble. Who wants that in their life? Besides, they're all older than me. This guy who spoke to me looks like he seems much older than he looks to be!" she argued.

"Shadra, this is your anxiety speaking to you. If only one person believes in you, it's enough to do something. And this person is me. As much as I don't like letting you go with them, I knew this day would come. I didn't know how exactly, but this is it. The balance isn't in its correct order at the moment. You know that. We have seen dead fish and reefs down in the sea. You can't pretend that nothing is going on."

Shadra looked at the sea—Ferguson was right. The sea was showing its first signs of imbalance. Whoever had the first seal in his or her hand had taken advantage of the first things and beings in the society.

"Fine. But I will come back and make sure I can see you once in a while. I need someone to talk to about how different the city is going to be for me," Shadra said. She smiled, leaning forward to hug Ferguson.

Maybe going with these people was naive, and maybe it was rushed. But deep inside, Shadra knew she could only find out if she was meant for this if she embarked on a new journey. Ferguson held the hug as long as he felt it was needed. Then he let Shadra go, and she left with the others.

***

"And since that, I tend to pick non-magicians once in a while." Kilian finished his fourth cocktail.

Relayne was on her second, but whatever Kilian had put inside it was enough to make her cheeks turn red. "Fascinating that someone who is so desperately against street magicians hooks up with humans. Isn't that complicated sometimes?" she asked.

"It's just building another illusion for them. They tend to ask the same questions after the show. How did I shrink the cards? How did I make the billiard ball disappear? And how did I turn from one corner to the other? It's cute and gives me a certain confidence. None of them knows that there's more magic behind it," Kilian said.

Relayne smiled a little. "It's good. It gives them hope and motivation to find out what is happening behind the stage." She could see how Kilian pulled off a good show, taking hundreds of people into a universe of hope and illusions.

"Did you know any of the magicians in the water tank?" Relayne asked.

"I knew some of their names, since they were all Tricksters. But I wouldn't call any of them a close friend. It must be horrible to forget what it's like to have magic and then die because of it. I don't wish that to happen to anyone, not even my worst enemies."

Both of them went silent for a moment.

"Have you ever finished the trick I wanted to show you years ago?" Kilian asked.

"You mean letting a billiard ball fly? No. It's hard for me to concentrate feelings on an object. Sometimes I move objects when I'm angry and focus my anger on something. But I'm better with people and their feelings. I mean, that's what Feelings do. That's our section," Relayne explained.

Kilian stood up and held out a hand.

"What are you doing?" Relayne asked.

"I'm gonna teach it to you now," he said.

"Kilian, you're drunk," Relayne laughed, trying to refuse his offer.

"Maybe, but if you're smart right now, you're going to oblige before I'm bitchy again." He winked and waited.

Relayne struggled for a second before standing up and taking his hand. He turned her around so she stood with her back towards him. He stepped closer and rested an arm around her, but just to put a billiard ball in her hand. Relayne took a deep breath.

"You need to feel the magic through your veins," Kilian began. "If you can be one with your element, you can also use your feelings to let simple things like this fly. A Trickster is born with it. I could probably let a whole house fly. But it's not about me right now; it's about you." It was probably the first time Relayne heard him talk in a calm, soft, and maybe even caring voice.

Relayne nodded and closed her eyes. When she opened them, they glowed red, and she tried to focus on the billiard ball in her hand. It didn't move at all.

"You can't force it. Think about something that gives you a strong feeling—whether it's anger, sadness, or something that made you feel very good," Kilian instructed.

Relayne thought about the last few days. The first thing that came into her mind was the breakup with Baelfire. They had been through so much more than what was happening right now. Why couldn't she understand this and be more patient? Why did she have to break up with her, as if everything was suddenly so different? Relayne swallowed and focused on the ball. She tried to concentrate, channeling more anger into her thoughts. It worked. The ball was now rising slowly up above her hand. Kilian started smiling, which she couldn't see. But so did Relayne. It was just a moment, but she had made it.

"Not too bad for a Feelings," he said.

Relayne turned around. "Not too bad for a Trickster as a teacher," she answered, realizing how close they were to each other. She cleared her throat and gave Kilian the ball. Kilian held her hand for a moment longer than necessary. Their eyes met. Neither of them said anything. Kilian simply took a wisp of her hair between his fingers and stood there like that. Relayne didn't find words, either.

And there was this feeling again. The little flame that blazed inside Kilian. It wasn't familiar, and it wasn't friendly. It felt forbidden.

"We're back," Jegor's voice broke the silence, and they stepped away from each other. Kilian looked at her once more before he stepped into the hallway to greet the others.

***

Shadra looked around when she stepped into her room. Together with Petyr's room, hers was upstairs. There was only one room left for the child they hadn't found yet. Light blue colours set the decoration in her room, and her bed was a giant shell.

"It knows what you love." Petyr interrupted her thoughts.

Shadra turned around and smiled briefly. "I like it. It makes me feel lesser parted from home. I guess your room has a certain nature vibe?" she asked. Even though this new journey was overwhelming for her, Shadra couldn't hold back her curiosity and excitement.

"Yes, indeed. My bed is up high, so I kinda get the feeling of being in a tree again," he answered, sitting on her bed. Curious as always, Petyr also looked around.

"So which part of your family have you lost?" Petyr asked, shameless in breaking the ice. He was older than all of them together and had no interest in beating around the bush like Jegor and Alicia when it came to their private lives and trust.

Shadra sat down next to him. Out of all of them, Petyr was the person who had captured her interest first and emitted a kind of trustworthy feeling. He was right when he'd said that nature magicians would understand each other. It was the connection that brought them together and gave them a sense of trust.

"I don't know my mother, and I haven't seen my father in ages. He is a pirate and a captain. He's probably challenging quests out on the sea. But I'm sure he'll come back with his crew, and then I can show him what I have done, hopefully," Shadra explained with a smile, as if it didn't bother her at all.

Petyr looked at her and felt a certain admiration in that moment. She was the youngest of them all, and she brought a certain bravery with her, for believing in hope. Maybe her father would never come back, but her presence showed that she was living with the fact, and no matter what, she was somehow getting through the day. A little smile spread over his face.

Shadra was about to say something when a scream broke the silence. It was Alicia. Within seconds, Petyr had left the room, Shadra following him. All of them went into Alicia's room. Jegor stood at her bed and gave a hand sign that told them to stay back. Alicia wasn't awake, but she was dithering on the bed and trying to catch something with her hands, as if grabbing after something or someone.

"What's happening?" Shadra asked. She had never seen anything like it.

"She's having a Vision—or a Dream, maybe an Omen. But something or someone is holding her in it," Jegor said.

"Can we wake her up?" Relayne asked. Alicia seemed to be getting paler every minute.

"We don't know what we're up against. If we try, it could kill her," Petyr said. He stood close to Alicia, while all of the other children stood at the far end of the room. He closed his eyes for a second, and in the next moment, ivy tendrils came out of the bed and wrapped themselves around Alicia's arms and legs so she couldn't move around.

"It doesn't hurt her, but it will help her control herself a bit more," Petyr said, trying to figure out if they were dealing with a demon or ghost.

"I can sense something bigger than a usual enemy here," Jegor said with a look at Petyr.

Relayne grabbed Kilian's hand and swallowed. Watching her and doing nothing was a horrible feeling that made her balance struggle inside.

Petyr spotted something around Alicia's shoulder. It was the same print she'd had after she was attacked in the Woods. The nature magician looked over to Jegor. "It's the Bogeyman. He's challenging her," Petyr said, his face blazing with anger. "He's testing her to get to me. But why? She was only a visitor."

"Not if anyone has touched the seal or even stolen it," Jegor said. "The second one is in the Woods, isn't it? Maybe he's trying to warn her or sees her as a target for a reason."

With a loud scream, Alicia woke up and ripped through the ivy tendrils. Her breath was coming fast, and her face was pale as a ghost's. Cold sweat ran down her back, and for a moment, she didn't know where she was—until she saw the faces of the others.

"He needs help," she said, out of breath.

Petyr took one of her hands to calm her with his magic. "Who needs help?" he asked softly.

"The Bogeyman," Alicia answered before she passed out.

***

After the incident, Petyr stayed with Alicia. He would look after her and make sure that she was okay when she woke up. The others went on with their tasks, and Shadra had gone to bed after everyone else. There was no report from the palace. They had no new clues for the last child, and Alicia needed to rest before she could tell anyone what she'd seen and how to act on it. Shadra realized now that this was much bigger than anything she'd been involved in before. In a way, it was scary, but she knew it was the right thing to do. People who were chosen in prophecies or legends never had it easy. Who would sign up for this journey when the price of losing someone was so high and the pain so deep? The legends always tried to tell people that a chosen one would be a hero, but maybe there were no heroes after all. Maybe they were all more like survivors, outcasts who had come together to make things happen when no one else would or could. She closed her eyes and drifted away into her dreamland, where everything seemed to be okay.

***

"Mum?" Shadra looked around. She was standing at the beach, and a feeling told her that she had just been with someone close to her. It was the same beach where she used to live, but besides her, no one was around. She turned, and suddenly she was in a whole different area.

This wasn't Icon—it was the human world. She stood in the middle of Trafalgar Square, and she could see the National Gallery in front of her.

"Help me," a voice whispered, and she turned around in circles to find its source.

There was no one, but her intuition told her that this voice was coming from the gallery. She walked closer, and the voice grew louder.

"You need to wake me up. It can only be you," the voice said.

Shadra went into the gallery. But she could only see darkness around her.

***

After the incident with Relayne, Kilian had made his way to the palace. He knew he couldn't avoid this meeting. Sooner or later, he had to see his father, at his stepmother's funeral at the latest. At first, he had thought of taking Jegor along, but this was something between him and his father, even though it was a family loss. Kilian took a deep breath before he opened the door to his father's room. Alegro was sitting at his desk. He looked up when Kilian entered the room and closed the door.

"I didn't expect you," Alegro said. His hair looked messy, and the dark circles under his eyes pointed out his lack of sleep. His crown was lying on the desk. Alegro had no need to wear it in the privacy of his study. As beautiful as it looked, it was just a symbol to him. Some days, it was too heavy to carry when he was on his own. The king yawned before he pointed to the chair next to him.

"Sit down and have a drink with me," he said to his son.

Kilian nodded and sat. His mind was racing, and he tried to find words that would fit the situation. But there it was—the struggle of their connection.

"As I can see, you are drowning yourself in work," Kilian said, trying to make conversation. Maybe he should have taken Jegor with him. But then, Jegor was even less social when it came to his father.

"The palace's work won't stop just because someone is gone. Synclair is covering for me at the council. Some are speculating that something else happened to my wife."

Kilian rolled his eyes. Most of the council members were too curious when it came to palace life. "You need to rest, Father," he said. "Take your time. I can finish the rest of the paperwork for tonight. The children are all together, and Jegor will inform me if something happens and I need to go back."

Alegro's eyes went to his son. Moments like this were rare between them. "Thank you, Kilian," he said, and meant it.

Kilian took his place, and Alegro went over to his other desk, where he usually stored alcohol and herbs. Sometimes, that was what he needed to get through the day. While Kilian worked through the papers, Alegro just watched him in silence. If only this was a normal situation—Kilian meeting his responsibilities towards the palace. Alegro hid his thoughts for tonight. He knew that another argument would come soon enough, and for now, he enjoyed being with his son. They didn't have to talk; just being there for each other was enough for Alegro. The loss of Tyana hurt less, even though it would only last for a few hours.

Chapter 12
Bond

Humans, so full of everything.
– F. F., "The Dollmaker," *The True Urban Legends*

Alicia woke up the next morning. It took her several minutes to realize that she was in her bed and had passed out after the horrible things she had seen. This time she wasn't sure what it was. She was used to Visions. But the situation with Flynn had been an Omen. This felt similar, but Omens were common for the Black League.

She glanced to her left to see Petyr lying next to her. He was sleeping and looked quite innocent. Alicia felt a tingle in her fingertips, an urge to run her fingers through his hair or touch his face. *Ugh, get yourself together. Just because you passed out last night doesn't mean I need intimate comfort.* Without making too much noise, she got out of bed and went over to her wardrobe. A shower was well needed, after the recent event. Moving quietly as she could, she went to her bathroom. All of them had their own little bathrooms. The house took their thoughts and wishes and made them into a perfect living area for each of them. A relieving sigh left her lips when she felt the hot water running down her body.

When she looked at her shoulder, she noticed a print like the one from when she'd first been attacked. This one was fading away as the water ran over it. This time, she also hadn't been attacked. She had seen something from the Bogeyman. However, it worked, she had seen who was coming for the seal.

It was a woman—a very strong, dark witch. Perhaps a Voodoo. The monster she had with her was even darker. It was over two metres tall—a giant wendigo with long black hair and gleaming, sharp teeth, not to mention the claws.

The Bogeyman had shown her a hint towards the second seal. She was the one who was meant to protect this seal, and the Bogeyman knew this. Yet she didn't trust this creature enough to be sure that he wouldn't choose her as a target. So many things were going on and she wasn't sure if someone was playing with her mind again. This was how she had lost Flynn, when someone had played with Kilian's mind. She didn't want to risk anything more.

"Did you really wanna go in the shower without me?"

Petyr was standing in the doorframe of her bathroom. Alicia chuckled and turned off the shower before she grabbed her towel and wrapped it around her body. She stepped out of the shower and looked at him.

"Didn't know I gave you an invitation," she said.

He smirked. "Next time, I guess. How are you feeling?"

"Good. I know who we're up against now. I'm just getting ready, and then we have to tell Kilian and Jegor. Maybe they know the person I've seen."

***

"The human world? But how is that possible?" Kilian looked at Shadra, eating his pancakes at the kitchen table.

Relayne wasn't really with them. Her first coffee hadn't kicked in yet, and the others didn't seem to be awake either. Coffee was one of the great inventions from the human world Relayne was thankful for.

"I have no idea, but she is female and trapped in the gallery. We have to go."

"It could be a trap. The gallery is full of ghosts, and some people are even trapped in the pictures in this gallery. I'm not sure what to think about this," Kilian said, sceptical.

"You had a Vision and knew it was me," Relayne pointed out.

"Yeah but it all happened in Icon. In the human world? Someone seems to be playing with her mind, if you ask me, and we need to be more careful after Flynn."

"But it could be possible," Relayne said. "Think about the balance. One of the seals has been taken away, so that means some gaps opened between their world and ours. We have to at least have a look. I'm going with her, and you should go too. If someone can manipulate and bring us in without someone seeing the magic, it's you, Kilian."

The Trickster rolled his eyes and sighed. "Fine. But if we have an encounter with any kind of monster like in Fear's shop, I'll be the first to leave you guys behind, because I told you so." He stood up and left the table.

Shadra gave Relayne a bright smile.

***

Together, the three of them travelled through a portal into the human world. Kilian looked around. They were in the middle of Piccadilly Circus when they came out on the other side.

"It's always so busy here. Can't wait for summer and all the tourists," Kilian said with a smirk. Tourists meant lots of beautiful people from all over the world with whom he could flirt and hook up with.

Relayne rolled her eyes. "We're not here for fun," she said, and Shadra agreed.

All of them started walking towards Trafalgar Square. It was a beautiful day, as if they had picked the right place and right time to come here.

"Do you know where we have to go?"

"It was an extra room. It wasn't open yet, probably for a special gallery," Shadra explained, trying to concentrate. The closer they got, the stronger the feeling grew inside her. It took them a while, but as soon as they entered the gallery, Shadra felt very warm inside.

"She's at the end of the first floor," she said.

"It's probably locked, so we have to see how we can get inside," Relayne answered.

"Leave it to me. I know how to get us inside. We just have to be quick," Kilian asserted.

All of them went up the stairs and onto the floor Shadra had described. They acted like they were really interested in the paintings, and Relayne could swear that some of the portrait's eyes were actually watching them. Kilian was right about the ghosts.

When they stopped in front of the door she had seen, Shadra looked at Kilian, who nodded.

"Both of you stand as close to the door as you can," Kilian said, and in the next moment, he took a little box out of his pocket and opened it. He took a pinch of red sand from within and threw it up in the air before moving his hand in a way that made the sand fly around the whole room. Shadra and Relayne exchanged a look, but they could see the effect almost immediately. Everything around them was moving in slow motion.

"It's one of the little helpers that make it possible to go from one point to another. The sand gives us five minutes until everyone is moving normally again," he explained.

"What about the alarm?" Shadra asked.

"It would take too long to turn it off, so we have to hurry. Even if any other security enters the room now, they won't be able to move. In reality, everyone will be confused and not remember clearly what has happened, and that's it," Kilian explained, and in the next moment, he opened the door.

The alarm went off, but all of them ignored it and closed the door behind them. No door was ever locked to a Trickster; it was one of the first magical tricks they learned in their first days of schooling.

"You were right," Kilian said, impressed. In the middle of the room sat a cluster of ice sculptures, obviously hidden from the public.

"That is the upcoming exhibition," Relayne said.

Shadra went straight to one of the sculptures—a frozen girl. She looked like she wanted to run, but to the human eye, it looked like she was jumping and not being captured by something or someone.

"It's her. I'm sure of it," Shadra said.

"Brilliant. Then free her before we get caught," Kilian answered.

"How? I've never done anything like it." Shadra looked at them.

"Ice is your element. Concentrate on it and set her free. I can help you with harnessing the strong emotions for it," Relayne said.

Shadra nodded and took Relayne's hand, grabbing the hand of the frozen girl with the other.

"Focus now," Relayne said, and her eyes went red. She started to give Shadra strength and confidence, and while the turquoise-haired girl could feel something warm inside, she focused on the ice sculpture. She imagined the ice was melting, the matter searing through her fingers, and a tingling ignited in her fingertips, ready to melt the sculpture. At first, nothing seemed to happen, but then, slowly, the ice began to drip away.

The girl who had just come to life took a deep breath and fell into Shadra's arms, still shaking.

"Thank you, Shadra," she said, holding onto her as if her life depended on it.

"Not to be non-romantic here, but we really have to go," Kilian said, interrupting the scene.

Relayne let go of Shadra's hand and put it on the girl's shoulder. With the ability of her Feelings magic, she helped the girl warm up. Once that was done, the three of them started to move.

***

After they had broken the girl out of the ice, the group returned to Icon, sitting in a café in Shoreditch. The newspaper would report that the statue had been stolen, but the cameras wouldn't show anything, since Kilian had tricked them. Relayne stood next to him now as Shadra tended to the girl. Relayne smiled. *I guess it's her Element, being so calm with the new girl.* Her thoughts were interrupted by a shiver down her back. Kilian was uneasy.

"What's your problem now?" Relayne asked him.

"Nothing. I would rather bring her to the house as soon as we can. Time is running against us, and I'm pretty sure that whoever is up against us knows that we're all connected now."

Relayne sighed—but he was right. There was no rest for someone with the weight of the world on his shoulders. Relayne's looked over to the television, which broadcasted current news in the magical world. Today was the day when new rules were discussed. Once a month, the important people came together and discussed what was happening in the magical world. Sometimes, residents of Icon could decide what the new rules would be, and sometimes it was only on the palace or the head council. The balance mostly benefitted the people in the higher classes.

"Kil, your father's on," Relayne said, pointing at the TV.

"Nothing new. He's mostly the one who has the last word when they make up new rules."

"Hear what he has to say. It might be important for us," she insisted.

Kilian focused on the words that his father was saying—not that he really cared; Relayne could see that. Mostly, it was political nonsense in Kilian's eyes. But this time, the future prince wasn't right. Relayne felt the tension in the room rising. Kilian wasn't uneasy anymore. He was on edge about something.

"Today, a new rule will apply to this city. Together we have discussed the current situation. The safety of our city is at risk, since the balance isn't provided anymore. My son and his cousin are, as always, investigating and are on the lookout for the people behind this. But for now, we have enacted a new rule that will help everyone and provide more safety—not only for this city, but even more for everyone who lives in a magical place and needs this balance. We can't risk staying silent about this any longer. The seals that provide our balance are in danger. Therefore, we've decided to send out a death threat to everyone involved in the crime that goes against the safety of this city and everything that is connected to the people who try to destroy the balance. Any activity or clue must be reported. Any activity that supports this person or group will be considered allies of the enemy. There will be no exception from now on."

Relayne caught her breath, hit by the wave of Kilian's anger.

"Kilian, wait—"

Relayne couldn't catch him. Kilian had left the café, leaving Relayne angry and frustrated.

***

"Is he okay?" Leyla asked Shadra.

Shadra shrugged. The last half hour, she had been focusing on Leyla, the girl she had set free from the ice. Shadra couldn't say what it was, but something was drawing her excitement towards Leyla. There was a calming aura surrounding her natural beauty. Shadra had opened up immediately, too excited to think anything through or hold back. This was their journey together and the young Element wanted to know more. Shadra had always found women more interesting than men—another advantage of living by the Seaside, which was famous in Icon for its gay bars and shops owned by the LGBTQAI+ community.

"I'm sorry if that has anything to do with me," Leyla said worriedly. The girl from Puerto Rico was a couple of years older than Shadra and, though the Element had asked Leyla a lot of questions, Leyla chose her words wisely.

"Don't worry about him. We just found out that a death threat has been announced," Relayne explained, sitting down next to them.

"Death threat?" Shadra asked.

"It's a doomsday rule. The last death threat was announced ages ago—definitely before we were all alive. It allows people to kill easier, kicking off a witch hunt and use some very dark magic. The death threat sets a bounty for a person. People are greedy for the money, so they can make it look like a defence kill against the magician that has the bounty on their head. No death threat had ever a good outcome in any city in New Born Kingdom ," Leyla said. Her tone made Shadra realise the seriousness of the situation.

"It's against the people who are fighting us. So even the smallest activity can cost someone his or her life. It's pretty serious by now. I don't know what to think about this. What if people use it for the wrong purpose and make it possible to kill their enemies?" Relayne sighed.

"That means we have to hurry even more," Shadra said.

"Leyla, do you remember how you got into the museum?"

"It was the night when the first seal got stolen," she started. "I was on the way to meet with a friend, and suddenly, I could feel something weird happening. Sometimes I have this sense that tells me something bad is about to happen. So I went on and tried to reach my destination before anything could happen. But when I kept on walking, I could feel that my legs kinda froze, and then I saw ice starting to build up around me. The last thing I remember is someone behind me, and then I was in that gallery. No idea how I got there."

Relayne mulled over her thoughts for a moment. "What were you supposed to do that evening?"

"I was meant to do a trick that night. Instead of my friend, I wanted to help her with the water tank trick. Shadra told me already that people have died over this," Leyla said.

"So you were supposed to do that magic trick. But instead, someone froze you and put you somewhere else? And in the human world of all places?" Relayne continued.

Leyla nodded. "I guess so. Whoever did this saved me. This person must have known me or is at least on our side."

Shadra felt her heart beating faster. This was just the beginning and she was part of it. No more swimming in the sea and drinking cocktails whenever she wanted to. This was her life now.

"You mentioned a sense that something bad is about to happen, right? But isn't that an Omen? I only paid attention once in class," Shadra said, biting her lower lip.

"It could be. The prophecy told us that all of us could have Visions, Dreams, or Omens. But not as we are used to having them. Shadra and I would only be used to having Dreams, but the things I've seen so far were either Visions or Omens. It's hard to tell when you haven't grown up like Kilian and Jegor have," Relayne said.

Shadra agreed, but Leyla's eyes showed only more worry. A story was hidden inside her. Gently, Shadra rested her hands on top of Leyla's.

"You're with us now. And whatever Omen may come, we will figure it out together," Shadra said, and Leyla smiled gratefully.

***

"Are you insane?"

Kilian threw the doors to the main room of the palace open. His father looked at him and sighed. Kalimba was with him. It seemed she'd already argued with their father.

"I knew you would be upset," Alegro began.

"Upset? Are you joking? You send a death threat out in the city? This will lead people to commit more crimes than ever. There is enough already happening in the Underground, and you literally just gave everyone permission to kill each other."

Alegro looked at Kalimba and told her to leave. Then he looked back at his son, now standing in front of the throne.

"I know it's hard with your mother passing away and all the pressure that is on you. But this is the exact thing that will lure them out of their caves. We need to see who we are up against, and this is a fast solution," Alegro explained calmly.

"Do you even hear yourself? This is the perfect advantage for too many people to kill each other and make it look like they were involved. You've helped these bastards, whoever they are!" Kilian couldn't help but scream at his father.

"Sooner or later, you will understand. Or are you upset because you know someone who is involved and you don't want to see that person on trial? You haven't complained about the fact that torture is still an allowed necessity in our system. So what's upsetting you now?"

Kilian rolled his eyes. "You're unbelievable, Father. Besides, she was never really my mother. My mother died on the day I got my magic. And honestly, I'd rather give up on this than fight the war you're leading us into. Wake up. The world is changing, and you just gave whoever's behind this the biggest advantage in this whole city. So when they come for us—for you—I will tell them to go on. Because you brought this on yourself. Just like you ruined our relationship the day you killed Mother."

Silence prevailed in the room, and Alegro looked at his son—perhaps for the first time—in shock.

"Synclair let me speak to her when I was old enough. I know that you killed her because she was more in love with him than she was with you. Jealousy? Really? I always wanted to hear it from you, but you never even thought about it. Instead, you came up with another woman and stole my childhood, bringing me to the edge of everything. So pardon me for living my wild, arrogant, fancy life. It was the only chance I had to survive this hell of a palace—just as Jegor chose his way." Kilian was furious. The feeling inside him was stronger than before, a wave crashing against his inner walls.

Alegro stepped forward. "It was an accident," he started. "A fight that ended in tragedy. How could I look into your eyes and tell you what I had done? You always loved her more than you loved me. It was easier to make you hate me than to try to put together the pieces. Don't you see that, Kilian?"

"I see a selfish king who never cared about his son. Now excuse me. I need to fix this damn balance before everything falls apart."

Kilian turned his back on his father and stepped out of the room.

***

After the argument with Kilian, Alegro went back to his room. Guilt swarmed him, and he could barely think straight. Alegro had just sat down when Synclair entered the room without knocking.

"You two are really stressful," Synclair began. "All the palace ghosts are asking me about the latest gossip on you."

He sighed and mixed two drinks, giving one to his brother before sitting next to him.

"Kilian knows. About his mother," Alegro began to say. He closed his eyes, feeling the tears swelling. Alegro hardly cried. But after all, he was just a magician with feelings like everyone else.

"I don't like to be that person, but I told you so," Synclair stated with a sigh. He took a sip of his drink and eyed his brother. A moment of silence passed before Synclair wrapped an arm around his shoulder.

"Sooner or later, he would find out. I know that you tried to protect him, but he isn't your little boy anymore. Prophecies happen. People die. But avoiding the tragedy in this family has never brought us anywhere. If you want Kilian to be on the throne one day, you need to open up as much as he needs to open up. You two are both stubborn. Kilian doesn't get that side on his own. Not to mention that he has her temper." Synclair let out a little laugh, and Alegro rolled his eyes.

He struck Synclair's hand away, just to empty all of his drink in one go. "Do you think I am a bad king?" Alegro asked his brother.

Now Synclair rolled his eyes. "Spare me with the questions of life, brother." He flicked his fingers and refilled their glasses. "I think you're a king who knows what he's doing. You have your ways. I have my ways. There is no good or bad when you have the weight of the crown on yourself. You will never be able to satisfy everyone. But you can learn from your past. It's never too late to be someone new—especially as a father."

Alegro didn't say anything. Pictures from the past were running through his mind. He could feel cold sweat running down his back. He felt a stitch inside him, as if someone was trying to pin needles into his heart. But with the words of his brother, he took a deep breath. The pain wouldn't just vanish, but Alegro would figure out how to deal with it.

"Thank you, Synclair. Now go and deal with the ghosts in the palace. I have duties to fulfil and rules to make."

Synclair obeyed, standing and leaving his brother alone.

***

Feardorcha Forbes turned the TV off with a sigh. The new rule wasn't something he had decided. Actually, he was one of the few magicians who opposed it. But obviously, the palace had enough supporters to follow the order of the current king. A knock on his door interrupted his thoughts. When he opened the door, a smile spread across his face.

"Hamlin, you old bastard," he greeted the person on the other side of the door.

Hamlin grinned and stepped inside. Hamlin was a thirty-year-old Jester who had failed his bloodline and wasn't able to do magic. It was a rare situation for someone to experience that kind of disaster in their life. Only a few people had suffered such a fate, and Hamlin was one of them. It happened before the end of the ceremony— the Leagues would deny the person of magic because their future was written in a dark cloud. Some people called it a protection system to see far into the future and try to avoid danger for the other magicians. Fear didn't thought much of to deciding whether a four-year-old boy was dangerous enough to not give him permission for magic. It was an early age, too soon in his eyes to decide if a magician was worthy of becoming a part of the society.

As a Jester, it was still possible to walk through the human and magical world with the use of magical artefacts. That's how Hamlin mostly went through his life.

"I think we should have a drink on the new rule, don't you think?" Hamlin asked. He wore his usual black hat and long coat. He was a man who proudly took care of his beard.

"Thought you'd rather hang out with a red-haired lady," Fear answered sassily.

Hamlin laughed. "You're right. I'm ready for some entertainment tonight, but first I thought I'd report to you the news you wanted to hear. The choice was mostly made by the politicians. I think Alegro is up to something. I'm not sure if it's good or not, but the fact that he is sending out a death threat sounds to me like he's up for another war. We haven't had a war in ages. That's more the style of the human world, don't you think?"

Feardorcha looked at Hamlin. "Careful what you spread around, Hamlin," he said, and his face didn't look so friendly anymore.

Hamlin giggled and took a little bottle of alcohol out of his bag. "Don't you worry. I might work for a lot of people, but I'm not stupid. Someone like you is rather my friend than an enemy. Which brings me to the point—I found something very interesting in the library. Since you told me that you had burned all the copies, I thought I'd show you this." Hamlin opened his coat and took out an old book; the title was hardly to be seen, almost faded away.

Feardorcha grabbed it out of his hand and opened the book. A little note fell from within, which read:

You're not the only one who has a secret. Stay away from her.

Feardorcha looked at Hamlin. "How did you get this? Was it just there? Have you tried to see who put it there?" he asked harshly, ill at ease.

"As you know, I am not that powerful. That's why I gave it to you. If someone knows who you are next to me, you should find that person and make sure they shut up—however you wanna call it."

Fear looked once more at the book before igniting it with magical flames. "Make sure no one finds any more copies. It seems like someone broke into my apartment, since this was one of my books. If they have a copy, I need to find it before everything blows up. Go now. I'll pay you whatever you want."

Hamlin laughed in amusement and rubbed his hands. "Give me all you got," he said.

Fear left momentarily and returned with a box. "That's the potion and poison box you ordered. Now go. We have work to do."

Chapter 13
The Bogeyman

Some saw him as a King. Others saw him as the monster he always had been.
– F. F., "The King of the Woods," *The True Urban Legends*

"She looked very pale and like a doll next to the monster. They seemed pretty close, and whoever they were I know that they're after the seal. That's why the Bogeyman wants me to come and find him. He wants me to help, I think," Alicia explained, sitting with Jegor and Petyr at a table.

Leyla, Shadra, and Relayne were in their rooms.

"If they have the seal, it could be a trick. That would mean they take you directly into his arms," Jegor said, looking at the Beastarium, which was open. The Bogeyman was depicted as a shadow, since he looked different to everyone. Some saw him as a ghost; others saw him as a person.

"I know, but he won't let me go. And if I don't do it, who will? We can't waste our time now that we're all together. It's about the seals now. We have to try and protect everyone," Alicia said. "My brother nearly died because of these people, and the death threat is out there. It's not that I really care if certain people get hurt, but there are still people who don't deserve to be in pain."

Jegor sighed, and in the next moment, Carlin set himself in the middle of the table. *I think she should go. You don't say no too often to a seal monster—or to a monster in general.*

"I'm going with her," Petyr said, and looked at Carlin, who seemed to smile as a thank-you for agreeing.

"Good. You two are going. I will watch the Woods and make sure no one else gets in the way. What magician do you think it is? Who is capable of dealing with a monster like that?"

"I could feel a sense of Voodoo. But that's very rare, isn't it? And most Voodoo magicians who are registered are male. Or am I wrong?"

Jegor nodded in affirmation. "I think I know who we're dealing with," he said.

"Do you? Then why are we not hunting her down?" Petyr asked.

"Because she was supposed to be dead," Jegor continued. "If I'm right, her name is Maddison. She and I trained together, and we used to be friends. Maddison was a loner, just like me, and she was never really into people. She knew how to play and manipulate them, but she never got close to anyone. She was her own person, and so she was growing stronger with the dark magic every day. If you don't meditate or find a balance, the dark magic can take over easily and do dangerous things to your mind—voices in your head, hallucinations, and all that crap. The range of damage is great when it comes to our League. Dark magic comes with a bigger price than the other leagues. That's why mostly males are known for this magic, because the female mind works differently and is, according to the council, sometimes too sensitive. We have to see—there are incredible women who've conquered that kind of magic. Maddison was born to be a dark magician."

And she was beautiful.

"Thanks, Carlin. That is an unnecessary fact," Jegor said.

"What happened to her?" Alicia asked.

"She had to deal a lot with the court and council. A lot of them thought she was going too far with her magic. She also wanted to earn another League, since she eventually got bored with her power. But then she found a very dark magic book. She and I had gone to Fear's shop. We were meant to pick up some potions. Maddison seemed to have a crush on this warlock for whatever reason. Fear was, in a way, interested in her too. But I don't know if there was anything more between them—it doesn't matter. When Fear went away and let us look over his shop, she found an old urban legend book. It was from Fear's collection, and there were some notes about Voodoo magic as well.

"I don't know what she found that day in the book, but whatever it was, she changed after that. She never went with me to the shop again, never spoke about Fear, and focused harder on her work. A week later, she tried to get a contract signed, to get permission to receive the abilities of another League. The council rejected her. But instead of being angry, she was scared. She never told me why. I'd never seen her like that before. The next day, I found her corpse in our practise studio. She had tried to do something to herself."

Jegor swallowed and held back for a moment. "She tried to make herself into a Voodoo doll. I have no idea why she did it. But something scared her so much that she tried to live forever. There's a spell that turns a magician into a Voodoo doll. It's one of the most complicated black magical spells in our range—that is, the essence of living forever. As a Voodoo doll, you are rarely capable of feeling anything. If you combine that with the sense that we have, it's a deadly combination that makes you immortal."

Petyr nodded. "I've heard that before. But has anyone ever made it? Turned someone into a Voodoo doll?"

Jegor's eyes went to Carlin, who seemed to grin.

"I made it, with Carlin. When I got him, he was just a normal Voodoo doll who could still speak but not feel or do as much as my little friend here can do now."

Jegor gave me the chance to understand this world better.

Alicia and Petyr exchanged a look.

"I wanted to find out what happened to Maddison, so I followed her path and figured out what she had done wrong. Maybe she did everything right, but wanted everyone to believe that she was dead."

Carlin looked at Jegor. *Can they see me for the real me now?*

"Carlin, it's not the right time. You know if it were legal, I would let you run around in your true form. But then, Kilian wouldn't be amused."

"The real him?" Alicia asked.

"If the spell works, every doll has a small form, which you can see now, and one that makes them look like us, but more like a monster."

I'm the most beautiful of them all.

Petyr giggled. "I think I like him more now," he said.

Carlin winked at him.

***

Jegor was on his way out of the house when Relayne stopped him, coming out of her room.

"Quickly. We have the clue where the next seal is and what's going to happen," Jegor said.

"I'm worried about Kilian. After we found Leyla, he went to the palace. And I haven't seen him since then. He got so angry about the death threat that I think it might have been a bit too much."

Jegor looked at her and sighed. "I don't want to be mean, but he's probably in someone's bed. That's what he does when he needs to distract himself. Besides, since when did you start caring about him?"

"We sorted it out, I guess," Relayne said.

"That's good. But don't break your thoughts and heart over him. He'll be fine; trust me. I sometimes don't see him for a week, and suddenly he turns up at family dinner."

Jegor continued to the door, but before he could open it, Kilian walked inside.

"I told you he's all right," Jegor said, and left.

Kilian closed the door and sighed. "I'm not fine, but thanks for telling me what's going on, cousin," Kilian said sarcastically. He looked at Relayne. "Were you worried about me?" A slight smirk crossed his face.

"I wasn't. I just thought I'd tell your cousin, so he'd know what happened."

"You were worried," Kilian said with satisfaction.

"Shut up." Relayne turned her back to him. Before she could walk into the living room, Kilian stopped her, and before she could blink, he was standing in front of her.

"Just because you're a Trickster doesn't mean you have to make a show out of it," Relayne said, avoiding his eyes.

"I always do a dramatic opening, just to be clear," he corrected her. "And something seems to be on your mind. So, I wanna know what it is, cherry." He took a strand of her hair between his fingers.

"Nothing. It's just a scary thought that magicians can now kill without getting punished for it. Everyone can make something up. What if suddenly my friends are in danger? Summer and Ashton."

"I don't think any street magician is capable of dark stuff like that."

Relayne pushed his hand away from her hair but held onto it. "Don't underestimate us. We can do more than you think," she said, her eyes glimmering with red.

Kilian swallowed as a warm feeling went through his body. The tension between them gave Kilian a certain urge to get closer to her than he should. It was the flame, the sense to cross a line.

"Goodnight, Kilian," Relayne said, and let go of his hand before she stepped away and into her room again.

Kilian took a deep breath, his heart still beating faster than usual.

Inside her room, Relayne sagged against her door and took a deep breath, too. This feeling was new. Different. A struggle in her inner balance.

***

"Petyr, we missed you. Where have you been?" one of the nature magicians asked.

"I've been busy, my love. But don't you worry. I'll be back soon," he said, smiling before he went on with Alicia and Jegor.

"I didn't know you were that famous," Alicia said sardonically.

"Don't worry. I actually don't care about most people here. The nature is more important to me. You know most of the magicians around here after one party. That's it."

Jegor looked around. "I'm gonna wait here for you. Carlin can sense if something goes wrong. Take care."

Alicia nodded and went on with Petyr into the Woods.

"In a way, I knew it had to be the evening or the dark hour," she said. "But honestly? How creepy can an area be?"

"Your head is playing games with you. If you grew up here, you would know it's not that bad. Don't you remember the good time we had here?"

"You found corpses near the lake. Absolutely romantic."

Petyr laughed. Alicia spoke with more sarcasm than Kilian, and yet that gave her a good sense of humour.

"How can I find him?"

"You can't. He will find you. And when it happens, you can't do anything about it. You don't know what he's gonna look like, what he's gonna do, or how he'll react. You have to be flexible and prepare for anything. Don't show him that you're scared. He smells fear like the humans smell perfume."

"Why do you know so much about him?"

"I live in this area. Or at least I used to live here. I usually don't get scared of anything or anyone."

Alicia nodded, and the further they walked into the forest, the more she had the feeling they were losing track and not following the path anymore.

"If you're right about this, he'll lead me into his arms. I'm pretty sure about it."

A crack next to them interrupted the conversation. Alicia looked to her left and felt the ground under her feet start to break open. Shocked, she started running and tried to not fall.

Petyr jumped on one of the bigger trees, grabbed her arm, and pulled her up. She was hanging in the air while the ground opened, slowly revealing a row of roots leading down into the hole, fireflies lighting the way.

Alicia's heart was beating faster, and with Petyr's help, she got down and stood in front of the hole in the ground.

"Thanks for catching me before I could fall down the rabbit hole."

"No worries. The bigger question is, are you ready to go down there?"

"I am. For the sake of my brother and whoever is in danger."

***

Down inside the chasm, only the fireflies lit Alicia's way. She looked around and spotted a door engraved with Latin words. A small sigh left her lips before she walked over to the door. She didn't even have to touch it, and the door opened with a little creak. Inside, she couldn't see anything. It was completely dark.

"I'm right behind you. Don't worry," Petyr said, and Alicia went forward.

As soon as she stepped through the door, it closed behind her, and for a moment she was surrounded by nothing but darkness. It was a weird feeling. She wasn't afraid, but she didn't feel comfortable either. Slowly, step by step, she went on. After a while, the darkness faded away, and she realized she was standing in the Woods. But this was the underground area—the upside-down one where the Bogeyman lived. It was a dark forest that children imagined in the Urban Legends. The fireflies had changed their glow into lilac. Trees and flowers glowed in the dark, growing in diverse directions. A melancholic feeling grew inside her as she remembered the night of the circus.

"It's the forbidden paradise," Petyr whispered. "One of the oldest legends that the Woods tell each other. It's hidden— everyone always wants to find out where it is, since it's the safest place in Icon. The rules are different here, made by him, the King of the Woods." Petyr couldn't hold back his fascination. For someone who was over three hundred years old, that was something special. Alicia had never seen Petyr that fascinated. For once, he found something that made him curious—more so than anything that had happened in the past days.

"King of the Woods? I think we have different legends. I have always been told that nature itself is leading this area, and not another king." Alicia looked around, searching for clues.

"That's because no one likes that there is more than one king. But no one knows who it is." Petyr grabbed a neon pink fruit from a tree with dark violet leaves.

"I wouldn't eat that if I were you," Alicia said.

"I am basically immortal, and rarely anything can harm me, since I am one with the nature."

Petyr wanted to take a bite, but Alicia threw the fruit on the ground. "We're not here to enjoy this. We have a task to complete," she said harshly.

"Fine. But if we get through this, I wanna have this fruit. And I'm gonna enjoy it."

Both of them started walking through the Woods. The deeper they went, the more fascinating it became. The trees didn't have normal branches; some of them curled like vines. Others formed the shape of a flower. The leaves had all different colours, and the trunks were mostly black. The grass was a dark blue. Nothing seemed normal here—in terms of how people would usually identify anything in a normal forest.

After a while, the two of them came to a glade. It was huge, the grass as crimson as some of the fruits. Alicia made Petyr stop. "I can feel it," she said, looking around. "He's here."

Neither of them could see anything.

"Didn't I mention that I only wanna see you here?"

Both of them turned around in shock at the scratchy, charming voice behind them. The creature was over two metres tall. They couldn't tell what it actually was; somehow it looked like a tree combined with the anatomy of a human. Little branches sprouted out of its left arm. Instead of a head with hair, the creature had a treetop, dotted with fairy lights. Hanging from the branches were leaves, teeth not identifiable as those of people or animals, and some small flowers. But that wasn't the only weird thing. Instead of a normal face, Alicia and Petyr stared up at a mask that reminded them of a plague doctor's.

"It's pretty brave to walk down here without an invitation, don't you think, my old friend?" The creature looked to Petyr.

"So it's true. It is you," Petyr answered seriously.

"Can someone explain to me what is going on?" Alicia asked.

"Your Bogeyman is the King of the Woods," Petyr answered.

The creature giggled and gestured for them to bow down. Alicia wanted to say something, but Petyr made sure she knelt first. There was no room for disrespect towards the King of the Woods.

"Some only believe when they see—especially you, Petyr," the creature said, allowing them to stand.

"Why do you want my help?" Alicia asked.

The Bogeyman grabbed one of her arms and looked at her, or at least it seemed like he did. "Because you're as much involved as I am in this. I am a monster to some and a friend to others. I've always been here to protect one of the seals. And you, my dear child, are written in the seal I'm protecting. Therefore, you are the one who can help me the most and help us all."

"Which seal are we talking about?"

"Saeculga—the seal that never seems to be in one place only. Everyone thinks I'm in charge of the seal that lies down here somewhere, but I'm not. I tend to have my place here, because I'm the king as well—which makes me realize that I've never introduced myself. Kingsley 'Bogeyman,' King of the Woods."

Alicia couldn't believe he was serious, but he didn't show any signs of joking. "Fine then...Kingsley...sir...King? How do I do this?" she asked, confused.

"Kingsley for you, King for anyone else. Now, can we continue business?" The beast's one hand swept upwards, and a dark cloud of fog appeared in the air, projecting an image in front of them.

"Maddison and Misfitress," Petyr said when he looked at the cloud.

"Exactly. These two are the people who are trying to steal it. Don't get me wrong. I'm strong enough to deal with them, but Misfitress is an old friend who I don't want to fight. However, she made it possible to control him and even turn him into a human. They're both very dangerous. But I saw something, like a Vision. There's a weapon as old as the urban legend itself. Have you ever heard about the sword of the runes? The legend says that only a magician born with the White League and under the name of the northern gods can lead it. Now tell me, who are you living for?"

Alicia swallowed. She understood. She was a God in the name of Tyr. "And I need this sword because?"

"You need to chop off Misfitress's head to turn him again. He will return after you've done it, but not as a human and no longer under her control. That gives her less power, even though she seems to be a strong magician. But if you can get her on her own, you can figure out who she's working with. That might help you and the whole world, wouldn't it?"

"How do we know you're on our side? The struggle of the balance can be an advantage for you, too," Petyr asked.

"That is a fair point. But the more the balance goes away, the fewer people listen to me. The corpses you found were on me. I do kill people who don't live under the rules of the nature in this area. But if everything gets out of control, every district will have their own war. And who would rule this area if I have to kill everyone living here?" The Bogeyman sighed.

"So you're letting me do the dirty work," Alicia said in a sarcastic tone.

"Pretty much. But you have no choice either. You are a chosen one. Now go and fulfil your duty, before I start torturing your pretty freckled friend."

Chapter 14
Omen

Only Acer could understand the King of the Woods, so they say.
– F. F., "The King of the Woods," *The True Urban Legends*

"You seemed pretty calm around him. Is there anything I should know about you and the Bogeyman?" Alicia asked and looked at Petyr.

"Perhaps there's a lot that you should know, but it's not the right time," Petyr answered. Being as old as he was brought not only a lot of stories, but also people and creatures that he knew longer than others. Kingsley had never shown his face to him before, but there were multiple situations where Petyr had had to face either his work, his loyal followers, or the brutality of nature that occurred when the King of the Woods was not amused.

"It's never the right time for anything. But I guess for someone who is over three hundred years old, there are right and wrong moments," Alicia stated. Petyr smirked. There was so much more for the stubborn White to understand who he truly was. Even though he had to admit that he was really starting to enjoy Alicia's company.

As soon as they arrived, Alicia went into the house and straight to her room.

Petyr sighed. At some point he would tell her, but there were other things they had to focus on right now. As long as he could avoid the darker parts of his life, he would do it.

"Where did you leave my cousin?" Kilian asked when Petyr walked into the living room, where Kilian and Leyla were sitting.

"He wasn't there when we came out the Woods, so maybe he went off when he saw that we came out together," Petyr answered, then sat down next to the others and told them what had happened.

***

Jegor had left the area when someone caught his attention. He had a feeling that something would happen while the others were in the Woods, and if he hadn't been so close, he wouldn't have followed her. Curiosity—and maybe the intention of Carlin—was leading him.

He was standing in a side street somewhere near the market square. It was quite dark, but light enough to see her.

"I knew you would follow me. Even though Kilian seems to be the one who is always curious, there's something inside you that wants to find things out on your own as well," the woman said with a smirk.

"Good to see you too, Maddison," Jegor answered in a dry yet polite tone.

Maddison's grin widened. Her skin was nearly white, but other than that, she seemed human. "Dry as always. Guess you wanna get some answers?" she asked the Voodoo magician.

She stepped closer. Even though they were already close, Maddison took her time, step by step. "I had to go for many reasons. All of them were ones I couldn't name in the moment. How could I succeed if anyone knew? Or is it the fact that I should be dead when I am indeed alive?" Her voice sounded comforting, but there was a tone to it that made her words more mysterious.

"Wherever you want to start, if you want me to protect you from the palace," Jegor replied.

"I don't need your help or anything else. I've changed, and so have you. Something is coming. You might be able to see and even understand it. I'm not so sure about your cousin. Who knows which side you're standing on, at the end of the day," Maddison explained, focused wholly on Jegor.

Jegor was calm. He always tried to understand the case as best he could and why someone acted the way they did. But the Maddison standing in front of him was a different person than the woman he'd known before.

"Give me answers, and I won't have to fight you," Jegor said.

"Don't worry. I will tell you things, since I still like you. You were always honest with me and different from all the classic magicians that exist in this world. You might be smart enough to join us and do the right thing that helps everyone," Maddison continued.

"Who are you with? And what do you know about the seal situation?" Jegor asked.

"I know enough to tell you that something is coming—a revolution, something that we all need in this society. Flip the balance, flip the rules, and recreate them. Have you never thought about this? You, as second prince, should know how wrong the system can be. Or do you wanna tell me that you were always happy in the place you grew up?" Her voice was serious rather than mocking.

She dragged one of her fingers over his face. Jegor let her do it before he grabbed her hand. From the shadows, he could hear a snarl, the kind that didn't sound friendly at all.

"You don't wanna hurt me. Trust me," she said, and freed herself from his grip.

"The more you tell me, the more likely I'll have to mention your name to the palace and the current death threat. But you're not my enemy," Jegor said. He didn't want to deliver her to the palace. Jegor wasn't fond of the death threat, by which anybody could deliver anybody if only the story behind it seemed logical. Besides, Maddison wasn't wrong. The past days had shown him the horror in the streets. The council collected more corpses, the missing posters started to duplicate. The underlying message of something much bigger to their understanding was there. The system had gaps and he—*they*, as the chosen children, needed to do something about it. There was no way for Jegor to oversee the obvious.

Maddison laughed. "Sooner or later, you will understand what I have just told you. Go now and think about my offer. The world will change. We will make people think. And it is just the beginning," she said, and stepped into the shadows.

Once she had walked away, Jegor was sure he saw white eyes in the shadow that looked like they belonged to Misfitress.

His eyes went down to Carlin. "Perhaps it's time for you to walk around, too."

***

"And you think he's gonna buy that?" Baelfire asked Pieotr.

The two of them had been sitting on a roof near the street where Maddison had just seen Jegor.

"I don't really care, but I think I know what we're up against next," Pieotr said with a yawn.

"And what is that?" Baelfire wasn't sure if she wanted to hear the answer.

"Maddison is pretty much doing her own thing at the moment, and that will cost her something sooner or later. You know that the boss mentioned that before, and apparently it's my job to tame her," Pieotr sighed.

"At least you get to speak to him. My patience isn't really capable of waiting any longer to hide my true form or the fact that my girlfriend is running around with this prince," Baelfire said, her voice ringing with anger.

Pieotr laughed in amusement. They were the complete opposite when it came to love and relationships, even though Pieotr could understand Baelfire. "Nothing better than a little jealousy, don't you think?" he quipped, aware that Baelfire would probably slap him any second.

"Is that why you run after Maddie?" Baelfire asked in return, sassy as usual. "She pays more attention to the monster than you." She was the one who looked amused now.

"Very funny. Speak of the devil, your girlfriend is walking through the streets. Seems like she wanted to speak to Jegor as well," Pieotr said. He pointed down the street.

Baelfire leaned over to see if Pieotr was right. "That's weird. Why would she run around on her own again?" she questioned.

"Dare to find out?" Pieotr asked.

And before Baelfire could say anything, Pieotr had kicked her off the roof, and Baelfire was down in the street. With a dull noise and curse, Baelfire crashed to the ground, capturing Relayne's attention immediately.

"Baelfire?" she asked.

"Surprise." Baelfire tried her best to not sound pissed off while standing up.

"Are you stalking me?" Relayne asked, somewhat confused.

"Not really. I was actually hanging on the roof with a friend. Why are you running around here?" Baelfire tried to change the subject.

"I was looking for a friend," Relayne replied.

"Cool. Go on then. I'll be fine," Baelfire said, realizing that her ankle felt anything other than fine. The roof wasn't that high, and as a magician, it was hard to get hurt. But since

Pieotr had caught her unprepared, Baelfire felt that something was wrong with her ankle.

"You seem hurt. Let me help you," Relayne said, stepping closer.

"Sure your friend isn't waiting for you?" Baelfire asked in concern.

"Maybe, but the person I care about is more important," she said.

Baelfire bit her lower lip. She looked up to the roof and saw that Pieotr was still there. He nodded—the moment had come. Baelfire looked back at Relayne and smiled weakly. She had no idea what would happen next, but if the boss and Pieotr were right, it didn't matter and everything would eventually work out. "I guess I could use a little help. If you can get me home, I can help myself," she finally said.

"I have never been at your house or flat. You always came to my place," Relayne said in surprise, but she didn't look like she would say no. It was true that Baelfire had never taken her home, for good reasons. Baelfire had been good with finding excuses or putting her lips on Relayne's before she could even start an argument.

"I know. See it as thank you? Please." Baelfire took out a black key in the shape of a seven.

Relayne focused on the key for a moment. It wasn't an unusual key, since sometimes keys took the form related to the house of the magician.

"Fine. I'll bring you home, and then I'll go back," she finally agreed.

***

Together they entered Baelfire's room. Relayne let go of her. She wanted to say something, but standing here and seeing the room of someone she really cared about brought back emotions. The room was a bit chaotic—clothes on the floor and a giant king-size bed, the whole room a mixture of red and black. Baelfire had gone into the bathroom. Relayne stepped over to the small table next to her bed, above which a couple of pictures were pinned. She saw herself a few times, but one picture showed Baelfire and a boy in bed together. She raised an eyebrow. Her gaze went to the ground, where she saw the clothes. These were all male clothes lying around.

"Surprised?" Baelfire's voice interrupted her thoughts, and Relayne looked over to the bathroom.

The Baelfire she had known wasn't standing there anymore. Instead it was a guy—quite skinny, with short black hair streaked with red. He was slightly tanned and his arms were lined with tattoos.

"Oh, excuse me. Let me get a shirt," he said, plucking one from the ground and putting it on. When he stepped closer, Relayne spotted an eyebrow piercing.

"What's going on?" Relayne asked, crossing her arms.

"Everything I should have told you for a long time. But you were so happy that my curse attacked me in my mind, and I didn't wanna risk what we had," he explained. "Please hear me out before you run away."

Relayne swallowed. "It's quite hard," she admitted, taking a deep breath.

"I get that. I'm an Element magician who mastered two elements—fire and shadow. But I had to pay a price to get to this level. Have you ever heard of the Chameleon—the nature magician that no one really knows since he or she always has a different face? I admired them since I was small, and one day, I found them. This person told me how to be more than one person. So far, I have only two main appearances that I really like—the one I was with you and the other you see now. I am still getting used to my other two bodies."

Relayne remained silent.

Baelfire looked her in the eyes.

"Why didn't you just tell me? Do you really think I care about your gender?" Relayne asked in confusion and certain anger.

"Not really. There's more to it, and I did it mostly to protect you. We all have our secrets," he answered. He took one of Relayne's hands. "When I broke up with you, I did it to protect you. I have dangerous enemies, and you had so much going on. I didn't wanna include you in any more trouble. You're important to me, Relayne. This is why I am showing my true self now."

Relayne glanced at their hands before her gaze went back to Baelfire. "Did you watch me through the shadows? Or was it just a feeling I had?" she asked now, her anger nearly gone.

"Maybe...from time to time. Do you know how hard it is to see you next to a prince? Especially someone who dresses so well. The only thing I can show you are open shirts and tattoos," Baelfire said in frustration.

"You could literally dress up in a bin bag and I would still like you," Relayne said. "I still don't understand why you made it such a big secret. We used to tell each other everything." She was still processing, and it showed on her face.

Baelfire stepped closer, leaving only a bit of space between them. "Yes. But you told me you would still see me, and since all of this started, I rarely had anything of you. I admire you more than anyone. Don't forget that. So if you wanna go back to your friend to do whatever you wanna do, that's fine. Or you can stay with me. Just for tonight," he offered.

He slowly took her other hand. Relayne could feel how her body reacted to the closeness. A little shiver ran down her back, and she avoided looking him in the eyes.

"Tell me you missed me," he whispered in her ear. "I can make you forget everything for one night—all this pain, pressure, everything you're feeling right now. Just you and me."

Relayne could feel the tension inside her growing bigger. She had missed her girlfriend, who now seemed to be a boyfriend as well. She couldn't care less about the gender situation, since Baelfire had always gotten her attention with words and actions. Her inner struggle was on the edge.

"They need me, Baelfire," she whispered, still avoiding his gaze.

"I know. But so do I. And I'm selfish enough to ask you right now to stay with me." His voice was rougher, raising goosebumps all over her body. To see this side of the person who she'd always trusted the most—along with Summer— made her weak. It was confusing and attractive at the same time. One of Baelfire's hands went towards her neck, and slowly he touched it with two fingers. The tension grew even more. She could feel her skin burning just from the touch. He was using his fire element to break her last wall.

"Tell me you don't want this, and I'll stop and let you go," Baelfire whispered, knowing exactly what he was doing.

She could feel his voice so close to her ear that she bit her lower lip to resist. Under different circumstances, he would be on the bed by now, but she had some responsibility, and she could already imagine Kilian's voice and face when he found out. But then, who was he to tell her what to do? That was the moment her last wall broke. She grabbed Baelfire by the collar of his shirt and pulled him into a passionate kiss, one that he'd been waiting for. Hot kisses and moans followed as Baelfire led Relayne to the bed. There wasn't a second where he wasn't showing her that he had missed her. Relayne could feel the heat rising inside. Both fought for dominance until Baelfire eventually pinned her hands above her head, using shadow magic to hold them with black matter.

"Relax. I'm gonna make you feel good," he whispered into Relayne's ear. The Feeling bit her lower lip and closed her eyes when she felt Baelfire's lips on her neck, sucking, licking. Relayne moaned in pleasure, feeling the heat from every kiss, every touch. Baelfire pulled her shirt up, leaving marks on her belly, and kissed his way lower, teeth scratching over soft skin.

"Fuck." Relayne moaned and pushed her lower body against her lover. She could feel the heat in her lower body. The tension was killing her.

"Sorry, what was that?" Baelfire asked mockingly. He looked up to her, fingers teasingly wandering over the top of Relayne's jeans.

"Fuck—me. Please," Relayne repeated, cheeks red.

Baelfire smirked, not answering. His hands quickly opened her jeans, pulling them down along with her underwear.

"I mean, you know my name, so be nice and loud, babygirl," Baelfire said, then he spread her legs, putting his face in between them and using his tongue where Relayne needed it the most. Hot moans from the Feeling followed as she enjoyed the pleasure and pushed her hips towards Baelfire's tongue and lips. She had missed this, the lust whenever they were together. This was only the beginning of a very long night.

***

Leyla woke up and choked on her breath. Her blanket was on the floor, and her breath came fast. Shadra was lying next to her, looking worried. The young Element magician had spent more time with Leyla after they had come to the house together. She was the calm nature among the children, while Leyla was still the quietest but also the most centred. Leyla loved dancing, festivals, and had diverse music tastes. She was also interested in zodiac signs, something Shadra didn't know much about. Leyla had told her about the zodiacs, planets, and the meaning behind them. It was part of Leyla's job as a healer in the White League to deal with astrology and understand the magic of the universe.

"What happened?" Shadra asked.

"It happened again. I had an Omen," Leyla said, swallowing hard.

Shadra took her hand, looking Leyla in the eyes. She helped Leyla catch her breath, calming her slowly using her Element magic. "It's okay. You can tell me what you've seen," she said softly.

Leyla smiled. She knew she could trust Shadra; it was something she'd learned the moment they had found her. Leyla was a strong believer in connections and that some people were simply meant to meet each other. She was a very sweet soul who tried to see the best in people. Shadra was the wild one—open, loud, and ready to explore things. Leyla had told her a lot about her life and the things she could remember before the museum. It was a simple life, written by family and heart. Leyla was a person who satisfied with the little things in life. She didn't need much to be happy. The circle of her family and closest friends was enough for her. Right now, though, Leyla was far from calm and relaxed. The Omen was still inside her body, shaking her and leaving a heavy feeling.

"Come on, Leyla. If it's supposed to help us, we need to know," Shadra coaxed.

Leyla looked at the Element, panic in her eyes. She took a deep breath. "I saw Relayne," she began. "I saw how she hurt Kilian."

***

Jegor had just entered the house when Kilian opened the door of his room and looked at him. Something had happened.

"We need to talk. Now," Kilian said, out of breath.

"Can I at least make myself a cup of tea? I need to tell you something, too," Jegor said.

"The tea has to wait. I had another Vision," Kilian said tensely.

Jegor sighed and went into his cousin's room.

"I had a Vision about Relayne," Kilian continued.

"Please spare me the details," Jegor answered dryly.

"Not that kind of Vision," Kilian snapped, annoyed. "I saw her and me standing in the palace—in the main hall, and I was sitting on the throne. I was king, and we were having a discussion about something. And then Synclair showed up after she had left and told me that I was the only one who could save her if I didn't want to fight against her. What does that mean?" He nearly talked himself into hysteria.

Jegor took a moment to think. "It's an Omen," he began slowly. "Remember the lesson about the different types and which one the Leagues can have? Blacks have Omens. Whites have Visions, and Red and Green usually have Dreams. But the dream you just had was an Omen—an important message that something is happening in the future that can be changed. What you saw might or might not happen at all. It's in your hands. You can change the outcome. A Vision shows you something that might happen and a Dream is something connected to your past, present or future."

Kilian looked at his cousin before he started pacing up and down the length of his room. "What if she is the snake that the legend is talking about? She's from the streets, the only one," Kilian said, still tense.

"Don't talk like your father again," Jegor exhorted. "It could be any of us if we're talking about a traitor in our circle. We still don't know who we're up against, but I got a clue and an idea. I saw Maddison. She's alive and one of the people causing all the trouble with the seals."

"You spoke to her, and you did nothing?" Kilian snapped.

"Listen. She's only one person; we need to find out who the others are. Remember what we found at the place where the first seal was stolen? The word *Superbia*. I couldn't think of anyone who fits that description more than one of the Seven Deadly Sins."

Kilian stopped walking. "You think that's it? The bad guys are a group of sins?"

"Think about it. We're seven. So are they. It could be possible. That's how they can be in one place or another. Besides, they seem to have their own rules. Maddison was speaking of some kind of revolution," Jegor explained further. "If we can catch her, we can get something out of her. There's more to it, and I want to know what it is before we involve anyone else. The palace would initiate a trial to execute her. But that doesn't help us if six other magicians are out there who might be even bigger and better than she is already. Someone who tricked death is capable of anything."

She wasn't alone. Don't forget that.

"Carlin, this is a talk between grown-ups," Kilian hissed, and Carlin giggled in reply.

"Carlin is right. Misfitress was with her. I saw its eyes. She has it under her control," Jegor said, adding to the load of information.

"Oh fantastic, another monster that's going to kill us if we don't play along," Kilian drawled.

"We need to set a trap. We know where the second seal is, if Alicia had a Vision or a clue. As soon as we know, I'll make Maddison believe I'm on her side, and we're getting the seal together. Then it's on all of us to capture her, kill Misfitress, and get the answers we need."

Kilian nodded in agreement. "I can't believe I'm saying this. But I have a plan." He glanced at Carlin. "And you, my little annoying doll, are invited."

Carlin grinned mischievously.

Chapter 15
The Seven Sins

Seven children, born in misery.
- F. F., "Lucifer's Wish," *The True Urban Legends*

Relayne woke up alone in the king-sized bed. A look at the messy sheets told her that it had been a long night. All she wore was the shirt that Baelfire had given her afterwards, her clothes strewn somewhere on the floor. With a yawn, she sat up and got out of bed. Her hair was curlier than usual, and she definitely needed a coffee with some magical extra potion to get her through the day. She grabbed a pair of shorts from the ground, tugged them on, and went to the door. As soon as she opened the door, Relayne realized Baelfire's home wasn't just a simple house; it was a giant lodge, and Baelfire's room was on the second floor.

"What the hell?" she whispered. Portraits and art decorated the walls. Contrasting the chaos in Baelfire's room, everything was nice and neat. The floor, the walls, and even the carpets were white. The portraits accented the style of the house.

"Not exactly what you were expecting, right?" a deep but charming voice asked.

Relayne looked to the left, at the person who questioned her. "Who are you?" she asked.

"Rude. I asked you a question first," he said, and came closer. He was skinny, tall, and had incredible cheekbones. His dark blond hair was a bit of a disaster, but the black shirt and posh black trousers he wore made him look even more attractive. As stepped closer, Relayne realized he was nearly two metres tall.

"I guess Baelfire didn't give you the introduction that you deserve, my dear child," the stranger said calmly. "I think he went out to help Amber. But don't you worry about her. They are not together anymore. You look a bit pale. How about I make you some breakfast and we have a chat?" he asked.

"I don't think I should talk to a stranger who won't even tell me his name," she replied.

"Oh, pardon me." He cleared his throat and bowed before taking her hand and kissing it softly, holding her gaze the whole time. "Pieotr Polikarpowitsch," he said, and now she noticed the slight Russian accent.

"Are you his brother or something?" Relayne asked.

"Not directly. There is a lot that you need to know, but first—"

"Don't we have a rule to not bring anyone home?" a female voice interrupted them.

Pieotr rolled his eyes and looked behind him.

Relayne gasped.

"Surprised to see me?" Maddison smiled in amusement.

A second later, Misfitress approached behind her and Relayne took a step back. Did Baelfire seduce her to deliver her to whoever these people were?

"Maddison, get your manners together. Your toy shouldn't walk around like this when we have guests," Pieotr said in a harsh voice.

"He can walk around as he likes," Maddison argued.

Misfitress grinned and bared his teeth. "You heard her, Pieotr," he growled in a dark, dangerous voice.

"He tricked me," Relayne whispered, balling her hands into fists.

Pieotr focused on Relayne again. "Ah-ah! Don't be angry. There's an explanation for everything, and I bet that you're curious to find out now. Are you not?" he asked.

"Why should I stay with someone who's my enemy?" Relayne hissed.

"Very sweet. I like her temper," Maddison commented. She leaned against the banister of the stairs leading to the ground floor. She gave Relayne a little smile.

"We don't like the word *enemy* here. You are not ours, and we are not yours. If you hear me out and think for once, you'll see. Everyone has their reasons, and it's only fair to hear us out," Pieotr explained, reaching a hand out to Relayne, who didn't seem very confident facing a wendigo like Tress.

"Only if it's you and me," Relayne said.

Maddison let out a giggle, and Tress grinned.

"Don't make her fall for you. Bael doesn't like the prince. We don't need a fight between each other," Maddison said before Tress turned into a human and disappeared with her into one of the rooms. Relayne froze. It was true what Jegor and Kilian had suspected. Tress was able to change his form.

"If I run, you're going to hurt and torture me, right?" Relayne swallowed.

Pieotr sighed and rolled his eyes. "Don't be so dramatic. For now, I want to introduce you to our way of thinking. If you make a choice afterwards, it's on you if you get out alive or not," he explained with a smile that only made her more uncomfortable.

Relayne swallowed once more before she took Pieotr's hand, not shaking any less than before.

***

"You'd better give me a good reason why I was supposed to come," Baelfire said to Amber.

Amber smiled. "I wanted to see you. Is that not enough?"

"It's not, Amber. I told you that you have to stop. You're a danger to our mission," he said.

"I am? Who brought that princess in our house?" Amber snapped.

Baelfire rolled his eyes. "Have you drunken your potion? Your jealousy is getting out of hand again," he stated.

It wouldn't have been the first time Amber refused to take the potion that kept her balanced and in control over her Mind magic.

"So is your disgusting habit. Sleeping with her in our walls while I'm in the next room? I thought you had at least a bit more self-respect," Amber fired back.

"My privacy is mine. Get that in your head. Shouldn't you be in the council supporting someone?" Baelfire asked.

"He can handle it on his own. That's what the boss said," Amber commented, stepping closer, looking at Baelfire. "You know what we had was more than anything. Don't pretend it's nothing at all anymore."What can she possibly have that I don't?"

Baelfire struck her hand away as she reached for him. He was tired of playing this game with her. "For starters, a heart," he answered, and turned his back on her.

"If she doesn't join our side, there's no reason for me to be nice or friendly; maybe I'll even kill her," Amber said.

Baelfire froze and slowly turned around again. "You lay one finger on Red, and I'll break all ten of yours."

With these last words, he disappeared into the shadows, not giving Amber the chance to answer.

***

The breakfast table had everything that someone could have wanted on a morning like this, but Relayne struggled to eat anything at all. Pieotr sat at the opposite end of the table, drinking his tea and reading the newspaper as if everything was normal.

"You need to eat. Otherwise, you're gonna have a real bad day," he suggested.

"How can I eat when I am sitting in a cage?" Relayne questioned.

Pieotr sighed and put the newspapers away. "Seems like Baelfire didn't do his job right if you're still under so much pressure."

Relayne's cheeks started to burn.

"Now that's the colour I like to see," he said with a short smile.

"I want answers," Relayne hissed.

"And I want to marry Maddison, but she's more interested in the company of a monster. How tragic," Pieotr stated cynically before he took a sip of his coffee. "Have you realized who we are by now? What we stand for? Any clues?" He stared at her intensely.

"You're the group opposing us—the people who want to destroy the balance and flip the rules," Relayne said.

"In a way, that is correct. We are a group with our own principles and goals. We also have a legend, which is not completely written yet. Everything can be changed in one way or another. It always depends on the possibilities and choices we make. Seven children on each side. When we first found each other, we didn't know we were meant to find each other. Maddison was the first one I found. She never told me how she did it, but I found her on the edge of life. She escaped death in a way that I've never seen before. The others found me after. Baelfire and Amber were the last ones. They were a couple when I met them. I could already feel that they were not meant to be together. Have you ever looked more into the magic of the sins?" Pieotr asked.

"I only heard the urban legend about it. I never paid any more attention to it," Relayne answered.

"You should—especially as a street magician; the urban legends are the ones that give you power. The magicians who live in the upper class have the best teachers, but we have the legends. And when you figure them out, they give you what you need. I was looking for people who think like me and understand my anger. I knew I couldn't do it on my own—what I was planning to do. So I found them, and I found someone who is even more dangerous than I am. At least that's what they would call me, since everything that goes against the system is a threat. We all paid a price for what we got, but it was worth it. Maddison reached immortality. Baelfire can switch forms. Amber can make people lose feelings completely. We all have special abilities. All of you have them as well. That's why we're equal, and one of mine fits one of yours. That's what the legends both say."

Relayne remained silent. All this information was messing with her head.

"It's a lot to take in for sure," Pieotr said.

"So because you paid a price to use dark magic, you got access to the magic connected to the legend of the sins?" Relayne asked, trying to understand the bigger picture.

"Yes. Baelfire wanted to learn the shape-shifting. With that, they signed up in the name of the sin of lust. Like a curse that is now inside them. Amber needs to eat a human heart once in a while to maintain the balance between her envy and her ability," Pieotr explained.

Relayne was about to take a bite of food but dropped the fork, appetite lost again. "And why do you wanna change the system? Yes, it does cause a lot of problems, but people have died because of this, and most of them are innocent," she said.

"Every revolution comes with a price. Innocent or not, people may have to pay that price, and we have our goals. We don't want to destroy everything and live in anarchy. We want to change the system for the better. The system has a lot more room for improvement. And have you ever thought about the fact that we are not allowed to be with someone from the human world? They separate us, make us live in two worlds, and yet there are gaps. But if they find out, it's a tragedy. For what? Having feelings for someone who understands us and doesn't care if we're magical or not? Or the fact that there are people who seem to be not worthy of magic because their future looks too dark? How can you decide for a four-year-old child whether they're supposed to be an outcast? Sooner or later, there are ways for the evil ones. Letting creatures live in slavery and not alongside us? The only districts that have balance are the Doom and the Woods. I can give you a longer list if you want me to continue. But we want to make a system that's better for everyone—not just for the people up high. We want to make a better system and let the worlds collide. Let the folk decide and not just the council and people up high. People should have a right to vote and plan this life here as well. This is the balance we need."

Pieotr leaned back and took a deep breath.

"Stealing the seals brings a lot more chaos. How is that fair?" Relayne argued.

"It's not. People will die and get hurt. But see it as a kind of natural purge. People who know how to defend themselves against the struggle of the balance will survive. But it's a chance for everyone. When there are no rules, we make them. That's more needed than ever now. Or do you think the death threat is something that should exist?" Pieotr asked. "The Royals are afraid of us because we want to overthrow them. We reveal their secrets that they have been hiding all along. The moment they announced the death threat, people got triggered. Perhaps not in the finer districts, but the

Underground is rebelling. Arguments, fights—people are on edge. It's just a matter of time before words turn into actions and Leagues start to rise against each other."

Relayne shook her head. The death threat was something that only brought more trouble, and she didn't want to see the council's latest reports on dead magicians. "It's not," she said, remembering her mother's death. No one had given her an explanation or cared about the way it had happened.

"Have you seen the statistics on how many street magicians died that no one talked about?" Pieotr pressed. "Or the people who suddenly die and no one has an explanation for? This system is filled with gaps and the palace and council especially make us believe we live in a stable society. They make it look like everything is working, but it's not. At least fifty street magicians die each month, and no one seems to care. The list of missing persons just gets longer, and the council tells you they care, but they do nothing. How long has Shadra's father been gone?"

"Long enough to be a missing person," Relayne answered.

"You don't have to be a scientist to understand that he won't come back," Pieotr said, leaning forward over the table. "Think about it. Eat. Have a rest. You are our guest. Trust me to tell you that they don't need you in this moment, since they are on their next step already. Make a choice by the end of the day. It would be a pity to see you running into more tragedy than you need in your life."

He stood up and walked away, leaving Relayne with a million thoughts and two paths sprawling ahead of her, where only one could be the way.

***

"We can't wait any longer if we want to do this," Jegor said.

Kilian and the others stood together. Relayne was missing again, the only person they were waiting for.

"Shadra and Leyla, you'll stay here, just in case we come back quickly, and we need a Healer."

"That's fine. But Kilian, there's something you should hear first," Leyla answered.

"Not right now. Maddison has a routine, and if we don't catch her when she's doing it, we're going to miss our chance. We can't risk anything, even if Relayne isn't with us at the moment," Kilian said.

Jegor agreed. Alicia exchanged a look with Petyr, who nodded, ready to go.

"Let's go, before it's too late," Jegor said, and the group of four disappeared.

Leyla looked at Shadra, clearly worried. The impulse to scream edged up her throat. Was it the after-feeling of the Omen that made her think irrationally?

Leyla looked at Kilian. "Just be careful, Kilian," she said seriously before the children went on.

Shadra took her hand. "It's gonna be okay. Kilian and Relayne have a bond. No one can cut that so easily."

Chapter 16
Saeculga

One leader, in the faith for six.
– F. F., "Lucifer's Wish," *The True Urban Legends*

Leyla stood in a dark corridor. She looked around, but could barely see. It felt like she had been here before, but she couldn't tell when. There was an awful smell in the air, and she was sure it wasn't coming from something alive. She created a ball of light with her magic. The corridor wasn't dark, but the only thing she could see was how long it was. Looking down, she realized she was standing in some kind of skin, as if that of a snake's shed. But it didn't look completely like the skin of a snake. When she looked up, she saw Kilian and Relayne walking along the corridor.

Leyla raised her voice, but neither of them seemed to hear her. They were talking about something she couldn't clearly understand. A loud noise interrupted their conversation. Kilian looked scared while Relayne froze. They heard the noise again. But this time it was louder—as if it was coming closer.

***

Leyla woke up with a gasp. She had fallen asleep on the sofa while Shadra was making them some food. Still breathing fast, Leyla saw Shadra came out of the kitchen.

"What did you see?" Shadra asked.

"It was the same Omen again. But this time there were more details. It was in a dark place. Everything smelled disgusting, like potions. I don't know where it was, it seemed pretty serious. We have to warn them. If I sit around here any longer, I'll go crazy for sure," Leyla said. She was often taken as the smart, quiet Healer, but she had enough fire inside her to stand her ground. Whether that was for herself or other people. Though Leyla tend to choose words over actions. She knew when it was okay to step away from a situation.

Shadra walked over and took one of Leyla's hands. "Right now, we are saving society. You have to trust them, even if it's confusing and upsetting. Kilian is a strong magician, and so is Relayne. Everything will work out fine. I'm sure about that. Sometimes you need to have faith, even though that means you have to wait and can do nothing about it. Tell Kilian what you saw as soon as he comes back. But don't do anything that interrupts our current plan," she told her.

Leyla still wanted to do something. Sitting and waiting around could be harder than the actual task, dealing with the unknown. She took a deep breath and nodded. It was in her manner of magic to have faith and trust. But before she had been frozen into ice, she had been dealing with patience that needed her spiritual guidance. This here was different from her daily life. Everything felt more intense. And the fact that her family didn't even know about this, though for their own safety, also nagged Leyla inside.

"You're right. I hope it doesn't happen again," she said, trying to sound calmer. "Let me help you with the food before we prepare some potions. We might need them, to face whatever happens next." She smiled and placed a quick kiss on the cheek of the turquoise-haired girl. Shadra returned the smile and started preparing the potions.

***

"Just to be sure everyone knows the plan, I'll make sure that Maddison and this monster are following me to the seal. None of us knows where it is, but the seal Kilian created as Trickster looks exactly like Saeculga, right?" Alicia looked at the boys.

Kilian nodded, and the others agreed.

"Jegor is on his way to talk to Maddison, and as soon as they are on their way, you will go inside and pretend that you have just found it. We'll make sure that no one harms you, and when everything works out, it's on Jegor to capture Maddison while we knock out the monster," Kilian said, repeating the plan. He had no idea if it could work, but they needed to take the next step and see who they were up against. Sitting around and waiting for something to happen could damage society even more.

"Fine. Let's do this," Alicia said, and everyone took their positions.

***

After listening to all Pieotr had to say, Relayne went back to the room where she had woken up. Too much was going on in her head. But instead of leaving, she decided to wait for Baelfire. They had a lot to discuss, and he had a lot to explain.

The door opened, and Baelfire stepped inside with a smile. Before he could say anything, Relayne's first impulse was to throw a pillow at him, hitting him squarely in the face.

"Ouch. Hey! What was that for?" Baelfire asked.

"For the fact that you haven't told me anything about being one of the Seven fucking Deadly Sins!" Relayne shouted.

Baelfire froze. "Did you leave the room?" he asked.

"Of course I did. What did you think?" Relayne snapped.

"Who did you meet? I wasn't meant to stay away for so long. But I guess that was exactly what Amber wanted," he said. "Sit down. I'm gonna tell you everything that you need to know."

Relayne stepped back. "I don't wanna sit down. I wanna hear what makes you think that I can trust you ever again. Was that the reason you looked at me the first time? Because I'm the key you guys need? Is that the reason you disappeared all the time and didn't say anything at all?" She was nearly shouting.

Baelfire sighed but softened his gaze. "When I met you, I didn't know who you were as much as you didn't know who I was, okay? That night we met, I wanted to escape from Amber and her discussions. I'd had enough of her, and then I saw you. I couldn't resist saying hello," he explained.

"So you were still with Amber when we hung out the first time?" Relayne asked. It was hard to keep her voice down.

"Yes, but it took us a few weeks before I even kissed you. Do you remember that?" Baelfire asked, again trying to step closer.

"You lied to me!" Relayne screamed, and her eyes went red. She nearly punched the wall, but forced herself to be calm.

"As you might have realized, my life was complicated enough by that time. I just wanted someone who understood me and was there for me, without knowing too much," Baelfire explained, clenching his fists and trying to hold back his magic.

"So you didn't even think about telling me you were with someone, because it's complicated?"

"How do you think Amber feels now? She wants to kill you because of it, and that's my fault. I've been an idiot, and yes, I know that. But this is much bigger than you think. I couldn't just tell you all this from one day to the next. These people here are not my family. We have the same goal, but that's it. Pieotr is maybe the only one I really get along with. But the others are dangerous, and if you're not truly a part of it, you're a danger to our mission and success. That's why I always kept you out of this. I didn't wanna lose you over choosing a side—choosing between me or someone else." He looked her in the eyes. "I understand that it's a lot to take. What did you hear?"

"Pieotr explained what they want and why. Do you know how much pressure is on me now, knowing all this?" Relayne asked quietly, calmer now.

"I know," Baelfire murmured. "But sooner or later, you need to make a choice. Even someone as wild as you are, Relayne. Don't act like you haven't seen what's been going on in this society."

Relayne laughed bitterly. "Why did you join them? Just because you can live in two bodies? That's something that anybody could learn and do. You don't have to be cruel and kill people for something like that."

Now it was Baelfire who laughed. "Are you really that naïve, to think that our society will accept someone who likes to live as a girl and a boy? There's a law that goes against shapeshifters because they are scared that someone will use it against them. How many more examples do you need to see that this world we're living in isn't that perfect?" He couldn't hide his anger.

"Okay. Fine. I get it. I can see it now more than ever," Relayne said roughly. "That doesn't mean this decision is any less hard for me, okay?" She swallowed and looked down at the floor. Missing people. Corpses around the city. Oppression against species. Discrimination against people like Baelfire. These were just a handful examples—Relayne had realised that the moment Pieotr had told her his side of things. Nevertheless, she felt guilty for closing her eyes on something that shouldn't be.

She could feel Baelfire slowly wrap his arms around her.

"I know," he began to say. "But whichever way you're gonna walk, please don't make me fight you."

***

Jegor was standing at the exact point where the children wanted to start their plan. He was ready, even though the unknown of the following moments loomed behind him like a dark shadow.

"I am glad that you chose the right side," said Maddison, who'd just shown up.

They were somewhere in the Doom District—the best place to meet someone and still hide from the public eye.

"They don't know it, obviously. I thought it would be easier if I play two-faced. Kilian won't recognize it, since he'll simply think I'm not in a good mood, like always," Jegor said.

Maddison smiled slightly. "Let's have a walk before we go off and catch the next seal," she said.

Jegor nodded and they went along. He could feel Misfitress following them in the shadows.

"There's something I need to tell you," Maddison said. "From the day you saw me so scared about something."

"You never gave me a sign or clue about what happened that day that scared you so much," Jegor replied. Maddison was someone who never seemed to be afraid of anything or anyone—not back in the day and not now.

"It was the day I found out why Fear was so attractive to me. I used to think it was simply my hormones as the young girl that I was. But there was more to it. I'm not sure if you wanna hear this, but your friend isn't who you think he is. He's much more than that, and that was why I was so scared. I just wanted to have an inside look for some experiments, the Voodoo magic of course. Then I found this other book, and at first, I thought it was just another urban legend, but this one was different."

Maddison stopped walking and looked at him. "It was the story about how Fear had come to life. Some warlocks are so old that no one seems to know where they come from, right? Have you ever asked your friend where he came from?"

"He told me a lot about different cities and places but not the exact time or date," Jegor said uncertainly.

"He was one of the first magicians who ever existed. He must be so old that the old legends and gods must have created him. He always seems to have a solution for everything, right? That's because he's the balance between life and death. He *is* Death," Maddison said. "Ever heard of Death and his three muses? Death, in this legend, is cursed. He is captured in a human body, looking for love. There is a white muse, a red muse, and a black muse. All of them are different, and each has a different desire towards him and he towards them. I usually wouldn't have paid too much attention to this, but there was a note. My name was next to the note on the black muse. *I* was his black muse."

Carlin giggled, and Maddison raised an eyebrow.

"You're still living with him? Fascinating," she commented before she continued. "In the legend, the black muse is the only one to be with him, because the others get killed or take their lives before he has the chance to get to them. They end up as ghosts, and in some versions, some magicians ban them so they can't be with him in any way. Only the black muse has a tragic ending. With her hating him and in pain all the time, the two of them live forever. Do you wanna live in tragedy forever with someone?"

"I don't wanna live with anyone in particular, other than Carlin. So imagining living with someone in tragedy is not a pleasant picture for me," Jegor said. "But that's why you tried to escape and be immortal? So you don't have to die at all?" he asked. He was slowly beginning to understand her reasons, even though he wasn't sure if she was speaking the truth about Feardorcha. He was one of Jegor's oldest friends, and for sure there were many rumours and stories surrounding the warlock. But Maddison had always harbored a certain hatred towards society and magicians. "Even as a doll, someone can hurt you, if the person knows his or her ways around Black magic."

"You can rip me apart, and I can flick myself together. I had to escape before he would do something to me. The black muse has nothing at the end; that's why she stays with him," Maddison said.

"So you escaped before he could hurt anyone close to you? Do you have any proof that he is Death? Fear has never done anything to us. I have never seen him working against society or anything. At the end of the day, it might be just an urban legend."

Maddison smiled. "Tell me, Jegor, how many times have you worked for him?" she asked.

"A lot. What has that to do with it?" Jegor questioned.

"Death has a hangman—the one who is his helper without even knowing." Maddison turned around and looked into the shadows. "Come on, Tress. Time for you to get your snack."

Jegor looked after them, then down to Carlin. "I don't need to be anyone's hangman when I have you," he said to his doll, who smiled brightly.

***

"I'm staying behind to make sure none of them catch you while you do your work," Jegor said as soon as they neared the building where the seal was meant to be.

So far, everything was going well, and Maddison seemed to play along. A lot of questions were still open to the Voodoo magician, and Jegor needed to find out more about Maddison. This whole case was bigger than any other case they had dealt with before.

"That's fine. Misfitress goes inside in the shadows, so I have a backup there as well," Maddison said, and entered the hall.

Do you really believe what she just told you?

"I believe that she's crazy, yes. And we know her biggest fear now, which seems to be Feardorcha Forbes. As a friend of mine, he should help us as soon as we catch her," Jegor said to Carlin.

But can I not torture her and make her bleed?

"If she turned herself into a doll, there is nothing you can do—unless you want to date her," Jegor said sarcastically.

Kilian is here. I can sense him.

"Good. Then we can start our plan."

None of them knew that Pieotr had also joined the area.

***

Inside, Alicia walked towards the middle of the room. It was a giant hall full of boxes and junk, between which Kilian had placed the seal. Alicia was good at pretending she had just encountered this place, since she had never been here before and only had seen it in pictures Kilian had shown her.

Somewhere behind her, she could hear a noise that didn't sound human. She stopped and looked around before continuing. Alicia knew exactly where she had to go, but there was a feeling growing inside of her—a feeling she couldn't resist, leading her in another direction. The others were counting on her. But if she went another way, it would look more realistic, so instead of turning towards the middle, she chose to go left, hoping the others would still do what they were supposed to do.

It didn't take her long, and she ended up between another set of boxes. A closer look made her realise it was full of weapons. She took a sword out, then dropped it and by intuition grabbed another weapon. Alicia began to smile—it was an axe. But something was different about this axe. She could feel a connection. Someone had made her pick it up.

"Thank you, Tyr," she whispered, then returned to the middle of the room, where she saw Maddison and Misfitress leaning over Kilian's seal. Alicia should have been very comfortable, but something told her this situation was serious.

Saeculga moves from one place to another. You can never know where it will be next. It will show itself when the time is right and the chance is there. Alicia remembered the words of the King of Woods.

That's when Alicia realised: this seal was the real Saeculga. It wasn't a trap anymore.

"I'm impressed that you're facing me without any fear," Maddison said to Alicia, looking at Saeculga. "Since I don't have much time to be here, get her, Tress."

The wendigo sprinted towards Alicia, who dodged to the side. Tress crashed into a bundle of boxes as Maddison used a spell to release Saeculga. Alicia started running, darting between the boxes before she found a spot that had more free space. She swung the axe around. Tress stopped, observing her.

"It's been a while since I had some flesh that put up a fight," Tress stated.

"It's been a while since I chopped someone's head off," Alicia replied.

Again, she swung her axe up high before she crashed it against one of Tress's claws. Tress grabbed the axe and was about to push her back when Alicia did the exact same thing. The creature snarled, not expecting such strong power.

"Don't underestimate someone born with the gift of Tyr," she hissed, and pulled her axe back.

Tress struck out to strike her with his other claw, but Alicia was faster. She ducked down, out of the way of the claw, and swung her axe with full strength into one of the monster's eyes. Tress howled in pain.

Maddison whirled around when she heard Tress's howl. Internal struggle showed on her face.

"Damn it, this bitch is better than I thought," she swore, resisting the urge to rush to her monster's aid.

Petyr and Kilian blocked her way.

"Oh really?" she said, amused. "You two *really* think you can stop me?" They had no idea what she was capable of.

"Actually no, we're here to take you," Petyr corrected.

Maddison froze, and before either of them could do anything, she focused and stitches rose to the surface of her face, sewing her mouth shut. Most disturbingly, her eyes disappeared.

Kilian had to look away for a second, clearly disgusted.

"Out of my way," Maddison said, her voice in their heads now.

"Leave her to me. Look after Alicia," Kilian said, and Petyr went on.

"You look absolutely disgusting, my dear," Kilian said to Maddison.

Maddison made a screeching disturbing noise, and a giant cloud of black fog appeared, turning the whole hall into a hazy area within seconds. Kilian took a few steps back. She'd used the fog to escape, so he had to concentrate to figure out where she was.

Left, right, left, right. He deftly withdrew some cards from his sleeve and threw them in the direction he had spotted her. He could hear swearing, which meant he'd at least grazed her.

That was enough for Jegor, outside, to realize where she was. What Maddison didn't realize before was that Jegor had used his magic to connect himself to her—a tracking spell. The dark fog wasn't to her advantage anymore, and Jegor joined the fight.

Kilian was sure they were close to their goal, and that made him careless.

"You didn't think her monster was her only company, right?" The soft female voice came from behind him.

Kilian wasn't fast enough. When he turned around, it was exactly what she wanted. Amber pressed her hand against his heart, her lips formed to a sinister smirk.

"I'll make sure your heart is filled with jealousy towards the person you love the most," she said.

Kilian's breath came in short gasps. He couldn't move. Whatever she was doing, she was powerful. The few seconds were enough for her.

When Amber let go, Kilian fell straight to the ground. He tried to get up, but everything felt heavy, especially his heart. All he could do was lie there and hope he had enough breath to survive.

***

Alicia caught her breath as she jumped out of the way again. Tress had grown more aggressive after she hit his eye and damaged his sight. It was only a matter of time until Alicia would go succumb to exhaustion. She had underestimated the speed of the wendigo. There was a reason Maddison had him by her side.

Alicia had to keep going. The others were counting on her. Another jump out of the way followed, but this time Alicia didn't land smoothly and fell to the ground. Her axe clattered to the floor next to her. She grabbed it quickly and used it as shield to defend herself from one of Tress claws.

"There you go," Tress growled. In one smooth move, he smacked her axe out of her hands. It was too far away for her to reach. Alicia rolled out of the way, pushing herself up but stumbling. She faced the wendigo, who drew back one of his claws, ready to attack. Alicia didn't close her eyes, ready to face the stroke of his claws, when suddenly Petyr jumped in between them. screamed as Tress hit him full-on, claws penetrating deep inside Petyr's chest. The nature magician held on to Tress's claw with green matter, inciting a growl from the wendigo.

"Get your axe, Alicia," Petyr hissed. He wasn't looking at her.

Alicia ran to her axe as fast as she could. Adrenalin coursed through her body, pushing her further. She picked up the axe and ran back to the wendigo, jumping on Tress's back without hesitation and smashing the blade into his back. An unholy growl came out of the monster's mouth. He hurled Alicia off his back and she crashed to the floor with a loud groan. She pulled herself up again, stumbling over to Petyr. What she saw made her gasp and stagger backwards in horror.

***

Kilian was on the ground. Jegor had done his work. He and Maddison had fought, but with his advanced magic, it had been easy for him to win in the end. Nevertheless, it had been exhausting. Amber had disappeared, and there was nothing to be seen of Tress. The fog slowly dissipated. Alicia stumbled over to Jegor, Petyr leaning on her. Tress had attacked him and half of his face was deeply damaged, clearly struck by one of Tress's claws. His shoulder twisted at an unnatural angle, and he sagged over Alicia's shoulder like he was on the edge of dying which, in fact, he was.

"We need to go back to the house," Alicia gasped. "If he loses more blood, we'll lose him."

Jegor nodded and focused on Maddison. She would be knocked out for a couple of hours. He spotted Kilian a second later, hurrying to his side to pick him up. He too was unconscious.

"Let's go home," Jegor said, and all of them, together with Maddison carried by Jegor, went to their house.

After they left, Amber emerged from the shadows. They had also taken the seal, which was now a loss for the sins.

"Don't you worry. This is our plan." It was Pieotr, standing behind her. As usual, he seemed relaxed.

"I didn't know you enjoyed it when someone was beating up your love," Amber said.

"I had to control myself, but this is the best way to separate her from this monster. Tress is now damaged, and sooner or later, he'll be killed by Alicia. Maddie gains more power when she's hurt. Jegor only wants more information before they get her to the court, and before that happens, we can free her. None of them is capable of torturing Maddison enough to make her talk."

"I hope you're right about this. I would hate to see someone I care about suffer," Amber answered.

"Is that why you came here? For your own reasons once more, Amber?" Pieotr asked. He already knew the answer, but he wanted to hear it from her.

"Of course. If Kilian's heart is filled with jealousy, it will only take a few moments until he and Jegor get into a fight. I don't know who else Kilian really likes and could damage by the curse I've just cast on him."

Chapter 17
Turning Point

And because society would never accept them,
he created a new kind of magicians.
– F.F., "Lucifer's Wish," *The True Urban Legends*

Back in the Sins' Lodge, Relayne stared out the window. After the talk with Baelfire, she had asked him to leave her alone. How was it possible to make such a hard decision? Society was counting on her. After all, Pieotr and Baelfire had a point. The city was broken. But did that mean they had to incite a revolution to change everything?

The pressure didn't decrease even after hours of thinking. The sun was slowly going down, and she knew it was time to make a choice. One way or another, she couldn't step out of this house and pretend everything was going in the right direction. She walked away from the window and out of Baelfire's room, heading towards the living room. She passed two rooms she had not noticed before. One door was a soft lavender, the other a dark green. Relayne had noticed that each door of a sin member had a certain colour. Once in the living room, she saw Baelfire sleeping on the sofa, breathing softly. He had spent the whole day there to give her space. As for the others, no one was to be seen.

She knelt down and just looked at Baelfire. She still had mixed feelings. One day had changed everything between them. There were so many things that she knew now—so many secrets that had been unspoken. Gently, she kissed his cheek before she stood up again.

"Trust me, no matter what," she whispered before she walked out of the room.

She had made her choice.

Suddenly she felt a feeling rising inside her, so strong that she held on to the doorframe. It was overcoming her, growing rapidly. Relayne tried to breathe. She closed her eyes, counting to calm herself down. When she opened her eyes, her breathing was better but the feeling still lingered. Letting go of the doorframe, she kept on walking, and didn't turn around until she had left the mansion. Someone was watching her. Looking up to one of the windows, she noticed a shadow. A second later it was gone. Relayne turned away from the house just to stare into a silhouette that looked exactly like her, face warped into a frightening grimace. Relayne stumbled back, shaking her head and closing her eyes.

It's not real—you are overwhelmed by your emotions.

Carefully she opened her eyes again. The silhouette was gone. Relayne didn't wait any longer and started running away from the mansion, ignoring the growing pain inside her.

Chapter 18
Children of the Seal

One to lead. One to fall. One to be reborn.
– F. F., "Leaders of the Sea," *The True Urban Legends*

Immediately after Jegor had brought everyone back to the house, he left. He needed answers, and the others would take care of Kilian and Petyr. He crossed paths with Relayne returning as he left.

"I don't need an explanation about where you've been, but we have the second seal. It was a tough fight. And we also have Maddison. Kilian and Petyr got hurt. How has your day been?" Even though Jegor said he needed no explanation, he couldn't hide his sarcasm.

Relayne swallowed. Of course she felt guilty. "I'm sorry. I didn't mean to stay away for so long. Baelfire and I had a conflict—" she tried to explain, but Jegor interrupted.

"I don't care who you were with. I just want to know if I can trust you through and through. You have it hard with Kilian already. Don't give me a hard time, too." Jegor didn't sound angry. He was simply expressing his thoughts.

Relayne went quiet and nodded. There was nothing she could say to explain her situation and make it look right.

"Follow me," Jegor said, picking up his pace. "I don't think you can help, since Leyla is the better Healer. I'm on my way to Feardorcha. I need some answers."

"You look exhausted, Jegor," Relayne said, following him.

"Maddison is tough, but I'll be fine and can meditate later." He kept on walking. The fight had indeed been mentally draining. The way Maddison had looked at him when she'd realized he'd betrayed her had pierced him like a knife. After all, he was doing this to protect her. But Maddison wouldn't see it that way, and she wouldn't like what would happen next.

"Are they gonna be okay? Kilian and Petyr?" Relayne asked, trying to change the topic.

"Petyr, yes. But he'll live with something that will test his insanity. Tress marked him, which means he has wendigo DNA inside his blood now. He'll lose an eye, and depending on how quickly he heals, he might turn into some half-monster. He's a strong nature magician and immortal, which means, if he doesn't want to suffer in pain all his life, he will have to let nature decide what's going to happen. It's most likely that the nature will flow with his new DNA and make him eat flesh and meat like Tress does."

Relayne swallowed. She wasn't sure if she wanted to hear what had happened to Kilian.

"Kilian was asleep when I left them," Jegor said as if reading her thoughts. "Leyla said something is wrong with his heart, but we couldn't figure out what exactly. Someone must have damaged him in a very different way. I haven't seen power like that before. Even Maddison nearly caused me to wake up Carlin."

I honestly was waiting for it.

"It's not on you to decide that. Carlin, you know it. We can be lucky that the palace didn't show up. Usually, Alegro and Synclair are very good with sensing problems. But it could be that one of them was blocking it, or someone in the council is on their side."

"I'm glad it's not worse. How is Alicia?" Relayne asked.

"In the name of Tyr, she found an axe, which seems to be her personalized weapon. Sometimes it happens that the Whites, under the name of gods, get gifts that help them. It looks like a normal axe, but there's more to it."

Relayne saw Fear's shop as they turned onto the next street. "Jegor, whatever happens, I just wanna let you know that you need to trust me. I'm with the spirit of the legend. Don't forget that, whatever happens."

Jegor stopped and looked at Relayne. It wasn't clear what he was thinking. "You're a bit like me—an outcast with her own plans. All I'm saying is, whatever you're going to do, make sure it's the right thing for you and something you can live with."

***

"Good to see you two. What can I do for you?" Feardorcha greeted them with a smile.

Jegor didn't waste any time. "I need answers. Maddison is alive, and apparently you're the one she fears most. Death and his muses—anything that rings a bell?"

Feardorcha looked at them both before he giggled. "Sit down, kids. It's storytime," he said, dragging over two chairs.

They all sat. With a flip of his fingers, Fear locked the door to make sure no one would interrupt them.

"First, it's news to me that she's still alive. But then, I assume she was the one who got you and Kilian into trouble down in my chamber," he began.

"She told me you're one of the oldest legends that ever existed. Care to explain?" Jegor asked, making it clear that he wouldn't drop the matter.

"Many people have given me names. That shouldn't be something that worries you, my dear friend. Maddison was in love with me. She is good at telling only one side of the story.

She was trying to find a way to escape her feelings, not me," Fear said. "Did she mention any of that?"

"She did not. I have faith in you. That's why I'm asking. Go on then. Tell us your side of the story," Jegor said. Relayne remained silent.

"Only because I'm with people who I can trust," Feardorcha said with a sigh. They could see that it wasn't just a simple story like the ones he used to tell. There was more to it.

"I think she was one of the rare people who ever got my attention. It's not that I don't enjoy company, but I'm so busy with all this magical stuff that I rarely have time for anyone. Maddison always had a way of entertaining me. Instead of staying positive, she always had something negative to say, but in the most honest way. She simply didn't care. She knew her behaviour was horrible, different. But that was her character, and that's what I liked. She just did things, living her life. She never told me anything about her parents, but it was clear to see that she didn't know anything about love. Negativity had always been in her life, and she was living with it, instead of fighting it to be a better person. I think I was one of the rare people she gave an inside look of her mind, next to you, Jegor."

Jegor nodded. He agreed with some of the things Fear had just said. Maddison was different than most people—that's why they'd gotten along so well.

"She turned herself into a Voodoo doll. Do you know anything about this?" Jegor asked.

"Not that she wanted to be one. But as I said, she wanted to escape her feelings. I only know a few things, and she has been through a lot of pain. When she realized she liked me more than she should, she couldn't handle it. She didn't know how to cope with something like that. I tried to help her fight her inner darkness, but we ended in fights most of the time. The day she killed herself was as shocking for me as it was for you, Jegor."

"So she's angry at the world and everyone else?" Relayne asked.

"Yes. It was always easy for her to blame everyone other than herself. But she had suffered as a child. The Black League rarely accepted her because of her gender. A Voodoo magician and female? That was a scandal. Jegor was the only one who treated her normal. Besides that, she never knew her parents. She was raised in an orphanage. The children and people there were terrible to her, especially after the ceremony. It was her first time being a loner. She had to fight for something the day she was born. A black rose, blooming with tragedy."

The way Fear spoke about Maddison made Relayne feel sorry for both of them. Feelings were still there; she didn't have to use her magic to see that.

"Where is she now?" Feardorcha asked.

"She's with us. You're the only one who will get an answer out of her. Can you help us?" Jegor asked.

"Sure. But I need to be completely alone with her. There's more conflict than you've just heard. I will do whatever I can to get some answers."

***

Petyr woke up with a gasp, pain shooting through his body.

"Don't get up. You've just been fixed by Leyla," said Alicia, sitting next to him.

"I can't see from my one eye. Did he really damage me that much?" Petyr asked.

"Yes. You've lost it. There's also a giant scar around your shoulder. Leyla fixed you as well as she could. But you'll be left with some damage. The scar on the shoulder will remain, as well as the lost eye." Alicia felt uncomfortable telling him, but he just laughed.

"Why are you laughing? I've just told you that half of your body is ruined," Alicia asked in confusion.

"My body is just a body. The fact that, after all these years, I've done something that actually helped people makes me feel alive. I've done the right thing. Otherwise, it would be you who wouldn't have her true beauty anymore. I can live like this. You lost too much," Petyr said, satisfied.

Alicia looked at him, feeling a mix of confusion and something else she couldn't define. "Even if that means you're going to suffer from hunger like a beast?" she asked.

"I could turn into a full wendigo, and I would have to live with it. Sure, it will be a struggle, and it's not on my bucket list to have this form. But it was worth it, and that is all that matters," Petyr said, starting to smile. "Besides, I still look handsome, just a bit damaged."

Alicia couldn't resist and laughed. "You are really a one-of-a-kind person, Petyr."

***

Maddison woke up and looked around. The blurriness of her vision slowly subsided. She was inside a giant bubble protecting her from the water of the glass case they had put her into. Her wounds from the fight still hurt. Her feet and hands were bound with handcuffs connected to a giant steel track.

"It's a pity to see you like this," a voice she knew well said. Pieotr walked closer to the case until he stood in front of it.

Maddison didn't react.

"Before you get angry that I didn't help you out there, you brought this on yourself. I told you to stick to the plan, but you went away with your little monster. I bet he's a bit depressed, not knowing where you are. What a poor thing." Pieotr sighed as if he meant it.

Maddison pulled at the cuffs, but the steel track only rattled.

"I just want to let you know that I will help you as soon as they are done with you. I've told you that you can trust me, and that hasn't changed. But this is a lesson you need to learn for being so stubborn. You're in one of the darkest chambers of the Doom District, by the way. If that helps you, who knows."

Pieotr stepped back into the shadows, leaving Maddison staring at the spot where he'd just stood. The cuffs and steel track began to shake from the force of her emotions. Maddison let out a scream of pain that no one could hear.

***

When Kilian woke up, he felt drained and dizzy. He couldn't remember much, but the face of the person who'd touched him was clear. The girl had left a picture in his head. Even though the fight had drained him, he didn't feel too exhausted. He knew that he had to take it easy. Slowly, he got out of bed, went into the bathroom, and splashed cold water on his face. Noise from the bedroom prompted him out of the bathroom.

"Sorry. Jegor just told me to look after you." It was Relayne, who'd just come back from visiting Fear.

Kilian didn't say anything at first, then told her to sit down. "Wanna explain why you left us again?"

"It's too much for you to handle right now. But I wanted to see you and see how you're doing," Relayne explained.

"Fine, thanks. If that's all, you can go now," Kilian answered.

"Don't be like this. We all need each other right now," Relayne said, refusing to be pushed away.

"Then why did you not come with us? Have you been with someone else? Somewhere else switching sides? Tell me, Relayne. How am I supposed to trust you?"

Relayne took a deep breath. "I'm sorry for trying to care," she hissed.

Kilian sighed. He didn't know what was going on, but he felt angrier than usual towards her. For sure, it pissed him off that she hadn't been there with them, but someone like her would have a good reason. Right now, though, this wasn't enough for the prince to believe. There had to be more, and he wanted to know what—or who—it was. "Have you seen Baelfire? Or why is that name in your head?" Kilian asked her.

Relayne looked at him in shock before certain anger dawned on her face. "How many times have I told you to not read my mind?" she asked.

"Poor you. If you would be honest with me, I wouldn't have to do this," Kilian replied.

"Baelfire is not your problem. That is my privacy, and just because you're a master of the Red League doesn't mean you have to use it against me!" Relayne snapped, her anger rising, the feeling from earlier hammering into her system and pushing her boundaries.

"Bad for you. I'm doing it right now. I want answers. Otherwise, leave this room, and don't pretend to worry about me when you clearly don't," Kilian stated in a cold voice.

"I do worry!" Relayne shouted at him. "I'm confused, okay? But that isn't the point. All I did was for the right purpose. You have to trust me," she said in frustration. "Jegor trusts me. Why can't you?"

Kilian came closer until he stood in front of her. "Because after all this time, you're still from the streets. And even though she was never my real mother, Tyana was right when she said, 'Don't give your heart to someone who is from the ground. They have seen the worst, and they will do everything to take the best, not caring whether or not someone gets hurt,'" Kilian whispered, the coldness still with him.

Silence.

Relayne swallowed. Her eyes widened. There was no string connected to him anymore. She should have seen a black string, but there was nothing—not even a very weak string. She looked him in the eyes again. "It's okay. Go back to hating me for who I am. Go back to being the posh prince who doesn't care about people like me. But promise me one thing. Treat the people in this house like your own family. They'll be the only ones left when you're looking for love and no one else is there to give it to you."

Kilian didn't say anything. Instead, he grabbed her arms and pushed her against the nearest wall. The only sound in the room was their breathing. "Help me," he whispered, but it was as if something else inside him was speaking. His grip tightened, and his expression changed. "You would be nothing without me—nothing without the people who still give you the chance to live here. Our world would be a better place if people like you wouldn't destroy the balance."

Relayne shoved him back. "You don't have to tell me that I'm not good enough. That is something I've lived with every day since I was born. You're just another person, just another voice in my head," she fired back. She needed to get out of this room. She could feel her breath getting short, her heart aching, and her bones burning. Something inside her wanted to fight back.

"Do you love her?" Kilian demanded. His voice was calm but filled with the same coldness that he had shown her in the last minutes.

She looked over her shoulder to Kilian as she strode to the door. "It doesn't matter," she said, her voice breaking. "You've got what you wanted."

Relayne left the room and closed the door. She took a deep breath and swallowed hard.

Jegor came over to her, noticing the pain on her face.

"Something happened to him," she whispered. "Someone cut off our connection. It's his heart. Something dark has gotten inside his mind and heart." She could feel tears in her eyes, which only made her struggle more. Kilian's words had been nothing she hadn't heard before, but hearing it from him had struck her deeply. "Fix it," she said to Jegor. "Fix it, or we are all lost."

Relayne walked away. Once in her room with the door closed, her legs buckled and she fell to the ground, cold sweat trickling down her back. She pressed her hands against her head and closed her eyes. She had no idea what this feeling was, but it felt like she was going to be burned alive.

Chapter 19
Family

There are no heroes. Just survivors, as they say.
– F. F., "The Leaders of the Sea," *The True Urban Legends*

"Stop running around. You're making me nervous," Pieotr said to Baelfire.

"I've heard nothing from her since she left. What if she's against us now?" Baelfire asked. There was no reason for him to be calm.

"Then we have to fight her. So live with that."

Pieotr stood up from his chair to lay an arm on Baelfire's shoulder.

"She will find her way to us sooner or later. Have trust in her like she has trust in us," Pieotr said, trying his best to calm Baelfire.

"Maybe I should have told her who her sister is." Baelfire sighed.

"Don't. Her sister doesn't know it either yet," Pieotr warned.

"You didn't tell her? Where is she anyway?"

"No. I didn't. It wasn't the right time. And right now, she's learning a lesson that she has to learn," Pieotr answered with a sigh.

Baelfire wasn't satisfied. "Where is Tress? What happened after the incident?"

"He went away. If it's true and he got hurt really badly, he will go somewhere to get back his energy. A wendigo his size and with his power is pretty tough."

"You would love it if he were dead," Baelfire said with a grin.

"Of course I would. But right now, we can't do more than wait."

***

"How are you feeling?" Jegor asked, slipping inside Kilian's room.

"Drained, but I suppose good for someone who got attacked by one of the Seven Sins," Kilian answered.

"Everything okay with you and Relayne?"

"Yeah. She's unimportant as always, just like my father," Kilian grunted.

Carlin looked up at Jegor with a concerned expression. Kilian's voice seemed different.

I can feel it. Something's inside him, like a virus.

"Can I give you a check-up, just to see if something is wrong?"

"Sure. No worries. I know that your magic is a little bit better when it comes to checking on conditions for people."

Jegor stepped over and put his hands on Kilian's shoulder before he closed his eyes. He concentrated on his powers, and a few seconds later, he got an inside view of Kilian's body. A black cloud surrounded Kilian's heart. Jegor let go, startled, and looked at his cousin. "You got influenced. What can you remember from the fight?"

"Only that this girl touched my chest, and then I fell down. I felt heavy, and then I woke up here. But honestly, right now,

I feel fantastic—better than ever. I'm gonna go to the palace today. It's time to talk to my father."

"To Alegro? Since when do you want to go to your father on purpose?" Jegor asked.

"I need to discuss things with him about my future. What about this influence?"

"Something happened to your heart. It looks like it's blocked," Jegor explained.

"It doesn't cause any harm, does it?"

"No, it doesn't—at least not to you. But it's there for a purpose. Let me take care of this first, and then we can go to the palace together," Jegor said.

Kilian shook his head. "No. it's fine. If it isn't any harm right now, you'd better look after our prisoner. We need answers. Also, the others need you. You're the leader for them," Kilian said.

"You don't sound jealous for once. Usually it's you who wants the best position when it comes to leading," Jegor said in concern.

"I'll have to wear the crown one day. That's enough leadership for me," Kilian said, and with that, he left the room.

* * *

Maddison slowly opened her eyes when she heard footsteps. For a second, she thought it was her mind playing tricks on her, but the person in front of her was real. Jegor was paying her a visit. With help of his magic, he undid her chains, but Maddison was too weak to do anything. A few minutes later, she sat on a chair, still bound.

"I'm surprised that you really tricked me," Maddison said hoarsely. "I trusted you. You were among the handful of people who I thought would always be by my side."

"You have your goals, and I have mine. If you answer my questions, I'll make sure you recover and make it safely to wherever you go. I'll make sure you get a trial and don't receive a death sentence. I still care for you, but sometimes you have to do things to achieve the bigger picture."

Maddison coughed and smiled briefly. "You mean using your best friend to get the answers for the palace? I have nothing to lose. You nearly killed my monster, and no one else matters."

"Everyone has someone important to them—even me, even you," Jegor corrected her. "I get that you're trying to start a revolution, but it's not worth the price. You wanna change the rules? There are other ways to give people a better life."

"Voting and waiting? Nothing will ever change if we don't do something. You should know how wrong the system is. What have they ever done for you? You suffered more pain than understanding. They looked at you like you're a monster just because the Black League chose you. Someone like me, a monster to them, won't get a trial. They will kill me regardless."

Jegor looked at her. "What is holding you back?"

"My loyalty. Believe it or not, I have it. And we all made a pact to not say anything at all. You can't kill me either, since I'm a living doll. If that's the only secret you wanna know, fine, I'll give it to you. But you won't get any answers out of me involving my family."

Jegor raised an eyebrow. Did she just admit that these people were like a family to her? "I told you everyone has someone they care for—even you, Maddison. But if you don't wanna talk, you don't give me any choice." He stood and walked over to the door.

Maddison looked after him in confusion, then watched as someone stepped out of the shadows. At first, she thought it was Pieotr, returning to mock her. But it wasn't him. It was worse—*he* was worse. She gasped and tried to jump off the chair, but the chains restrained her. Panic flooded her body.

"You can't do this, Jegor! Don't do this to me!" she begged.

Jegor didn't turn around. He had never heard Maddison so afraid, but if this was the only way to get answers out of her, he had to do it.

"Don't worry, Jegor. I'll make sure she speaks," Feardorcha said, his eyes fixed on Maddison.

Jegor had barely left the room when he heard her first scream.

Chapter 20
To Be Human

And there she sat, bonded to the chair,
suffering, drained, and crying.

She had never wanted to be one of them.
Never feel, never breathe.

But even Pride could not run from Death.

And so he took it,
flaying her while the wolf was watching.
Stitch by stitch,
leading the needle like the bow of a violin.

Tears were drying and screams were fading.
There was no one there to save her.

What's left was the empty shell,
a deserted soul in a world full of misery.

Chapter 21
Of Lovers and Losses

All he ever wanted was acceptance.
– F.F., "Lucifer's Wish," *The True Urban Legends*

Leyla was back in the dark corridor. But this time, she could see by the light of hanging torches. She looked around. Kilian and Relayne were not here with her. Her intuition led her towards the end of the corridor—something was telling her to go there.

She took a deep breath and started moving. It took her a long while until she neared the end of the corridor, where she could see a big room. There he was—Kilian, on the ground. He looked anything other than good, like he had just been attacked. Blood covered him and spattered the entire room, but Leyla couldn't tell if it was his.

When Kilian opened his eyes, he seemed to look right at her. It took all the energy that he could muster. "It was her," he whispered.

Leyla looked at him, helpless.

"It was her after all," he repeated, and everything went black.

***

Leyla woke up with a scream. It didn't take Shadra long to burst into her room.

"What happened?" she asked.

"I had another Omen. It was Kilian again. I need to speak to him, now!"

Leyla was already at the door when Shadra grabbed her arm. "Kilian just left with Jegor. Petyr and Alicia are the only ones here," she explained.

Leyla swallowed. She had a bad feeling that wouldn't let go. "I need to do something now. I have no time for hiding anymore." She hurried downstairs.

***

Alicia woke, too—only she hadn't seen an Omen, but rather an invitation. She looked around and saw Petyr still sleeping. He needed to rest. Even if she wanted to trust him, she had a feeling he would change. Becoming a wendigo was something else—especially considering that it wasn't just any wendigo, but the one who was supposed to protect one of the seals.

Alicia stood up from the chair she had been sleeping on and walked over to the window. The view was beautiful from here; she could see nearly the whole city. Everything was so magical about this town. She had never thought it could turn around. In the last days, she had lost more than she ever had thought she would lose. Alicia closed her eyes. She could see her brother as a memory returned. They used to be so happy together. Nothing mattered, not even the fact that they'd nearly gone their whole life without parents.

That is because I was always by your side.

"Tyr?" Alicia opened her eyes, and she saw a reflection in the window.

He had tattoos, a beard, and was quite muscular.

You've always been one of my truest believers. Even if you didn't go to most of the ceremonies, I could always reach your thoughts. You're not a person who gives up. You always found your way of getting through things. Therefore, I showed you the way, where only the true believer can go. You proved to be worthy.

"But what is this place, and why now? I have the weight of the world on my shoulders."

That is correct. That's why I gave you the chance to be one of the strongest of them all. You can't see it right now, but you will. It's a chance to be better than all of them. They need your power for what's coming. Think about it and choose the right way. You will not regret it.

The reflection disappeared and left Alicia with her thoughts. What she had seen in her Dream was leading her to a secret place. Sometimes the League, especially the ones under the name of gods, sent magicians on trials or tests. These chosen ones had a choice to participate. Some of the trials could cost them their lives. But if they went and came back, it was the key to more power, strength, and wisdom.

Alicia remembered the words of the Bogeyman. Without Petyr, she wouldn't have won the fight against Tress, even though she hadn't been scared when she looked the wendigo in the eyes.

"Alicia? Can you come back here?"

It was Petyr calling her.

"Yeah, sure. I'll be with you in a second."

She looked once more down the skyline of Icon before turning away.

***

After the encounter with Kilian, Relayne left the house. She wouldn't go to Baelfire, but she needed some space to clear her head. Kilian hadn't been himself, and still his words had hurt her. There was no connection at all, and she had seen it disappear.

Just as she rounded a corner, someone grabbed her from behind, and was suddenly in a different place.

Turning around, she raised her fist, ready to fight. But her captor was faster.

"Nice try," Calligan said with a cheeky smile.

"Rose? What do you want?"

"A lot. That's why I've taken you to my home. I can only assure within my own walls that nothing's going to happen to you. I've watched your steps lately. You know who they are. How do you feel about that?"

"Why do you keep on watching me? I am not a child that needs protection."

"That's true, but you are lost like me, and that is reason enough to help you."

Relayne looked at him, outraged. "You don't know anything about me."

"That is wrong. But you and I have the same issues. That why I like you."

"Issues? What is going on?"

"The voices in your head. I have them too. Let me explain everything to you, and then you can go. I need you to know that I am on your side, no matter what."

"Oh wow, great. I have a fan that I didn't ask for. Will you at least tell me where we are?"

"Not in Icon. I can't tell you anything else. Sit down now. I don't wanna bind you to a chair."

Relayne sighed but went to the sofa.

Calligan sat next to her and sighed as well. "I know a lot of this doesn't make sense to you, and I do seem like a crazy stalker. But everything I've done was always for your safety. I made sure Summer and Ashton are okay. They miss you, but I've told them that you have a lot of stuff going on. They know about the situation."

"Thank you. But there must be a reason you're doing all this. No one does anything for free."

"I suppose that's true," he said. "It was your mother. She gave me the connection to you. I come from an orphanage. When I was younger, I used to help in the markets. Most of the people didn't treat me well, since I was a Ghost from the streets. They always said I was meant to be a crazy person. Ghosts and Feelings are the most likely to go mental, next to the Voodoo magicians. Did you know that?" He laughed, but it wasn't bitter. "One day, your mother took me with her, and that was how I got to Icon for the first time. She was so caring and nice. I'd never met someone like that before. She was pregnant with you when she took me to Icon. I met you when you were just born. I could sense it—that we would have a connection. Not a romantic one. Or at least not until now."

Relayne had been silent until then. "A romantic one?"

"Yeah. I like you. But that's not why I brought you here."

"Don't get me wrong, but how can you like me if—"

"If I never really spoke to you at all? If I never took the chance to ask you out?" He smiled. "Did you ever have a crush on someone and prefer to keep it to yourself because everything was perfect as it was? I saw you and Baelfire together. You love them. There was no reason for me to not let you enjoy that happiness. Besides, I am more than just a little broken." He cracked another smile and looked into her eyes.

"You are so honest—perhaps the most honest guy I've met in a while."

"Now you're making me blush."

"Stop flirting and get to business," Brixton interrupted.

Calligan glared at him, while Relayne looked like she just had seen a ghost. "I mean, I know that animals can talk in the magical world. But why is your cat wearing heart-shaped sunglasses?"

"Because I was once his best friend and always had more style than he had. He can tell you the rest of the story when you two end up in bed together."

"Enough, Brixton. Go and watch Netflix. Let the grown-ups talk."

"Is that why you're wearing socks with avocados on them?"

Relayne laughed. These two were like a stand-up comedy programme.

"Sorry about that. He does what he wants. I'll bring you back before the night ends. They need you, and I know that, whatever you do, it'll be the right way. Keep in mind that I'm watching you and that I'll be there if you need me."

"It's still hard for me to understand why you're doing all this just for someone like me, who has never spoken a word to you."

"Sometimes you don't need a reason. Sometimes loyalty is enough to make you do things. And maybe you don't see it, but you are a queen to me."

***

"How long have you been staring up that window, Quinn?" a rough voice asked.

Quinn glanced at the guy standing next to him, almost a head taller. He had black hair, lots of tattoos, and an eyebrow piercing. His skin was pale as a ghost.

"I'm making sure Cami is not gonna kick his ass, Crush," Quinn answered the older hunter.

Crush chuckled in amusement. "You're paranoid these days. Let Cal have a little fun. The world is going to burn sooner or later," he said with a grin.

Quinn rolled his eyes, then squinted up at Calligan's house. "Cami is going to chop off his fucking hand if he doesn't pull himself together. Once a hunter, always a hunter. You don't stop being one of us just because you have a crush on someone."

"I'll cover for tonight," Crush said, giving Quinn a high-five.

"Thanks, Crush. I knew I could count on you."

***

"Have you ever thought about the fact that it might be one of them? Do you really want to kill your own son if it has to be that way? Or your daughters?" Synclair looked at Alegro.

The king sighed. "Of course I have, and the thought scares me—realizing that my own son might join the other side. But what other choice do we have to save this balance?"

"Make better rules and laws. We are close to anarchy if people like them, whoever they are, destroy the balance. The system is lacking, and you know it."

"It's natural selection. Not everyone can have the same standards; this is not how it works."

"Not even when it comes to knowledge and learning? Most of the street magicians go mental because they can't control themselves or because no one believes in them enough to help them. The orphanages are one of the places where crime happens the most, and we pretend everything is all right. Do you know how that is? No, you don't. Because you're not one of the magicians who have to pick up their souls when they're lost. I'm the one who sees ghosts!" Synclair's voice rose to a scream.

"I understand your anger. But this is the best way. This family has seen enough tragedy. Let's pray it won't see anymore," Alegro answered.

Synclair wanted to react, but the door swung open and Kilian and Jegor walked into the room.

"Pardon the interruption, but I'm here to talk about business, Father." Kilian looked at Alegro.

"Business as in...?"

"As in the future for me. I know you've wanted this talk for a long time. Let's have it now."

Synclair raised an eyebrow and looked at Jegor. Since when was Kilian so fond of his future? Jegor just nodded as a sign that it was okay.

Alegro looked at his son, noticing happiness for the first time in a while. "Follow me to my room. Synclair, be so kind as to update Jegor on the latest news."

As soon as they left, Synclair went straight to Jegor. "What's going on?"

"Kilian and his stubborn head. I have no idea what has gotten into him either, but if he wants to speak about the future and how he'll rule one day, I'd be the last one to try and talk him out of it. Sooner or later, he has to face it, whether he wants it or not."

"I still think you would be a better king, you know."

"Kilian has the better social skills. How are you doing?"

Synclair laughed. "Let's sit down and have a drink. I need to tell you a lot."

***

Alegro closed the door to his private room behind them. It looked empty, and Kilian could see that he had removed the pictures and paintings that his stepmother had chosen.

"I still have everything that she put up in this room. But for now, it was better to take it down."

"I get that, Father. No worries." Kilian walked over to one of the shelves near the bed. With an easy gesture, Kilian prepared a drink and send it flying to his father.

"Cheers," he said, and drank the whiskey shot in one sip.

Alegro set down his emptied glass. He didn't say anything at first, just looked at his son. Then, "I have always waited for this moment, when you would come to me and take responsibility," he said honestly. "I know I've never given you the easiest life. I could have been a better father to you. But my priority was always the kingdom and the world you would live in one day. My position isn't easy; it never was. I made many choices in the past that were not good everyone. But sometimes that's how the world works. People need to die to make it easier for people like you and me."

Kilian nodded. "I understand, Father. You're a politician through and through," he said, stepping closer. "That's why I want to discuss the formalities. Introduce me to all the important things and rules I need to know. We found one of the people working against us, so it's just a matter of time until the others come out of their hiding place."

Alegro laid a hand on Kilian's shoulder. "I am very proud of you, my son. After all this time, you're still the person I wanted you to be."

That was the moment something in Kilian's eyes changed—not their colour, but a little glimpse inside that showed his father something was wrong.

"I'll let you go with the words you always wanted to believe," Kilian whispered.

Alegro didn't realize what was coming quickly enough. Only seconds later, he was on the floor, drowning in his blood. A dark cloud left Kilian's body and he sank to the floor as well. Now in shock, he looked at his father and all the blood. The ace of spades in his hand made him realise what he had just done. He had slit his father's throat. Unable to breathe for a few seconds, he just stared at his father. How could this have happened?

Alegro looked at him, but it was clear that these were his last seconds. Broken bones and psychological pain could be fixed, but a deep cut like this could not. No White magician would be fast enough to fix this.

"It wasn't you," Alegro whispered, and took his last breath.

Kilian was still frozen. His father was gone. Silence followed before Kilian let out a horrible scream.

Chapter 22
Broken Pieces

Magic was never free.
– F. F., "Sacrifice of Magic," *The True Urban Legends*

"Are you actually insane?" Baelfire screamed, pushing through the doors to Amber's room. Overrun by his emotions, he nearly broke the door off its hinge.

Everything inside the primarily green room was nice and neat. Along with a golden statue of a snake, the mirror hanging above her dressing table was framed by golden snakes.

Amber sprawled on her bed, reading a magazine. "What happened to you, little lover boy?" she asked, not looking up.

"Put on the fucking TV, and you'll find out!" Baelfire hissed.

He didn't look like he was in the mood for a joke, so Amber grabbed the remote and turned on her telescreen, which was perfectly placed to watch movies before she went to sleep every night. As soon as it flickered to life, she saw the breaking news. Every channel was broadcasting what had happened in the palace. The king was dead.

Amber raised an eyebrow. "The king is dead. Why should I care?" she asked in confusion.

"Because the official statement was that the son, Kilian himself, was possessed by a very dark force that made him do this. There is only one person other than you who could have made him do this, and I'm pretty sure it wasn't him. So what on earth were you thinking?" Baelfire nearly screamed in rage.

After everything they had been through, Baelfire had never thought Amber was capable of such a thing.

Amber stood up, eyes on the screen. She went silent for a couple of seconds before her gaze returned to Baelfire. "I don't understand it. Yes, I cursed Kilian's heart with my dark magic. But he wasn't meant to kill his father. He was meant to kill Relayne. Or Jegor. I thought those two were the closest to him," she started, trying to explain herself. She began to realise that this was a bad situation, indeed. And worst of all, it was her fault. Her face paled as she avoided a book that Baelfire threw at her.

"Fix this shit on your own, Amber!" Baelfire shouted. "I'm not gonna save your ass this time when you need to explain yourself in front of the boss. You've got us all in trouble, and with Kilian soon on the throne, we are screwed!" He left the room without looking at her.

Amber swallowed and slowly sank onto the bed. She continued watching the news, and the more she saw, the heavier the guilt settled on her shoulders. This time, she really had messed up. It was an act of jealousy, something that she'd been dealing with her whole life. But this time, her dark magic, the envy inside her, had taken over. The resolution was something she wouldn't be able to fix—unlike the mistakes she had made before. Amber closed her eyes, knowing that she was now completely on her own.

***

Kilian woke up with a loud gasp. He nearly fell out of bed, but his sister Kalimba stopped him from falling.

"Easy, big brother," she said calmly. "It's all okay. You're in my room. You passed out for three days."

Kilian realised that it was her room as soon as he felt the climate. Kalimba's room was designed like a tropical jungle hut, always warm, with a diverse variety of plants.

"Did I really kill him?" Kilian asked.

"It wasn't you. Something was inside you. Jegor is trying to find out what it was. Synclair took over and made a statement. They doubled the death threats and made an open call for an audience for anyone who has any kind of clue leading to the enemy. The dark magic inside you made you do this. Don't even think about feeling guilty. No one saw it coming. Jegor thought it was a curse that would harm you at some point, but not anyone else," Kalimba explained, keeping herself as calm as she could. She had lost both of her parents, now, too.

Kilian swallowed. Even if there had been something inside him, it didn't change the fact that he hadn't been capable of fighting it. "I know what I felt, when I did it. Jealousy. But I don't know why. I understood the anger I was feeling. I understood the pain. But—"

"Jealousy comes to life when there is love. Whether you like to hear it or not, you loved Father—even after all he did to you. In some way, you respected him. That's how this magic got you. Destroy what is closest to you. This is how it works," Kalimba explained further.

The two siblings had always had a good connection, even though they were completely different. Kalimba had seen Kilian in different situations—his rage, anger, sadness, love—but she hadn't seen him like this before.

Kilian looked at his sister. "You're good with working things out. You should work in the political section," he said with a smile that quickly vanished.

"I'm too much of a nature lover to do that; you know that," Kalimba said with a grin.

He nodded. "What's going to happen now? Did the crown ceremony already happen?" The trouble inside him raged like a hurricane. But if he gave in to it, he would lose it entirely.

Kalimba shook her head. "No. It didn't. Mainly because the current king was still asleep," she said carefully, ready for an outburst.

Kilian raised an eyebrow. "Are you serious? Why isn't Synclair taking over?"

"Father wanted you to be on the throne sooner or later. Right now is the time to do exactly that. If we give the position to someone from the council, worse things might happen," Kalimba clarified.

"But won't it look like I've planned this all through?" Kilian argued.

"No, the head council has already seen that it was a trap," she assured him. "You're in the safe zone. But they've sent some patrols out to see if they can find someone connected to that. They will start with the Doom District, since they think it's most likely they come from a darker area."

"It can be any area if they go after that," Kilian said, slightly annoyed. He had never been fond of the council. Even though some of the members seemed all right, most of them still adhered to older ways and rules. Alegro had often agreed with them, which had been the primary reason he and Kilian didn't get along. Not to mention that the head council—the main leaders—were all different kinds of politicians, including Feardorcha Forbes. Fear was one of the resistant members of the head council, but his followers always voted him in. Kilian already had a headache thinking about dealing with these people in the near future. This was exactly what he had been running away from.

Kilian sighed. It was the least he could do to face his father's death honourably. Kalimba was right—a part of Kilian had always loved him. Alegro had never been the father of the year, but sometimes there had been moments when Kilian could see that Alegro at least tried to understand him. Sometimes trying was better than ignorance.

"Kilian?" Kalimba prompted her brother, who seemed to be elsewhere.

"Sorry. Just thoughts. I need to speak to Jegor." And with that, he got up and left the room.

***

After Calligan had explained more of his crazy connection to her, Relayne slowly accepted his words. He had been a stranger to her. She hadn't even known his proper name until recently. A bit of dramatic Shakespeare; that was for sure. But on the other hand, she could live with the fact that someone would help her no matter what. It was hard for her to understand why he saw her without flaws—or maybe he did see her mistakes, but simply didn't care. That didn't change the fact that Relayne was sceptical, and a whole new bundle of information had entered her life, including information related to her mother and past.

"You should see this," Calligan said.

Relayne turned to watch the news on TV, where Synclair relayed a message to the magical world. The king was dead. Relayne's eyes widened, and she gulped.

"How could that happen?" she asked, not sure if she wanted to hear the answer.

"How do you think it happened? It was just a matter of time until they attacked the palace. But it is actually sooner than I thought it would be. We're close to a war," Calligan said.

He was so calm that Relayne had a feeling she would lose her mind. After all, she had only known the real Calligan for a couple of hours, and she was sure that there was more to his story than he was telling her.

"I need to see Kilian," she said quietly.

Calligan frowned at her. "And what? He's okay, as they said. You can't do as much as the others," he countered roughly.

"Spare me your jealousy. I am a child of the seal. That means I have a job to do. And if you're always watching me, as you say, then you should also know that I know what I'm doing," Relayne fired back, standing up.

Calligan looked after her. "There's so much more that you have to learn, little rose," he whispered.

***

Pieotr looked out of the window. The manor of the sins had never felt so quiet and empty. It wasn't that he was missing a certain person, but simply the fact that Amber had messed up their plan so badly that they had to go Underground. The boss had been angry, and all of them were now trying to fix the pieces that Amber had left them with. Maddison was still with the children of the seal, learning her lesson, as he had told Baelfire. Amber would try and convince one of the others to get her out of this misery and away from the punishment awaiting her. The boss wouldn't like that. The sins didn't have rules to play by, though there were lines that shouldn't be crossed. Amber had been struggling in the last few weeks, seduced by her thoughts and overcome with jealousy. Love was a complicated thing.

"Can I come in?"

"Since when do you ask, *chameleon*?" Pieotr answered, amusement in his voice.

Baelfire let out a little laugh. "I wanna discuss a few things. One of us has to talk to the boss, since Amber has made a big mistake."

"Sounds like you can't wait to drag her name through dirt. Did you speak to her?"

"I made her realize what she has done. The media doesn't know what we know, but it's clear that this was her work.

Kilian would never kill his father, even though he hated him. She did it because of me, to make Red go away. Little did she know that this brought her perhaps even closer."

Pieotr turned around to scrutinize his friend. "I haven't seen you as a lady lately," he said.

"Things have changed, I guess. Besides, why do you care?" Baelfire asked.

"Just being curious. But since you're here, you're welcome to go and speak to the boss. If you do that, I'll make sure we get Maddison out of trouble, and then we'll all have to hide for a while. Which means, if she doesn't show up sooner or later, she isn't one of us and is on the other side."

Baelfire frowned. Pieotr was right—Relayne needed to be with them. Otherwise, the prophecy would change, and she couldn't be around him anymore. They would turn into enemies, and the thought of that reminded Baelfire of how important this mission was.

"Don't make such a face. There's enough time left. Besides, three faces are unrevealed. They have no idea how powerful we actually are," Pieotr said, strolling over to the shelf where he kept cigarettes and alcohol.

"Fine. But how are we gonna get out of this situation?" Baelfire asked.

"Easy," Pieotr said, swirling the rum in his glass. "We deliver them Amber."

***

Maddison. Maddison, wake up. Wake up, darling.

Maddison didn't know if the voice was part of a dream or reality. It took her a moment before she could open her eyes completely. She was still in the chamber where Jegor had left her with Feardorcha. She felt dizzy, like someone who had gone to a party and had to deal with a hangover—not like someone who had been tortured by a dark magician. When she looked around, she realized she was on a chair. But something felt different. It was her skin. Her eyes widened, and that's when she remembered what Feardorcha had done to her. He had made her human again.

"Before you say anything, you're welcome," a voice whispered behind her.

A shiver ran through her body. She was unable to see Fear, but she knew he was hiding in the shadows of the room.

"I told you, you will never be able to escape me. Sooner or later, you will come crawling back to me. Until then, I'll wait."

The voice disappeared, and Maddison screamed. She tried to get off the chair, but she was too weak to do any kind of magic. Tears burned in her eyes and a small whimper escaped her lips. Then the door opened and Jegor stepped in the room. He stopped when he saw Maddison.

"I guess Fear has done his job," he began.

Maddison faced him, anger blazing in her eyes. "You have no idea what you have done to me. What you let him do to me," she screamed. "It took me long enough to hide from him, and now you have made me his meat, his doll to play with! All I wanted was to escape." Her voice broke, and she sobbed.

Jegor came closer to her.

Maddison didn't look at him. "We are all damned in this society. Some of us are born with tragedy. But it is in our hands to make our choices and to create new ways," she whispered. "You have no idea what you brought to life, but you will soon see." She raised her head and looked him in the eyes.

"You need to come to the palace with me," Jegor said, undoing the ropes that bound her. "The king is dead and it's most likely that one of your friends—or whatever you want to call them—is involved in this."

That's when he realized Maddison was human again. Whatever Feardorcha had done, she was breathing and living. Her eyes looked empty and for a moment, Jegor just looked at her. When he'd let Fear go to her, he knew he would use his ways to make her talk. But he hadn't known that he would end up doing something like this. Yet it was too late to apologize. The damage was done, and for the first time in a long while, Jegor had underestimated the circumstances.

"I am only going to tell you something when you help me to escape him once more," Maddison said. "I will tell you everything I can. But don't ever let that monster near me again."

***

"I can't find Jegor. Do you know where he is?" Kilian asked his uncle, who was sitting at his desk, surrounded by piles of paperwork.

"I didn't think you would be awake already—though I can admit that the last three days have been quite mental. Have a seat and take a deep breath. Do you want to drink something? Or can I offer you some food?" Synclair asked.

"I'm fine. I need to talk to my cousin. I know what happened is terrible. But when I let my thoughts in, it will get us nowhere. Kalimba mentioned the coronation. And yes, I will fulfil my duties. Father always wanted that, and even though we had our differences, this is the least I can do for him—and for my mothers. Unless you have a very good argument or wanna take over," Kilian said. He still looked exhausted.

Synclair let out a laugh. "You're still the same—which is good. We need a strong palace bond. Your little sister is damaged, but she will live with it. Don't take it personally if she doesn't want to talk to you right now. She doesn't understand that kind of magic. A lot is happening on the other side right now, too." He sighed.

Kilian looked around. Synclair's room was messy—documents, books, parchments, and other paperwork strewn around the room. His uncle had already had duties to the palace, but right now, it seemed to be an extraordinary amount of work.

"Don't worry. I know how to handle it. As you know, I'm never alone." Synclair smiled.

But there was something else. Maybe it was the bitterness that he had lost someone so close. Since he was a Ghost, he had to sort spirits out before they could go to the other side.

Kilian didn't say anything. He walked over and gave his uncle a hug. "I think you needed that," he said, and he couldn't see it, but Synclair smiled. Maybe Kilian needed this hug, too.

"You're very strong, Kilian. They would be proud—especially your real mother," Synclair said softly.

Kilian nodded. He felt the need to let his thoughts go, but then he took a deep breath and ended the hug. There was no time for emotions. They had to handle the situation as quickly as they could.

"What do I have to do for the coronation? I know I have to fill out a lot of papers and undergo a trial. The longer we wait, the greater the chances that something else will happen."

Synclair nodded. "Sit down then, and we will cover the formalities."

***

Baelfire closed his eyes and tried to focus. It wasn't the first time he had come down here or talked to his boss. But this time, he wasn't bearing good news, and therefore wasn't sure how well he would handle it. The room was the lowest, down underneath the house, an extra chamber. Most of the time, the boss wasn't to be seen unless he wanted to be seen. Baelfire had only once questioned his power, and that had left him with a scar around the back of his neck.

"Yo, I'm here for a talk. Newsflash, the king is dead," Baelfire said outside the door, trying to sound as casual as he could.

For a moment nothing happened, but then he could hear something inside. And then the door opened. Baelfire knew what he had to do. He walked into the living room of the chamber, designed like any other room in the mansion.

"Speak," hissed a voice from the corner of the room.

Baelfire began to tell the story. He conveyed Pieotr's plan.

A couple of minutes passed before the voice spoke again. "I always knew that Amber was a danger to us. But not you, boy—with your beautiful faces and interesting sexuality. I always liked that." They laughed and Baelfire felt touched in a way that made him uncomfortable. "But you know what happens when someone goes missing?"

"Enlighten me," Baelfire answered.

"There is a gap to fill. And for the sake of all of us, I hope your little red rose finds her way to us," the voice said.

Baelfire gulped. Sooner or later, he had to face the fact that Relayne might not join the Seven Sins. But right now, it was hard to imagine. "I am sure she will do the right thing."

"Of course she will. Now leave. I need my beauty sleep. And no interruptions anymore."

Baelfire left the chamber and went up to his room. There was no rest for the wicked; he saw Pieotr sitting in his chair and Amber lying on his floor. One of her eyes was missing, as well as one of her hands. Baelfire looked over to Pieotr and saw a little blood around Pieotr's mouth.

"It had to look real," Pieotr said with a smile, and Baelfire felt the urge to vomit.

***

Maddison stopped as soon as they entered the palace. Jegor wanted her to move, but she looked at him. She could feel something was off.

"I have an odd feeling," she said, glancing around. The entrance hall seemed normal.

I can feel it too.

Jegor looked at Carlin. When his Voodoo doll had a feeling, it usually meant something.

In the next moment, Maddison fell down and started spasming like she was having an epileptic attack.

Jegor bent down and held her, trying to impede her movement.

Someone is trying to get into her mind—that kind of magic wants to steal something from her.

Jegor nodded and closed his eyes. When he opened them, they were black. He needed to stop the process before the magic could get through and damage Maddison. He placed his hands on her arm and focused, mumbling a few words in Latin. While most of the Voodoo magic used in Icon was based on rituals and preparation, Jegor had learned how to use his magic in situations like this—dark magic working against another dark magic.

Minutes passed until Jegor felt that he had prevented most of the attack. Maddison lay there, not breathing for a few seconds before she woke up and let out a frightened gasp.

"What happened? Who attacked you?" Jegor asked as the black faded from his eyes.

Maddison didn't seem to remember what had happened. "It paralysed me. Someone knows I'm here."

Jegor pulled her up. He couldn't lose more time. "Time that you talk, before anything else happens," he said, steering them towards the palace.

Maddison felt too weak and frightened to resist.

Jegor took Maddison to Kilian and Synclair. Entering Synclair's room, he saw Kilian lying on the sofa. Synclair's gaze went over to Maddison and Jegor.

"I was just waiting for you," Synclair said.

Kilian looked at his cousin. "Just in time," he said, still a bit pale, as if he had seen something terrible.

"What happened?" Jegor asked, gesturing for Maddison to sit down.

"I had an Omen. It was just as we started to fill out the papers for the coronation," Kilian began, slowly sitting up.

Jegor looked at his cousin. "What kind of Vision? A seal?" he asked.

Kilian nodded. "I know where the next one is and how we can hide it."

"Then why are you so pale?" Jegor asked.

"It's the Crimson Eater," Kilian said, his face riddled with terror. "He is protecting the seal."

Chapter 23
Treason

The moment of betrayal is something you can never see coming.
– F. F., "The Leaders of the Sea," The True Urban Legends

Again, Leyla walked through the dark corridor. She knew the way. She knew the smell. Still nervous, she walked along until she reached the room from last time. But there was no blood now, and the room seemed bigger, as if it was a whole underground system.

"Leyla," a voice whispered, and a shiver ran down her back. It wasn't a human voice. It was in her head, and it sounded like the monster under the bed that every child was scared of. "You might see what's coming, but none of you are ready when you are in my territory."

Leyla tried to ignore it.

The scene was interrupted by a piercing scream. Leyla wanted to turn around, knowing it was Relayne, but when she did, she looked in its eyes and couldn't move at all.

***

Leyla woke with a loud scream and nearly fell off the sofa.

Alicia and Shadra were at her side within seconds. Shadra knelt next to the sofa. "What did you see this time?"

"The Crimson Eater. He's after Kilian. I've seen it," she said breathlessly. "It's protecting the next seal. We need to do something. Kilian can't go alone." Leyla pushed to get up, but Shadra held her down.

"Take it easy. You know this stuff is messing with your head," Shadra murmured.

"Shadra's right. Besides, just because you see it doesn't mean it's coming true," Alicia stated. Magicians could tell when it was a mundane dream, but the difference between a Dream, a Vision, and an Omen in the magical world was something else.

"I agree with Alicia," another voice said. Relayne had just entered the room.

"I'm not gonna ask where you've been. I'm just glad you're here," Alicia said sincerely.

"Let's get Leyla something to eat, and then we'll figure out a plan. Alicia, get Petyr out of his room, even if he's still unstable," Relayne instructed.

Before they could do anything, though, the front door opened and Jegor and Kilian entered. Relayne looked at Kilian. Neither of them said anything, but the tension stretched between them.

"We can talk later. Right now we have a seal to find," Kilian said before she even had the chance to find words. He strode past her.

"You missed a lot," Jegor said. "Now catch up and help."

***

All of the children had come together. Petyr was still very pale, but none of them seemed bothered that his damaged eye had gone white and scars lined half his face. The healing was a process, but day by day, Petyr was getting better and adapting to his new form.

"You were not the only one who had a Vision or Omen; we realise that now," Kilian started to explain. "What we need to find out is the location of the seal. It seems to be somewhere underground, but with the help of Petyr and Jegor, we should be able to find it. Besides, I can also help with my coordinates magic, and all together we should find what we are looking for."

"Who is going as soon as we have found out what we are looking for? Not all of us can go. Maddison is still in the palace, and we don't know who killed your father, Kil," Jegor said.

"We're gonna split. Four of us are going for the seal. The other three—you, Jegor, and two others—will go to the palace to figure things out. As soon as we have the seal, we'll go to the palace, too. If nothing else helps, Maddison will be executed," Kilian replied.

"A public execution?" Shadra asked abruptly.

"It's going to be a trap. I'm not gonna be the king who kills people like in the revolutionary times," Kilian assured her.

"Okay, but how do you know that someone is coming for her?" Alicia asked.

"Everyone has someone they care for. Maddison might not have a social circle, but she must have someone who looks out for her or who she is useful for. We might get her wendigo to us as well," Kilian said, reinforcing his current plan. There was a certain scepticism in the round of children, but time was against them and Kilian was serious about his plan.

"I'm taking Leyla and Shadra with me," Jegor said. "Alicia, Petyr, and Relayne, you go with Kilian. Maddison knows me, even though she might not trust me anymore. If someone gets something out of her, it might be me." The others agreed.

"I might not be interpreted as a threat by the Crimson Eater, thanks to the lovely wendigo who bit me," Petyr said. "These seal creatures won't see me as an enemy unless I give them a reason."

"Maybe the gods will give me a sign, too," Alicia added.

"Good. We've talked about this—now let's do it," Kilian said.

***

Relayne took a deep breath before she knocked on Jegor's door. The others were getting ready, as was Jegor himself when he allowed Relayne inside his room.

"What's up?" he asked, packing his necessary things.

"I need to tell you something before I go with Kilian. I could tell anyone else, but maybe you know someone who knows this person. Does the name Calligan Rose mean anything to you?" Relayne asked.

Jegor stopped and faced Relayne, frowning. "I've heard of that name. But only in a past form. Why? You have been out a lot lately; we've all noticed that. Does that have anything to do with your family?"

"Yes. But I don't wanna go into detail. We don't have time for that now. How do you know the name?" Relayne asked, unsure if she wanted to hear the answer.

"He was once a Ghost magician who worked as a hunter in Icon. Does that ring a bell?"

"A hunter? The kind that is now forbidden in most cities?"

"Yes. Hunters would kill people, magician or not, for money. Some of them had groups and worked for a higher person. But most hunters worked on their own. It's against the law now. Since the circle of hunters died, crime decreased. This society isn't some kind of mafia we live in, even though some groups still believe in that," Jegor explained.

Relayne nodded, but she had an awful feeling. "My mother used to help this boy called Calligan Rose. She looked after him. That's why I was asking."

"I understand. But you don't have to worry about that anymore. Calligan died in the Woods. Maybe Petyr has information, if you want to know more."

Relayne just nodded. "Thank you, Jegor. Good luck with your mission. Don't forget you can trust me, no matter what." She left the Black magician's room.

Jegor glanced at Carlin.

Don't worry. I thought the same. She lied.

***

Maddison kept looking at the wall. They had put her in a completely white room. She knew it was enchanted against magic. There was no chance of escaping the palace, and she could only wait for someone to come and get her. Pieotr had said it was punishment, but he didn't know exactly what was happening and what she was going through. He didn't know that Fear had that kind of power, like no other magician in this godforsaken town. Maddison had never told him. She closed her eyes—crying wouldn't help either. She felt numb, and the food that Jegor had given her wasn't appetising. As a doll, she'd never had to worry about food. It was more a luxury; if she wanted to eat, she could. If not, that was fine too. So many things had been easier, especially the feelings inside her. Maddison gulped. No one hated being human as much as she did.

The door opened, and Maddison looked over to Jegor, who closed the door behind him immediately.

"How blessed I am to see you again," Maddison said sarcastically.

"Cut the sarcasm. This is your last chance to help us before we need to make a choice. According to the law of the old king, you have a death threat on your shoulders. But if you speak up, I can help avoid execution—because right now, I can see that you fear death again," Jegor told her.

Maddison frowned, feeling an impulse to scream. Instead, she sighed. "What are you going to do with me if I help you?"

"If you tell me what happened with Fear, I can make it look like you just wanted to escape him. Therefore, you ended up in the middle of the conflict with the Seven Sins. We all do things to survive in this world. There will still be consequences; the politicians will probably want you to stay human, so that you'll lose your place and abilities."

"You wanna make me an outcast? Just like the people who have no choice if the ceremony doesn't choose them? I don't see how this is a great option. This world is everything I have!" Maddison shouted.

"You've done it your way. Now you need to see what's happening because of that," Jegor argued.

Maddison couldn't see the struggle inside him. One part of him still hoped to save his best friend; the other was the investigator who had to solve this case and save society.

"This Icon is going to die," Maddison said numbly.

"Someone attacked the palace. If you're connected to it or the people you're with are, you need to find a good alibi as to why this isn't a strike against the palace and society."

"It must have been a mistake," Maddison said.

She's not lying.

Jegor looked at Carlin and then again to Maddison. "So what happened?" he asked.

"I have no idea. But since Fear has taken my abilities, how can you still look at me, when your friend seems more like the subject that's involved in this as well?"

"I am concerned about Fear as well, but one step at a time. Right now, I have to find a solution for you. Can you help me with this? Or are you going the hard way? At the end of the road, death is waiting for you, Maddison. I can imagine better things than seeing my ex-best friend getting killed again." Jegor had raised his voice.

That was the moment Maddison realised—he still cared for her. That's why he was here. Any other person would have brought her to the executioner already. But some part of Jegor was still there for the Maddison he had become friends with.

"I tried to escape him—not because of the love we had, but because of what he was. He is not the person you think he is. If he sees you as a friend, that is something good indeed. But it's maybe the only good thing left in him. He is someone much darker and older than you can ever imagine. I know his secret. I found it out back in the day, and it scared me so much that I tried to escape. But how do you escape death? I played along in a very sick game, just to end up as a doll with no heart, no feelings, no worries, and no sorrow anymore. When I found Tress, it was the first time I could properly interact with someone again. Humans, even us magicians, care so much about feelings and relationships. That was something I never had to worry about when I was a doll. I was free."

Maddison looked like she was somewhere else for a moment.

"What did he want from you? Why did you do all this?" Jegor asked.

"Remember when I told you about the Death and the three Muses?" Maddison asked.

"I do remember. It's one of the four urban legends that got banned from society. According to the law, there were elements that could be used for much darker magic," Jegor said.

"It's not just that. This one has something to do with me."

Jegor went silent, then sat down next to Maddison. "Speak. I need to know everything," he said, and hoped that he could look Fear in the eyes after whatever he was about to hear.

Chapter 24
Death and the Three Muses

"Once upon a time, in a land of darkness and misery, there was a man who was Death himself. No one knew his name, but they didn't have to, because just his presence itself was a name. He lived in a giant house on top of a hill of the village the people lived in. Every time someone died in the village, the people whispered that it was his fault, as if he were the devil himself. Yet the village couldn't exist without him, since he was a wise and helpful man. He could be a loyal friend if you did him a favour. But if you betrayed him just by whispering the wrong words, it would stir his anger, and he would make sure you'd regret it.

"One day, a magician came to the village. After a long journey, he wanted to rest and have something to eat. While most of the people in the village were scared of magic, the man on the hill didn't seem to fear the magician. He invited him as his guest and let him feast and drink as if they had been friends for ages.

"'I shall thank you for your kindness. But something tells me that isn't the only thing you long for,' the magician said to the man, who smiled.

"'Indeed, it is not. I was born selfish, and for my kindness, I want something in return. I'm an immortal man. I have already the gift of life. But therefore, I am lonely, and love doesn't seem to come my way no matter what I try. I wish to find love, like other human beings.'

"The magician laughed and clapped his hands. Of course it was a lack of love—one thing so powerful that it couldn't be missed. Not even by Death himself.

"'If that is your wish, so shall it be. But remember my words: Love comes with a price. You can't just take it and let it live by your side. You shall have three muses that cross your path. One pure, one wild, and one just like you, nearly the same. If you're able to understand them, so shall Love stay in your life.'

"Death, convinced of his power and charm, agreed without a doubt. The next day, he met the first muse. The white one was small, beautiful, and every man's desire. Her eyes were clear as the sky, her skin soft, and her voice like that of an angel. There was no evil in her. She was a pure, virgin soul, as if she had been drawn by a painter. And as soon as they met, they fell for each other. It was a quick, rushed, but beautiful love. Nothing seemed to worry them. There was no harm, no rumour that could go against this love.

"But one day, Death followed her to the lake, where she always picked the fruits for their kitchen. Blind and in love, he wanted to surprise her. But what he discovered was something else. His muse was swimming in the lake, but not alone. A lady was by her side. Shocked and furious, he confronted his muse that night. The white muse didn't deny it. Rather, she tried to explain that there was more than one person she would fall for, since this was her true nature. Unable to understand and accept this, Death was taken over by jealousy, and he murdered the white muse with his bare hands. He buried her in the lake where she had betrayed him, and never returned to her watery grave.

"The second muse met him a few days after the death of the first. She crossed paths with the village returning from a hunt. She was the leader of a wild group living outside the village. They always warned against visiting the village, but she didn't listen. And so the red muse came to the village and met Death, falling without hesitation.

"Soon, the white muse was forgotten. Everything was wild with this woman—the life, the love, the times she acted like a storm. But he loved her for that.

"One day, when she was going to her people, Death followed her. Again he discovered something that twisted his mind. He saw his beloved muse with another man, kissing her before she could let go of him. The red muse turned away and returned to the village. But not Death. He followed the man to his tent and murdered him with his own axe.

"Proud and sure of his doing, he went to his beloved to tell her what he had done.

"The red muse couldn't believe him. 'You murdered my first love,' she whispered, unable to face him.

"Angry and furious that she wasn't happy that he had helped her, his emotions overcame him, and the axe he'd used for her first love ended the red muse as well. Another love had gone. He took her into the backyard of their garden and burned her to ashes, which he blew into the night sky.

"Bitter over his loss, he stopped thinking about love. He had forgotten the words of the magician, blinded by negative emotion. That was the moment the last muse entered his life— the black muse. She was beautiful in her own way, pale as a ghost and soul dark as hell itself. Where the others had left him, she picked up the pieces, and they both understood each other, growing from pain and misery.

"But one day that didn't seem to be enough for Death. He wanted to be with her for eternity. So he brewed a potion that would make her immortal, just like him. The black muse had no idea what he had given her. The milk tasted different, but it seemed nothing to worry about. So she drank the mixture and gave up her humanity without knowing.

"*The moment she found out what he'd done, the trust between them broke. Death couldn't understand her fury, since it was an act of love. The black muse tried to kill herself, but no matter how often she tried, she always came back, damned to be with him always and forever.*

"*Living in his own tragedy, Death returned to the magician, living as a villager.*

"'*You told me love would come if I understood it. But you never mentioned the cheating, the lies, or the loss of love,' Death complained.*

"*The magician laughed and put a hand on his shoulder. He nodded. 'That is true. But love comes with a price, just like magic itself. If you're able to share, you are willing enough to go through hard times. The white muse was never cheating on you; the lady in the lake was no more than a friend. The red muse was struggling from a broken heart, not yet ready to love you like you deserved. Patience is key. And your wife, the black muse—she was so broken that her only happiness was finding someone she could spend her life with until the end of her days, not forever. Honest love doesn't come from pressure, distrust, or possessiveness. That, my friend, is your lesson. And now, farewell until forever.'*

"*Death turned his back on the magician, knowing he would now live forever in tragedy, but happily ever after in his eyes.*"

***

"And you're one of these muses, I assume?" Jegor asked after Maddison had finished the tale.

"There's no proof for sure that anything in these urban legends happen in our world," she replied. "But the way he always acted around me, as if he never wanted to let me go, that was the moment I knew something was wrong. And then I found the book. I confronted him, and at first, he denied it. But then he got so angry about all my questions that I believed since that day it was true. I was his black muse. And according to the legend, he tried to make me immortal. He used me for some experiments, but I was so in love that I didn't believe he had anything bad in mind. That's when I escaped and made myself immortal by turning myself into a doll. I couldn't give him the power over my body, my life, and everything connected to it."

Jegor nodded. He could understand her actions. "But you still stand for something much darker and dangerous in this society. I will let Kilian decide what happens to you. If you're lucky, he won't want your head. Until he's back, you will live in these four walls," Jegor said. "I hope you don't have to leave me again."

Chapter 25
Crimson Red

A colour to destroy.
– F.F., "Lucifer's Wish," *The True Urban Legends*

"I can't believe you didn't take the others with us," Relayne said to Kilian.

"Someone who is turning half-wendigo isn't a help. Besides, I spoke to Alicia, and she mentioned something connected to her magic. She has a mission, and so do we. Or are you afraid we won't make it together?" Kilian asked, but didn't look at Relayne's face.

"I'm not afraid. You're the one who can't stand this creature," she snapped.

"Shush now. I need your help. According to the Vision, the chamber and the seal are somewhere underground. We need to find where," Kilian said, closing his eyes and moving his hands in a certain series of finger clicks and movements.

When he opened his eyes, they glowed lilac, and his hands were surrounded by a similar-coloured fog. "I'm using one of my tracker spells to find the entrance, but it's costing me a lot of energy. You need to help me, to make it stronger," Kilian commanded, and Relayne touched his arm without hesitation.

She closed her eyes and let Kilian's fear inside her mind. By now they shared a connection good enough for them to work strongly together. Relayne opened her eyes, now glowing red. She could feel every bit of Kilian's fear. He had been confronted with this creature many times in his childhood.

"I can sense it," Kilian whispered, releasing Relayne. Seconds later, the lilac fog vanished. "Come. We can't wait any longer, in case any of our enemies are on it too." He took Relayne's hand.

Together they walked a while until Kilian stopped in front of a backyard, facing a door. It was nothing unusual in appearance, but this door wasn't any door. Relayne gulped. She remembered what had happened here before.

"It's the back entrance to Fear's shop," she whispered.

Kilian nodded. "Another reason we can't wait." He stepped forward.

***

Both of them had made sure they were quiet when they entered through the back door, but Fear didn't seem to be around.

"There must be something, like a hidden door, that leads to a deeper path," Kilian whispered, igniting lilac fire in the palm of his hand. It wasn't real, just an illusion, but it was enough to light the way.

Relayne focused, feeling a warm sensation inside her fingers, channelling her inner magic to lead the way. They stopped in the middle of the corridor.

"Do you trust me?" Relayne asked.

Kilian rolled his eyes. "I think we're way beyond the point where we have to discuss this now, *partner*," he answered.

"Don't say later that I didn't try," she said, and pulled him closer.

Kilian wanted to say something, but instead, the ground began to open. Seconds later, they fell a few metres before Kilian's magic stopped them.

His breath was coming fast. "Next time, a little warning would help," he hissed.

"I tried to tell you," Relayne said with an annoyed sigh. She pointed at the walls. "We're a few metres under the earth. Have a look at that." Slime and skin coated the walls.

Kilian gulped. "It's as disgusting as I imagined. Let's find the seal before it finds us," he said, taking her hand again.

This time, she could feel he hadn't done it to walk faster. Kilian was scared. Relayne felt the urge to tell him that everything would be okay, that he should trust her, but she couldn't say anything at all. It would just lead to another discussion. It was easier like this. The further they walked, the longer the hall seemed to be.

"We need to use another spell. Otherwise we're going to walk around here forever," Relayne said. She stopped, but Kilian didn't let go of her hand.

"Okay, can you use your magic? Try to memorize what you saw in your Vision and let the emotions lead you towards the seal," Kilian said.

Relayne nodded, closed her eyes, and focused once more. The image of the creature, along with the seal, came to her mind. Her body started to shake, and it took her a moment before she could sense something.

"Kilian," she said as quietly as she could.

She didn't have to continue to make him realise that they were in danger. When he looked up, he could see it—the end of the tail of the creature he had feared all his life.

"Run!" Kilian said, yanking her with him.

A loud crashing noise followed them, as if something was smashing against the walls, but neither of them turned around. They ran as fast as they could before the hall branched off in different directions.

"We need to split up," Relayne gasped, out of breath, as the creature drew closer.

"No. I can't. I—" Kilian stuttered. Fear was taking over his mind.

"Kilian, get it together. Whatever happens, trust me. We need to find the seal. Now go!" Relayne shouted with all the courage she could muster. She pushed him away and ran towards one of the left corridors, while Kilian went the opposite way.

"Come and find me, bitch," Relayne hissed and used her magic to lure the Crimson Eater towards her.

She could hear an awful, loud, reptilian noise behind her. She came to another giant hall, but this time, statues lined each corridor, and the room was much bigger. Relayne stopped and looked around, hectic and panicking.

"It's here," she whispered, sensing the seal. She hid behind one of the statues, startling to find Kilian already crouched behind it.

"How in Merlin's name did you get here?" she asked.

"It's an illusion labyrinth. It makes us think it's bigger than it actually is, but I think it's just the hall. It's the protection of the seal. It must be in one of these statues. I just haven't figured out which one yet," he explained.

Before he could continue, the creature entered the room.

I can smell your fear, royal son, the Crimson Eater said. The voice sounded deep, with an undertone of something that would scare any magician, no matter their age. Just like every monster of the seal, it communicated within their heads.

Relayne pressed one of her hands over Kilian's mouth, using her magic to reduce his fear.

Someone was here before. I don't see a reason I should give you the seal. Any of you little wimps could be a so-called child of the seal.

"Trust me," Relayne whispered in Kilian's ear, then stood up and emerged from their hiding place.

Her view of the Crimson Eater wasn't clear at first, but with the help of Kilian's magic, the room lit up. In the lilac glow, she could see the full size of the creature, filling out enough of the room to make her gasp. He was huge, with dark crimson skin, long, strong arms, dangerously clawed feet, and sharpened teeth dripping with blood. He had no eyes, but a long tongue slithered between his teeth. Long enough to reach Relayne and stopping infront of her.

You're neither good nor bad. Therefore, I can't harm you.

Kilian rose from behind the statue. "What does he mean by that?" he asked tentatively.

Oh, hello, little prince. You—well, you I can harm.

The Crimson Eater swung one of his claws, and Kilian and Relayne dodged at the last second. At the other end of the room, Relayne discovered the seal.

"It's the middle statue. Distract him. I'll get the seal," she said.

Kilian gulped but knew she was right. Not waiting for a countdown, both of them started running. Kilian used his magic, and hit the Crimson Eater in his back, while Relayne slid between the monster's legs to get to the other side. The creature let out a terrible noise before following Kilian into one of the corridors, smacking Relayne with the back of his tail and throwing her to the other side of the room.

Relayne screamed as she hit the ground. She could tell at least one of her ribs had cracked, but she had to get up. With all the power she had, she got up and ran toward the statue. She took the seal from the hand of the statue and closed her eyes, whispering the words of the legend of Merlin to show her worth. Then she heard Kilian scream.

Without hesitating, she ran towards the scream and stumbled into the big room she had been in before. She saw Kilian lying on the floor. Blood was everywhere, and the Crimson Eater crawled on the ceiling, letting his tongue glide towards Kilian, ready to feast. Relayne grabbed Kilian's arm and began pulling him away, then noticed the deep gash in his chest.

"Enough!" Relayne screamed and used her red magic matter on the monster, attacking it on the inside. With the seal in her pocket, power surged through her.

The Crimson Eater broke down with a nasty scream, trying to fight against the Red magic, with no choice but to obey. Once, twice he tried to bite, but then he crashed fully to the ground.

"You won't touch us until we're out of here," she said.

Kilian, draped halfway over her shoulder, whispered something like a thank-you.

"Shut it until we're out," Relayne said harshly, and together they escaped the illusion labyrinth of the Crimson Eater.

Back in the backyard outside Fear's shop, Relayne settled Kilian on the ground. He had lost a lot of blood. She was covered in scratches and the pain in her side lingered. She tried to ignore it.

"How did he get you?" she asked.

"Illusions. You were the only one able to get into the seal room," Kilian answered quietly.

"But I saw you there with me," she said, trying to staunch his bleeding.

"Everything you saw in there was an illusion. He had me from the beginning, but that's okay. You have the seal, so we made it," he said, his voice getting weaker.

Relayne could still feel the seal inside her pocket. Yes. She had made it.

"I'm proud of you," Kilian whispered. "After all, this seems to be a win for us."

"Don't be. At least not yet. There's much more I have to do. Nothing is finished yet."

"What do you mean?" Kilian asked, slightly confused.

"You will see. All you have to do is trust me, no matter what happens. Trust in the person you know, not the person society wants you to see. Be a better king," she whispered, taking away his pain. A few tears streaked her cheeks.

"Relayne, are you—" But he couldn't finish his sentence. Exhaustion overcame him, and he couldn't help but close his eyes, passing out seconds later.

Relayne sobbed as she stood. She knew that the others would find him. He wouldn't die here. But for now, their paths would separate.

"I have to do this. Don't forget who I am," she whispered, even though he was asleep.

She looked at Kilian once more before she walked away, and the clouds over Icon darkened. Something was happening—an eruption in the magical world. Relayne had saved the seal, but not for the children. She had chosen the path of the sins.

Chapter 26
Believe

And who do you see, when you look in the mirror?
– F. F., "A Tale of Roses," *The True Urban Legends*

"Wake up, Petyr," Alicia said.

The magician blinked, looking at her in confusion. Alicia was sitting next to his bed. He was still resting, trying to heal and get used to his new standard of life. So far, he hadn't had a problem. But he knew it would get harder, especially when it came to the hunger he'd soon have to face.

"Are you coming for another cuddle?" Petyr asked with a grin.

"No," Alicia said, smiling briefly. "I am here to say goodbye for now."

Petyr sat straight up and looked at her. "What do you mean? You can't leave the children just like that."

"I can. It has something to do with this whole journey. Tyr is calling me for something much bigger. I'm one of the rare believers who can go somewhere to gain more power, knowledge, and energy—all of which we need. I could barely face Tress. This war is just on the edge. A revolution is coming, and we all know it. I need to find more strength, but I need to go somewhere else to do so," Alicia explained.

Petyr took her hand. "So while I turn into a beast, you're just going away?" he asked.

"Yes. But I wanted to tell you this in person, before I go. The others got a note. You're the only one who gets a personal message," Alicia said.

"So this is some kind of special treatment? I feel honoured," Petyr said, and couldn't help but smirk.

"I will miss your stupidity and grin, I guess," Alicia said. "I have no idea awaits me, but whatever it is, I will think of you and how I'll kick your ass when I'm back." She grinned.

Petyr pulled her closer. "I was close to kissing you, but then you underestimated my power, Alicia," he whispered against her lips.

Alicia pulled back with a laugh and ran her fingers through his hair. "This is not a romantic goodbye. This is a may-we-meet-again."

"I know you will do amazing. Whoever crosses your path, make sure they know your name. And when you come back, we're going to change the world together," he said, smiling one last time before she stood up.

She had packed her bag already, and now slung it over her shoulders.

"May the northern gods never let you lose your beauty, Petyr," she said.

Petyr grinned, which showed one half of his human grin and the other side of his new personality, already forming into the silhouette of a wendigo.

***

Kilian woke up with a scream of fear. Jegor held him down so he wouldn't fall off the bed.

"It's okay. You're with us. You're in the palace. You're safe," Jegor said calmly.

Kilian took a moment to calm down, then sat up. "Where is she?" he demanded.

"Kilian, you need to calm down before you do anything," Jegor warned him.

"I don't care. Where is Relayne? What happened?" he looked down at himself and saw bandages around his chest. He remembered the fight with the Crimson Eater. He had lost against one of his biggest nightmares.

"Relayne isn't with us. But you have to calm down before I tell you more," Jegor said.

"Where is she?" Kilian demanded again.

Jegor took a deep breath. "She is with the sins now. She is not one of us anymore," he began to explain. "I knew it the moment the second seal was found. There was another eruption. So far it only seems that most of the magicians who were affected fell asleep, but we might have to deal with amnesia and other memory loss when they wake up."

"So she betrayed us," Kilian stated. "I should have seen it coming. She kept on repeating this stuff—about how I need to trust her no matter what. She's just running to these insane people." He couldn't tame his anger. After all he did to try and understand her, to get a better connection to her, she had done this to him. He ached from the damage she had caused his inner balance.

"We don't know why she left. Relayne has been out a lot compared to the rest of us. She could have met anyone. Maybe one of them offered her a deal. We can't say for sure," Jegor said. He wasn't any less angry than his cousin, but they had different ways of showing their anger. While Kilian was more outrageous, Jegor felt guilty for not having kept an eye on Relayne when he'd had the chance.

"If she is one of them now, her case falls under the death threats, just like any other magician connected to these freaks. My father died because of them. So did both of my mothers. Do you think I'm able to take any more pain? Do you think I'm okay with the fact that she just did that?" Kilian shouted, partially sobbing. The ache was getting worse. He couldn't say what it was—the fact that she had left, the fact that he had lost his father, the fact that this whole system was leaking on all corners. He was exhausted and a big part of him wanted to scream and rage and *do* something about it. He couldn't sit still anymore. He was angrier than he had ever been before.

Anger had been one of his biggest weaknesses all his life, and now he had to deal with another loss. He knew he felt more connected to Relayne than necessary. There was no one else to blame for this feeling—for the connection he had made. Kilian pressed his hands to his face, crying in silence. The future king had thought that there was something between them. She had felt it too, he was sure of that. How could she leave him alone with this mess? He didn't want Jegor to see him like this, even though it had happened before. Jegor had been there for him whenever Alegro let out his anger on the prince.

Jegor remained silent until he heard that Kilian had stopped crying.

"No. I don't think you're okay," Jegor answered. "But neither am I. Anger will lead to more pain, and if you don't learn to control that, we'll have more problems. Keep your balance together, Kil. Kalimba was affected by the last eruption. She is in her room, sleeping for now. When she wakes up, we can see what happened as a result of the second seal. For now, you need to get better. The Crimson Eater bit you. You will be left with some scars. I reduced the poison as much as I could and gave you back some blood through my Voodoo magic. You might have to deal with some other effects of the Crimson Eater."

Kilian removed his hands from his face and nodded. "Thank you, Jegor. Can I be alone now?" he asked quietly. Kilian was sure that this feeling inside him wasn't the side effects of the Crimson Eater, but he didn't dare say it out loud.

"Sure. But there's something else you should know. Relayne asked me about someone named Calligan, who seemed to be connected to her family," Jegor said.

"As in Calligan the serial killer?" Kilian asked.

"Yes. According to what she said. I have a feeling he isn't as dead as we thought he was. Or it's a new clue."

"If that's true, we have another case to work on—finding the murderer of Synclair's wife," Kilian said.

Jegor nodded in agreement.

***

Relayne slowly opened her eyes, staring at the ceiling. What she had seen and felt down in the chamber under Fear's shop still haunted her, threatening insanity. Maybe there had always been a part of her that wasn't completely good. Now she had made a choice that she couldn't take back. With the last bit of her adrenalin, she'd made it to the house of the sins. It was Calligan who had helped her find the house again. Relayne couldn't explain how he knew its location, but for now, she had other things to worry about. She had chosen a side. That would soon be public. It was just a matter of time until her face would be all over the media. And people wouldn't understand in the slightest what was going on. They would just see what they wanted to see, no matter whether it was fake news or not. Leaning towards the dark side of your inner balance was forbidden. It was one of the oldest laws and had never changed since it was created. The reason why Jesters existed.

Relayne took a deep breath and went into the bathroom. She found a pair of scissors, and without thinking twice, she cut off her hair. She didn't stop until it was level with her chin. It didn't seem like a big difference, but to her it meant something. Longer hair only meant a disadvantage in fights, and she had known fights were coming since she'd grabbed the seal and left Kilian behind. She knew the next time she faced him, he would look at her with hate. That was the price she had paid.

Once more she looked in the mirror, threw away the shorn locks of hair, and left the bathroom. The house of the sins felt empty, not familiar in any way. Was her room back in the children's house empty now? Her mind didn't stop thinking.

"I thought I saw a ghost last night." Baelfire's voice interrupted Relayne's thoughts. He leaned in her doorway, looking as if he had just woken up.

"I am a ghost. I walk through walls if I want to," Relayne answered, rummaging through the familiar clothes in the wardrobe—ones she had left in Baelfire's room.

"I prepared this in case you wanted to stay here. You deserve your own room," Baelfire said.

"I don't deserve anything," she snapped. "But—"

"Oh shut it, Relayne, will you?" Baelfire walked over to her and grabbed her arm. He realised she had cut her hair.

"Please tell me you did this for yourself," he said, gently touching her face.

"Of course. Do you really think I dress to impress someone else? That counts for my hair too," Relayne said, avoiding his eyes. She was still angry for the lies he'd been hiding the whole time they had known each other.

"Good. And you deserve everything in this magical world we live in, okay? I know that people always tried to take you down, but look at you. You are still here, and even though you paid a price, you are following your own goals. I can see it. You don't have to speak to tell me that something is going on—that you have a plan. Because I know you. I have always known you. There is no one I trust as much as I trust you," Baelfire said.

"But you had Amber," Relayne answered, still averting her gaze.

"Yes. But she belongs to my past. Besides, she never had anything on you. How could she? Have you seen yourself? You're different. But you're the good kind of different—the one the world needs. Maybe you don't see it, but for me, you are more than enough. You will always be enough to me." Baelfire finished his pep talk.

Relayne gulped. She could feel tears in her eyes, and quickly pressed herself against Baelfire.

"It's okay," he whispered, gently stroking her hair. "Sometimes we need to hear these words out loud, to heal." He let her cry for a moment before he pushed her back and wiped away her tears. "I came for a different reason, though."

Now Relayne looked at him. "Let me guess. It has something to do with the seal I got you guys?"

"Yes. Our boss wants to meet you. I guess you've impressed him. Besides, there's something else," Baelfire said, biting his lower lip.

"What is it?" Relayne asked.

"Pieotr told me not to tell you. But out of everyone in this house, I think I should be the one. He is currently helping your sister escape the palace's death threat," he confessed.

"My sister? I have a sister?" Relayne asked, confused.

Baelfire nodded and grabbed her hand slowly. "She doesn't know it herself. That's why I have to tell you this. Coming here meant you paid a high price, but maybe this will make things easier for you."

"Right now, you're the only person I can think of being around," she said to him. "But who are you talking about? Who is my sister?" She had learned a lot over the last weeks, including her connection to Calligan. But this was another revelation entirely.

Baelfire took a moment, just looking at Relayne. "It's Maddison. Maddison is your sister."

***

"Maddison Dorothea Parker, you are free to go," Jegor to Maddison, who was sitting on the floor.

Confusion twisted on her face, but before she could say anything, Pieotr appeared next to her. "Let's go home, darling. They found the real murderer," he said, sounding like a caring boyfriend.

Maddison got up and hugged Pieotr, quickly grabbing his hand to walk with him.

"What happened?" she whispered.

"Just what happens when someone betrays us. Justice will strike," Pieotr replied, and together they left the palace.

A moment after they had left, Jegor had refilled Maddison's place in the cell. He looked at its occupant now. It was his job to deal with her as soon as she was awake. Of course, he would—for Alegro and especially for Kilian.

Amber would die.

Chapter 27
Before the Storm

And when we rise, we shall drown them.
– F. F., "The Leaders of the Sea," *The True Urban Legends*

Leaving wasn't easy. It never had been, but Alicia knew she had to do this. Gods rarely sent signs. They had different ways of speaking to the magicians who believed in them. This was a task and a chance Tyr had offered her, and as much as she would have liked to stay, she knew she couldn't. She had lost her parents and her brother, and therefore, even though she had grown closer to the children, it wasn't enough to keep her here. She wasn't going on this journey just to prove her loyalty to the White League. She had to go for everything she had lost; she needed to find herself.

Alicia looked around. The day was clear, no clouds in sight. Yet the sun wasn't showing its face, as if it knew that something was going on. The nature magicians had felt it first when Alegro was killed—something unnatural in the balance of society.

"I'm here to go on this ship," Alicia said, pointing at the Viking ship in front of her.

Tyr had shown her the ship in her mind, and she had found it, following her instincts.

"Are you sure about that? You don't look like the typical guest we have on this ship," the young man said. He looked quite fit, with light brown hair and a few freckles, and seemed like someone who knew how to sail.

"And you don't look like someone who can judge me just by my looks," Alicia answered tensely.

The man looked at her, raising an eyebrow and smirking slightly. "And why should I let you through?" he asked.

"Because Tyr sent me. And if you don't, I'll sadly have to kick your pretty ass," Alicia replied with a friendly smile.

The man went silent, then let out an amused laugh. "All right then. Come on board." He let her past.

Alicia nodded and stepped onto the boat. She didn't know where it would take her—all she knew was that she had to go on this boat. A few other people were already aboard, and none of them looked like they knew where they were going, either. Together they looked like a diverse group on a tourist trip. Alicia sighed and sat down. She didn't turn around again. From now on, she would only look forward.

***

When Amber opened her eyes, she had no idea where she was. The last thing she could remember was Pieotr attacking her. When she looked down, she could see the damage he'd done. One of her hands was missing, and she could only see through one eye. She seemed to be inside a cell, but she couldn't piece it together. Pieotr and Baelfire had taken her somewhere—but where?

Amber had just stood up when someone opened the door. It was Jegor, but this time he wasn't alone. Carlin hung from his belt. Amber froze, realising where they had brought her.

"So the rats actually delivered me like a piece of meat," she began, her spite clear to hear.

She and Pieotr had never connected, but the fact that Baelfire had delivered her just like that made her angry and upset.

"Is that a surprise for someone who murdered the king?" Jegor asked.

"It was an accident," Amber said, defending herself. "I was meant to kill someone else."

Jegor seemed amused for a moment. "Since you don't even deny your crime, you can hope for your league to give you another chance on the other side. Your execution is tomorrow."

"Execution? Where are we, in medieval times?" Amber shouted. "They wanna make it look like I'm the bad guy here. But I'm not alone in this. I'm not alone, and you know—" Before she could continue, a horrible pain shot through her back, as if something was reminding her not to talk about certain things.

"Baelfire is your ex-boyfriend and Relayne's partner, apparently. We have nothing on Pieotr. So enlighten me, if you have something to say about him," Jegor said.

If she does, something is going to break her. I can feel it.

Jegor looked to his Voodoo doll and then to Amber.

"If I do, I'll die. If I don't, I'll die as well. I'd rather have the execution when these bastards show me that they have used me again. Revenge isn't worth it."

Amber wanted to sit down, but Jegor walked over to her and turned her around so her back faced him. She sighed painfully—Pieotr had done his damage perfectly.

"Pull your shirt up," he said.

"Excuse me? If you're going to touch me—"

"Pull your shirt up, or I'll do it myself. There's something going on with your back, isn't there?" Jegor asked.

Amber had no choice but to pull her shirt up.

"Talk about them," Jegor demanded.

"The Seven Sins," Amber began to say, and she could feel the pain coming back, already cramping her body a little. But Jegor held her so she wouldn't fall.

While Amber tried to speak, Jegor found something moving along her back. It wasn't a parasite, but it looked like a symbol, a faded tattoo that was moving and eating her from inside.

"Please stop. It's a curse, a pact that we made since this happened," Amber begged.

"Happened? You mean the Seven Sins? Who is a part of it?"

"I can't say anything more. It will kill me," Amber whispered.

Jegor released her and stepped away. "If you can't tell me, you will have to tell my friend," he said without emotion. He looked at his Voodoo doll, who looked back at him with a devilish grin. Jegor very rarely used Carlin, only when it came to intense fights or when he needed information.

"This is illegal. I have rights," Amber said, backing against the far wall.

"You broke those rights the moment you killed my uncle and used dark magic that breaks every rule that exists," Jegor explained.

Carlin jumped off his belt and walked closer to Amber.

"What the hell are you doing with this thing?" Amber hissed.

I would say I feel offended, but I actually don't. Carlin grinned at her.

"His name is Carlin, and you and he are going to have a little chat."

"I was only doing what I thought was right. We all have our own goals in life, don't we?" Amber said, panic rising in her voice.

Jegor wasn't listening anymore. "Let her live, Carlin. But make sure she speaks, even if it breaks her."

Jegor left the room and Amber knew that this wouldn't end well. No one would save her. She had brought this all on herself.

What happened then was something that she hadn't seen coming. Carlin began to make noises that sounded like bones breaking inside the little Voodoo doll's body. But instead of getting more wrecked, the doll began to grow, bigger and bigger, until he was nearly two heads higher than Amber. It took her breath away, and she pressed further against the wall. What she was seeing now was pure evil. There was no joy, no happy smile or grin to see. The stitches weren't just stitches anymore. He looked like a combination of human and doll. His fingers were sharper, like knives, and along his body there were needles, knives, and other sharp things either connected to his body, tucked in, or protruding from it. His left eye seemed pressed in, as if it had never been there at all. The right eye looked like a giant human eye, but instead of a normal iris, it had a giant button.

I don't have to hurt you if you would just speak.

Amber pressed her hand against her head. This thing could speak in her mind. That made everything worse. And the moment Carlin walked closer, Amber screamed—a sound that no one would hear or care about.

***

"You're still sitting on the bed," Baelfire said, snapping Relayne out of her thoughts.

After Baelfire had dropped the bomb that Maddison was her sister, she hadn't said another word. Suddenly, her world seemed even more chaotic than before, and she still wasn't over the fact that the children would see her as a traitor.

"Sorry that I didn't join you in the shower," Relayne answered with certain sarcasm.

Baelfire smirked and pulled on a pair of shorts and a black top. "You can ask me anything you like. I told you I will give you the answers you want to know," he said, sitting next to her.

"I know, and I really appreciate that. But can't you see that I'm trying to hold it together? I lost everything, and I don't even know for what," Relayne said, chewing on her lower lip.

Baelfire froze for a moment, then impulsively grabbed her hand. "You have me, Calligan, and others behind you who will always follow you," he told her.

"How do you know Calligan?" Relayne asked.

"Who *doesn't* know him?" Baelfire questioned.

"Jegor mentioned that he is some sort of killer and supposed to be dead. Is that true? Did he used to be a hunter?"

Baelfire focused on her face, searching for answers—ascertaining if she was really so uninformed. "I think you need some strong alcohol if you have no idea who he is. Even though I get you. He has a pretty face, and I'm actually not even mad if you hooked up with him—"

"What the fuck? Baelfire, you're unbelievable!" Relayne could feel her cheeks redden. Baelfire had shown once more how shameless he could be.

"Don't get me wrong. I would probably hook up with him myself, but I have you," Baelfire answered with a grin, and the next second, a pillow smacked him in the face.

"The world we live in is a mess, and you're asking me if I hooked up with another guy?"

"I'm trying to get my girlfriend back and help her to fix her life. What do you think I'm doing here?" Baelfire said. "I know how confusing this might be, but all the answers are downstairs. The boss will give them to you. You will still have your own choices, just like we all have, but you will understand why we are doing this and why you came here."

"He probably only let me in to be another Amber," Relayne answered sarcastically.

"Amber is still alive, though not for long. No one can replace her. Besides, you're so much better than her. Amber drowned in her own darkness, while we all learned to balance it. She knew what she was getting herself into the moment she agreed to this. But as I said, you will understand as soon as the boss speaks to you. The fact that he wants to speak to you is a big thing. Do you think you're ready to go? He wanted to see you as soon as he can. Maddison and Pieotr are probably coming here soon as well, and then you can sort the family stuff out, too."

Relayne went silent, trying to absorb all this new information. "How are you all always so informed? You seem to be always a step ahead. Is it because of the boss? Or am I missing something here?"

"Have you seen all of us yet?" Baelfire questioned.

Relayne looked at him as if something had just clicked. "Two are missing," she said, and Baelfire nodded.

"We have two people who give us all the info whenever we need it. Then there are people like Calligan, who are—by accident—obsessed with someone like you," Baelfire said in amusement.

"He isn't obsessed with me," Relayne said defensively.

"Well, his flat tells a different story, if you had looked around. But I can't blame him." Baelfire shrugged. "You are amazing, Relayne."

"Well thanks, idiot," she answered with a sigh, then got up from the bed. "Don't wait for me. Maybe I'm gonna hook up with your boss, since you seem to be pretty chill when someone else has an eye on me."

Baelfire laughed. "You really need to get your facts straight about Calligan. I'll see you later." He blew her a kiss, which Relayne returned with an extended middle finger.

***

After Jegor had left Amber to Carlin, he had gone to the house of the children. He and Kilian and had made a plan for another group discussion.

When he arrived, they all sat together.

"Amber shouldn't worry us anymore. That still leaves us with the rest of them," Jegor said.

"Maddison is one of them, isn't she?" Shadra asked.

"Yes and no. She had more something to do with a friend of mine, Feardorcha Forbes. Therefore, we had no proper proof that she is a so-called sin," Jegor explained.

"But she tried to steal one of the seals and got control over the monster," Leyla argued.

"Yes. But if she has problems with Fear, he'll be the one to hunt her for us. Maddison is a normal magician again, which means she has a lot more problems than she had when she was undead. Letting her run around will lead us to the others at some point."

"I also agree with this choice," Kilian said. "My father's death threat is still in effect. But I'm not sure if I should let it continue. My father and I didn't agree on a lot of things, and I can't deal with people trying to bring me people for me to chop off their heads, as if we are in *Alice in Wonderland*." Kilian sighed. "I will find a different solution. For now, we also have to deal with the fact that Relayne betrayed us. She isn't our ally anymore, and we can't trust her." When he said this, Kilian the pain from his scars burned like a reminder.

"Are you sure about that?" Petyr asked. "You were the only one who was with her when it happened, the stealing of the second seal. What if she had plans?"

"Then she could have told us. We are a family," Kilian said, but paused when he realised what he had said. That's what these people had become for him, no matter the short amount of time—family.

"I don't have time to read mixed signals from Relayne, when we were figuring other things out. Besides, Amber got delivered by someone called Pieotr and Baelfire. The last one is our lovely Red's lover."

"We also have to wait until Alicia gets back. She trusts the gods, and I trust her. From what she told me, there is something connected to the legend in terms of why she has to do this. That means we are kind of safe for now and have more time to figure things out," Petyr offered.

"Which brings me to the point that I accepted becoming king. The coronation will be in two weeks. I want you all by my side. Being king means I need a new recruitment as well, and in these times, I see a huge reason to make you all a part of it. Relayne might have betrayed us, but I trust you and the future that lies ahead of us. We are the future of this city, the society, and whatever comes with it. If someone is going to change something about it, it's us. Merlin brought us together. Now it's time for us to make a statement and show our faces—that we are not afraid," Kilian said with a serious expression on his face.

Shadra put out her hand and looked at them. "Let's bond together—in the name of not only the elements, but also of every magic in this society."

Leyla and Petyr followed suit before Jegor and Kilian put out their arms, too.

Shadra closed her eyes and murmured a spell that made them feel their different energies—a bonding, something that would bring them even closer together. From now on, there was no single movement anymore. They were together, a team—ready to face whatever would come for them.

Chapter 28
Dance with the Devil

Some say he was the devil. Some say he was just a child.
– F. F., "Lucifer's Wish," *The True Urban Legends*

Two weeks later

"Wake up, girl. We are nearly there."

It was Taylor's voice that woke Alicia from her dream. It felt like yesterday when she had closed her eyes to take a nap on this Viking ship leading her towards an unknown destination. But when she woke up, she knew that something was wrong. Confused and groggy, she looked at Taylor. He was the man who had allowed her on board.

"How long have I slept?" Alicia asked.

"As long as any other person on this boat. It's been two weeks since we left Icon."

"Two weeks?" Alicia nearly shouted and jumped to her feet, struggling to keep her balance.

"Easy, Missy," Taylor said. "Everything happens for a reason, and you will soon find out why. For now, look in front of you. We're nearly there, and you should get ready." He didn't seem surprised by her disorientation. It seemed like he was used to confused people on this ship.

Alicia looked in the direction Taylor had pointed. She could see a skyline at the horizon, and upon looking around, she became sure that this wasn't the human world. The sea was lilac, and the sky so orange that it looked like Van Gogh had painted it.

"Daarcemking," she whispered to herself, a warm feeling spreading inside of her—a feeling like home. Of course she had heard of it before, but so far, her journey had only led her around the United Kingdom. She had never had a reason to go anywhere else, since she loved the United Kingdom, no matter how much pain she had experienced there. But seeing Daarcemking on the horizon gave her a different feeling; something inside her had awaited this exact moment. She took a deep breath.

She couldn't see it, but Taylor was looking at her with a certain knowing; she didn't know it, but he did—she was born ready for this journey.

***

"Fear? Feardorcha Forbes?" Hamlin asked loudly. He looked around. The shop was still nice and neat, which meant that Fear still used magic to keep everything in order. But no one had seen him for weeks. The people in the council were saying that he was on some kind of journey, doing some business. But if anyone knew better, it was Hamlin. He knew something was going on, and he had a feeling that it had to do with the story that had been haunting Feardorcha.

Looking closer, Hamlin found a note—to his surprise, it was addressed to him. Was Fear watching him, this very moment? Hamlin looked around once more, then began to read:

My dear friend Hamlin,
Today I have to tell you that I will be gone for a while. When you get this note, you found the right moment to enter my doors, and so I shall welcome you. I can't say how long I will be gone, but I know if someone can deal, sell, and tell,

it's you. The shop will get used to you. Therefore, it shouldn't be a problem to handle it. Eyes will be on you, however you're going to tell them, that I'm only far away for a while.

Be aware of Jegor and Kilian.

Farewell,

Fear

After Hamlin finished reading, the note burned itself and a smug smirk widened on his face. After all the up and downs of the last weeks, this seemed like the perfect win. He could finally make a move for his business. Fear had just offered him a chance. Finally, it was time for revenge, and he knew exactly where he would start.

***

"Are you two still not talking?" Pieotr asked.

The girl with the dark red hair just shrugged, standing in front of Maddison's door. Since Relayne had chosen the sins, her style had changed, and not only because she needed it to.

"I think there are two types of people coming to terms with the fact that they have a sibling." Relayne stepped away from the door.

"For someone who just began to play with the bad guys, you are doing very well, my dear Red," Pieotr said, draping an arm around her.

Relayne rolled her eyes. "It's been two weeks. I've had enough time to figure everything out. Besides, I'm not a teenager anymore. I was lost then, but I am not lost now. I know what I have to do and what I want to do. Today is finally the day I can speak to our boss. How is that going for you, big bad wolf?" Relayne asked.

Pieotr whistled and grinned brightly, revealing sharp teeth. "I like the sass. Seems like you and Baelfire are in balance again," he assumed.

Relayne didn't give any kind of sign in answer. Pieotr was just curious, but he was also good at saying just the right words so people would tell him what he wanted to hear.

"Give Maddison some more time. She has a lot to process." He changed the topic now. "There's much more going on than she would like to admit. I think she's trying to bring that bastard back. If you ask me, I wish he was dead. But she has a thing for him, so I'm trying to find Tress with her," Pieotr said with a despondent sigh.

"It's okay. She can speak to me whenever she wants to. If you'll excuse me, the boss isn't someone you leave waiting. You should know this." Relayne made to walk away, but Pieotr stopped her.

"There's something else I have for you. Since you haven't heard of your personal stalker and Baelfire told me that you still want information, I have found a way for you to find Calligan. I had to dig deep and go to some nasty places, but I got what I wanted." He took a small note out of his pocket and gave it to Relayne. She looked at it and raised an eyebrow.

"This address is in Madness. Are you telling me that's where he lives?" Relayne asked.

"I'm telling you that this is the key you need to get more information about your personal serial killer. Now good luck with our wonderful boss, may he let you live." Pieotr winked and turned around, leaving Relayne with more questions than before.

***

"Are you nervous?" Shadra asked.

"Are you not?" Leyla questioned in reply, checking her face in the small mirror again, trying to look as calm as she could.

"It's not our coronation. He is just going to say our names, and then we have an official position in the palace—which means we also have two homes, and I think that's pretty cool," Shadra said, grinning widely.

"Coming from someone who lived at the beach, yeah," Leyla said. She laughed nervously.

"We've been in worse situations. This is just a small audience," Shadra said, still not worried. Throughout this journey, she had learned that there was always a way to face things. She was a big believer.

"And a live-stream for the whole magical world," Leyla pointed out.

"We will be fine," Shadra said stubbornly, giving Leyla a quick kiss. "Trust me, and if anything goes wrong, I'll be there with you."

Leyla looked after her, smiling softly. Among all the chaos, someone good had come into her life. She didn't care about the age difference; it was just the character, the natural aura that had taken away Leyla's heart. Even though Shadra seemed younger and wilder, they were a good match for each other. And the day they had announced their status, the boys had only grinned—or nodded, in Jegor's case—because they had already known.

***

While Relayne was on her way to meet the boss, Baelfire had gone for a walk. It was just a feeling he had. He wanted to see the current news reporting the new coronation. But then, he also didn't want to see it—Kilian's face all over the screens. Even though Red was now on their side, Baelfire couldn't let go of his jealousy towards Kilian. That was probably because he would either try to kill Relayne or try to rejoin them if he ever forgave her. Neither of those things could happen. Baelfire sat on a bench near the house of the sins. Enjoying the moment, he took out a cigarette, but before he could light it, a stranger appeared next to him.

"Cheers, mate," Baelfire said to the stranger—black hair, pale. He blinked a few times, waiting, but they didn't move.

"I know, it's shocking how two of us can look that good, especially since you decided to stay in your true form," the stranger drawled.

Baelfire couldn't tell if there was irony in his voice or if this was just his way of speaking. They did have similar style—he wore ripped black jeans, a band shirt, and a leather jacket that seemed all too familiar.

"At least I caught you on your own, for once, Baelfire," the person continued.

Baelfire dropped his cigarette. "How do you know my name?" he asked.

"I'm Crystan, in short, Crush," the man said, ignoring the question and allowing a dramatic pause. "I'm your big brother, Baelfire."

***

Kilian took a deep breath. This was his moment. He had always known it would come one day, but he had never imagined that it would happen like this—his father gone, cursed by dark magic. His family was counting on him—and not just them; Icon was counting on him, too. He folded the paper with the speech he had prepared. He had always been quite confident in his skin, but today he felt anxiety crawling on his neck, warning him not to enter the room where everyone was waiting for him. But there was no turning back.

Was this the way you imagined me here, Father? Is that the dream you have been seeing between all these lies and madness in Icon?

"Are you ready?" Jegor asked, standing at his side.

"Let's do this," Kilian answered, and stepped into the throne room.

A small audience—including his sister Kennady, the politicians, and other important people—stood in respect as he entered. Synclair was waiting next to the throne, atop which the crown sat.

"Today we officially crown the new king. Before this happens, Kilian shall speak the words of true honesty to impress you all and make you fond, aware, and furthermore believe that he is the one true king," Synclair explained, waving his hand in a gesture for Kilian to step up.

Jegor nodded to his cousin. Now was the moment that everyone was waiting for. If he didn't earn their respect, a conference would decide to search for another king, if needed.

Kilian took another deep breath and looked at his notes. His gaze wandered over the audience. He focused on his sister, his well-known friends, the politicians, and some faces he had never noticed before. But then his gaze went to the children—Leyla, Shadra, and Petyr. One seat was empty. Even though it was meant for Alicia, he imagined Relayne sitting there.

He ripped apart the note and began to speak. "Thank you for your appearance today. I prepared a speech. But to be honest, I have to speak from my mind and heart. I always tried to run away from this. No one could ever tame me, not even my own parents. I have always told them who else could or would be king. I have done everything to avoid my tasks and duty, and yet I am standing here in front of you to tell you that I am the one. But that is not because of my name, the legacy, or loyalty that my family boasts. It is because I am part of a movement, a revolution that is well needed in this city.

"My cousin and I have always fought crime in this magical world. In the last weeks, the fight has been more real than ever. A group who call themselves the Seven Sins have caused trouble in this society. They've stolen two of our seals and created chaos that we are still trying to fix. Some things will never be fixed, like the loss of my father.

"I have been angry with him most of the time, but by now I know better. I know that there are other ways to save this society, without causing any harm. We have rules, laws that we live by. This law will continue, but it will also change, with the help of my family, friends, and true believers. It is time for a change that doesn't cross lines but brings people together. I am not perfect. None of us are, but I can work on myself every day.

"From now on, I will lead an open, honest kingdom that will stand against everything that breaks our law, our rules, and our freedom. I will do whatever I can do to protect my people and this society. Have faith and trust in me, because I have it in you too, that in the end, good will succeed. Together we stand against crime; together we rebuild. If anyone can't agree with that, he or she or anyone in between may now speak up or stay silent forever." Kilian could feel how rapidly his heart was beating.

The audience seemed tense—until Shadra started to clap. Leyla and Petyr joined, and shortly after, the entire audience was clapping and cheering. Kilian could feel the relief of pressure lifting off his shoulders, and he turned around. Synclair took the crown from the throne and slowly placed it on Kilian's head. Kilian then sat on the throne. It was an intense, overwhelming feeling. But in that moment, Kilian knew this was just the beginning of a war that was yet to come. And while the crown on his head shone, Kalimba woke from her sleep—eyes white, gasping for breath.

"Kilian," she whispered, clawing at the blanket underneath her. Even though she had opened her eyes, there was no light to be seen. Her eyesight was gone.

***

Relayne stood in front of the doors leading to the boss. The dark mahogany and golden handle revealed dark magic hiding behind it. The hallways of the manor and its shadows lurked at her back. The paintings on the walls seemed to watch her. Unlike the modern-driven area where she and the others lived, this hallway almost felt like a step back into Victorian times. She could feel her heartbeat increasing, mostly because she had no idea what to expect. No one ever said his name. How powerful must this person be? What was he doing that the others couldn't do?

Taking a moment to steel her nerves, Relayne opened the door. She walked inside and it closed of its own accord behind her. It felt like time was frozen in the room, and she couldn't help but stare at the person in front of her. He wasn't even looking at her, and all she could see was his topless back and the black skinny jeans he wore. No socks or shoes. The room itself looked like a giant sleeping hall; pillows and blankets were strewn across the floor. Relayne didn't know what to say. She could only stare at his back; it felt like she hadn't just entered a new room, but had also opened a new door for more answers. The walls were decorated with paintings and notes. There were symbols, too—one that looked like Baelfire's tattoo—alongside a giant map of Icon with ongoing illusion magic. He had always been a step ahead because he had been watching from the shadows, the darkness, the friendly spider on your shoulder. Relayne was stunned and fascinated at the same time. An inside look at his mindset and yet she was just scratching the surface. Her eyes were drawn to the fourth symbol. She gently touched the paper, feeling the connection, a whisper against her neck beckoning her closer.

Finally, the topless man spun to look at her. His slight, evil smirk gave her goosebumps. The confident mischief in his eyes melted with insanity and dazzled in a dark grey cloud. His aura was frightening and addicting at the same time as if he had poisoned her the moment she stepped inside the room. Relayne was wrapped around his finger—and he knew it.

"It is rude to stare, but I'll let you off," the man said. His voice was soft, inviting, but there was a certain undertone that warned her of impending rage. A soft sinister, taking her into his mind and leading her to the dance macabre.

Relayne couldn't move. She was rooted to the spot, her whole body enchanted by his presence. None of the others had lied when it came to his presence. It was different than any of the people she had met before. There was a darkness, so deep, like an ocean in which one could only drown. Indolence, taking her on and leading her to death.

He smiled at her. It was comforting and inviting. He gestured for her to sit, and so she did, giving in to his wicked wisdom and devilry.

"My name is Icarus. It is time that we have a chat."

Epilogue
The Rose

Calligan could feel that something was broken—at least two ribs. The bastard had taken control of the situation as if he owned this damn town. If it weren't for his best friend, he would have ripped him apart as if there was no tomorrow. Blood ran down his face, and fatal wounds decorated his body. But he wasn't easy to kill. It had been a fight-or-flight situation and his first impulse had been to escape to the mortal world. His aim had been the streets of Manchester, and he had landed in an edgy shopping arcade. The dusty floor underneath him was now coated with his blood. Though the humans around him looked like they were either scared or in shock, he didn't care. He got up from the floor, noticing the figure of Pan waiting for him. Calligan smirked at the god, leaving a trail of blood behind.

What an irony—a portal in the middle of an edgy shopping centre called Afflecks.

"Other side," Calligan whispered, and the eyes of the statue blinked before he fell through the portal and landed on the floor of his apartment.

Pain shot through his body, but he knew he was okay. Everything would be fine, and he showed that with a certain, insane grin.

"Shit! What have you done this time?" Quinn shrieked, but Calligan could only keep on grinning, as if he had no sorrow. Crush and Brixton ran up to him. Calligan had meant to meet them before he had gotten into trouble. He coughed, the pain taking over his body.

"They are coming," he whispered, chuckling weakly. "They're coming here. It's time. The thorns have been stretched, and they think I'm bleeding out." He coughed up blood. The pain was intensifying. Calligan looked up to his friends, his eyes dark.

"Cal, what the fuck happened? You need to tell us what happened," Quinn pressured. Crush was already mixing healing potions while Brixton came running with a band-aid.

Calligan grabbed Quinn by his neck and pulled him close. "Demons, Quinn. I fought against demons," he said, then fell back to the ground, coughing and laughing.

Quinn looked at his best friend in shock.

"What did he say?" Brixton asked.

Quinn shook his head, not prepared to process what Calligan had said.

Calligan looked at them, the insane smile plastered on his face. "The revolution is here, and we are a part of it." Then he passed out.

Glossary

Black League
The League created from shadows. It is said that the shadow created the first magicians in the physical form.
– You and Me, The Ballad of Magic

Bloods
Magicians who can control, smell, and use blood. Bloods are rare but essential for healing, crime investigation, and dark-magic-related work.

Ghosts
Magicians who can see and speak to ghosts. Ghosts are in charge of the balance between the living and dead.

Voodoos
Magicians who can do dark magic connected to rituals, blood, and shadows. Each Voodoo owns a Voodoo Doll that is registered with the council as their helper in life.

Green League
The League created from nature. It is said that the nature created the world in the form of earth, fire, air, and water.
– You and Me, The Ballad of Magic

Beasts
Magicians who understand animals or can morph into one. Crossings are a part of the Beast; they are half-human and half-animal, the form of which is chosen at birth.

Elements
Magicians who can control the elements: fire, water, earth, air, light, or shadow. Elements are registered with one Element

when the ceremony chooses them. Depending on their educational path, they are allowed to learn another Element.

Woods
Magicians who are able to use the nature around them. Most Woods are non-human species such as elves, dwarfs, nymphs, etc.

Red League
The League created from myst. It is said that the myst created the feelings, emotions, wisdom, and words. – You and Me, The Ballad of Magic

Feelings
Magicians who can sense and control feelings. They are also capable of seeing the bond between people in the form of colourful strings.

Minds
Magicians who can read, manipulate, and control other people's minds.

Tricksters
Magicians who can do illusions of different kinds.

White League
The League created from light. It is said that the light created the sky and weather. – You and Me, The Ballad of Magic

Gods
Magicians chosen by a god. Their power depends on their loyalty towards their chosen god and the path that they are willing to take, lead by the gods.

Healers
Magicians who can heal others with their magic.

Jester
A magician that has no magic. Jesters are rare in the society. Their magic was taken away by the ceremony of Merlin.

Urban Legends
Legends told throughout New Born Kingdom. Not all magicians believe they are true, but the basis of folklore and mythology is reality.

Death and the Three Muses
The Urban Legend that tells the story of Death falling in Love.

Dream
One of the three magical triangle skills common in the Red and Green Leagues. A Dream can show things connected to the past, present, and future.

Vision
One of the three magical triangle skills common in the White League. It shows an event that might happen in the future but which be prevented.

Omen
One of the three magical triangle skills common in the Black League. It shows an event that is going to happen in the future. A magician can't prevent it, they can only prepare for it. The outcome depends on the magician and how they handle the Omen beforehand.

Battersea and Greenwich
Districts and portals in London that lead to places in Icon.

Market Square
The heart of Icon and the most common area for its cultural markets, where magicians sell all kinds of artefacts and essentials.

Seaside
The sea district in Icon, home to a port, a beach, and various shipwrecks.

Shoreditch
A portal and district in London and as well as a district in Icon. The circus is the heart of Shoreditch.

Council
A political centre and workplace, including the circle, who is the heart and head of the council. The circle is in charge of the ceremony of Merlin and compound by eight members, two of each league in the society.

Doom
The darkest district in Icon, known as place of dark magic.

Woods
The nature district in Icon, home to Beasts and Woods magicians.

Acknowledgements

Welcome to the republishing of the first book, once called *Revolution Blue*. Over a year has passed since I wrote *Revolution Blue* and now I have come back with the solution that I was really looking for: an origin story that sends you into a universe full of diverse characters and stories. Footsteps walked on the same path as you and me. These footsteps wouldn't have found their better version if certain people hadn't helped me. Each word, each character, monster, or setting wouldn't have come to life if not for the life I am currently living with the people surrounding me and helping me every day.

First of all, I want to thank my team. No matter what I go through, they always have my back. I am grateful for each of you and what you bring into this project to make it happen. We started as a book series and have developed into a movement that will bring change to the world—I am certain. A big thanks to Abbyll on this side, my right-hand-kitchen-utensils-throwing assistant, who never failed to get me back on track. One of the most talented people when it comes to creativity. Also a big thank you to my manager, Sara, who never failed to keep me organised and made sure I would hit every deadline.

Each member of my team is so unique, so brave, so talented in their own way that I could fill a whole page with it. Thank you, Craig, Mika, Alice, Fanny, Hannah, Mariana, Jodie, Vee, Selina, Cathi, Lea, Kitty, Lisa, Mikey, Mephi, Lisa, Kimchi, Jessie, and Curt. Furthermore, I want to thank the people that I have collaborated with so far on this journey. Simon, Alicia, Leon; you guys have brought amazing colour to this project and painted it with your own ideas and input which I am incredibly thankful for. I am also incredibly thankful for

Atmosphere Press and their amazing team that helped this book come together.

Further, I want to thank my friends, who have never let me down. My little brother Cameron, who was one of the first people to listen to my story. I want to thank my music friends, the ones that I went to concerts with and dove into the night, and all my friends that Korean music brought into my life, by now being all around the world. Friendship has been one of the strongest leads during tough times and these characters wouldn't have the same energy if it weren't for the people that surround me with love every day. Also a special thanks to Bronnie and Zack, who are both beautiful, talented people in my life that came to me through the magic of music.

The biggest thanks goes to my parents. Thank you for believing in me and my work. As I said before, I don't think I have ever been this proud of something before. This story is the first of many that comes truly from my heart and wouldn't be the same if you hadn't shown me love and support over the years. Thank you.

And not to forget my grandparents. Grandpa, I know you are watching me and still waiting for grandma. Grandma, thank you—rocking over 90 years of life is something I truly admire, and you have never failed to show your support and wish me the best.

Lastly, I want to thank you—the reader. A story is not a story if it's not read and told. You are the one that brings it to life. I hope that *Melancholy Vision* and its future brothers and sisters is going to bring you the spark and joy that it brought to me when creating it. Take the magic inside this universe and make it your own. Enjoy the journey. Love like Relayne. Hope like Jegor. And rebel like Kilian.

About Atmosphere Press

Atmosphere Press is an independent, full-service publisher for excellent books in all genres and for all audiences. Learn more about what we do at atmospherepress.com.

We encourage you to check out some of Atmosphere's latest releases, which are available at Amazon.com and via order from your local bookstore:

The Short Life of Raven Monroe, a novel by Shan Wee

Insight and Suitability, a novel by James Wollak

It Starts When You Stop, a novel by Johnny Abboud

Orange City, a novel by Lee Matthew Goldberg

Late Magnolias, a novel by Hannah Paige

No Way Out, a novel by Betty R. Wall

The Saint of Lost Causes, a novel by Carly Schorman

Monking Around, a novel by Keith Howchi Kilburn

The Cuckoo of Awareness, a novel by Andrew Brush

The House of Clocks, a novel by Fred Caron

The Tattered Black Book, a novel by Lexy Duck

All Things in Time, a novel by Sue Buyer

American Genes, a novel by Kirby Nielsen

Newer Testaments, a novel by Philip Brunetti

Hobson's Mischief, a novel by Caitlin Decatur

The Red Castle, a novel by Noah Verhoeff

The Farthing Quest, a novella by Casey Bruce

About the Author

L. C. Hamilton is a twenty-five-year-old writer and artist living in London better known as Laura, Lola, Charles, or lchamiltonarts. *Melancholy Vision, a Revolution Series Awakening* is the first novel in the Revolution Series. Hamilton is also the owner of REVMentoring and runs two podcasts called Solution Pink and Gigi and Sagi. In her free time she enjoys all kinds of books, TV shows and films as well as travelling around the world and inspiring people.

Lightning Source UK Ltd.
Milton Keynes UK
UKHW010638120421
381850UK00002B/551